ANNE MELVILLE

The House of Hardie

This edition published 1993 by
Diamond Books
77-85 Fulham Palace Road
Hammersmith, London W6 8JB

Copyright © Margaret Potter 1987

Set in Times
Printed and bound in Great Britain by
BPCC Paperbacks Ltd
Member of BPCC Ltd

Contents

PROLOGUE

One
1874

'Boy!'

Gordon Hardie hauled himself to his feet and staggered towards the cabin, clutching at every handhold as he went. His erratic course was caused partly by the rolling of the ship but even more by his own weakness. He had not eaten – had not *wanted* to eat – for three days of sickness and misery. The books which tempted him to run away to sea had described marvellous adventures in exotic places but had omitted to mention the spitefulness of the sea itself.

'Boy!' The naturalist's voice was fiercer this time, reflecting his impatience. Fortunately for Gordon, even the great Sir Desmond Langton had succumbed to sea-sickness in the Bay of Biscay, requiring no meals and very little service from his cabin boy. But to judge by the bellowing of his voice as he repeated the summons for a third time, he had found his sea legs now. Gordon presented himself groggily at the cabin door.

Ten minutes later, Sir Desmond appeared to be approaching the end of his tirade. 'A pigsty!' he shouted. 'Can you give me a single reason why I shouldn't order the mate to give you a whipping that you'll never forget?'

Gordon licked his dry lips and pressed them together to prevent them from quivering. With his hands behind his back he grasped the frame of the door lest hunger and fear should combine to make him collapse. Sir Desmond, who had been pacing up and down the cabin, turned to stare at him when his question elicited no answer. White-faced, Gordon stared back.

'Hm,' said Sir Desmond. 'Been ill, have you?'

'Yes, sir. I'm very sorry, sir. I'll try to do better.'

'See you do, then. I want this cabin shipshape by noon. To start with, clean my boots so that I can step along to the captain.'

'Right away, sir.' Gordon set to work with as much energy as he could summon, breathing and brushing and buffing. Aware that he was being watched, he kept his eyes down. But his master's silence made him uneasy. Slowly he raised his head.

'When did you last clean a pair of boots?' demanded Sir Desmond.

'They're very damp, sir.'

'Answer my question.' But the answer must have been obvious, because he gave an exaggerated sigh and sat down. 'Leave that alone and look at me,' he commanded. 'Now then. When that boy of mine broke his leg in Southampton and you appeared at the last minute like a gift from the gods, you told me that you were sixteen years old but small for your age. For good measure, you added that you were an orphan. You said that for two years you'd been employed at an inn, doing general work around the place. All lies, I take it, and more fool me to be taken in by it, just because you looked willing and not completely stupid.'

'I *am* willing, sir.'

'That's not enough. You need competence as well. Now then, let's start again. How old are you?'

'Fourteen,' mumbled Gordon.

'Speak up. Orphaned?'

Gordon shook his head.

'Family know where you are?'

10

'I wrote from Southampton with the name of the ship. I said I'd be away for three years and they weren't to worry.'

'Fat lot of comfort that will be to your weeping mother. Why did you want to run away from home?'

'I'm not running *away* from anything. I'm running *to* something.' With this positive statement Gordon straightened his back and raised his head. It was time to put behind him the misery of the past few days. He had been homesick as well as seasick, but that was something he had no intention of admitting. On the day he signed up for this voyage to the South Seas he had put his childhood behind him, and from now on he must behave like a man.

'Running to what?' asked Sir Desmond. 'Not just to life as a cabin boy, I take it.'

'I want to be an explorer.'

Gordon had never said that to anyone before. At home, in Oxford, it was taken for granted that he would one day own and manage the family business. Had he ever hinted that he had other ambitions, he would have been regarded as both foolish and disloyal. He could never have hoped for permission to take even a short period off for adventure.

For as long as he could remember he had been a wanderer. His very first memory was of the day when – only just able to walk – he had tottered away from his nursemaid as she sat mending his clothes in the shade; across the lawn, through the rose garden, around the shrubbery and to within a foot or two of the River Cherwell, which bounded the grounds. Snatched to safety by a gardener, he had been puzzled by his mother's extravagant hugging and the tears of his nursemaid, whom he never after that day saw again. Even at that early age he had formed the impression that when he wanted to

11

stretch the boundaries of his small world and explore some new territory, it was better not to let anyone find out. But Sir Desmond Langton was himself an explorer. He, surely, would understand.

Certainly by now the anger had faded from the botanist's expression, but he looked curious rather than sympathetic. 'What put that idea into your mind?'

'I've always wanted . . . I read a book, years ago. About Marco Polo.' For months as a seven-year-old Gordon had repeated silently to himself the phrase 'The Great Silk Road', thinking the words to be the very stuff of romance. 'It made me want to go to China.'

Sir Desmond exploded into what was more of a hoot than an ordinary laugh. 'China! You don't imagine that the *Periwinkle*'s going anywhere near China!'

'No. The South Seas. I know that. That's exciting enough to start with, while I'm learning to explore.'

'You don't learn to explore, boy. You explore in order to learn.'

Gordon puzzled over this and failed to understand.

'Put those boots aside and sit down,' said Sir Desmond. 'Let me tell you about my first expedition. Ever heard of an illness called malaria?'

Gordon shook his head.

'Unpleasant disease. Hits you in steamy, tropical kinds of places. Not in England. But our soldiers in India and Africa, they get it. Die of it. There's a medicine which cures malaria, called quinine. It's not new. We've known about it in Europe for a couple of hundred years or more, and the natives who first discovered it, in Peru, may have been using it for centuries. It's made out of the bark of a tree called the cinchona. No secret about that, either. The people in Peru have been quite happy to grow the trees and powder the bark and sell it to anyone with the money

12

to buy it. But they weren't going to let anyone else get into the market by establishing a cinchona forest any- where else in the world. You following me so far?'

'Yes, sir.'

'I went out there twenty-odd years ago, with a compan- ion. To explore, you might say, in Peru and Ecuador. But not simply for the sake of exploring. We had a target – to find the cinchonas and collect seeds. Not just a pocketful. We brought out a hundred thousand in the end. Now, lad, I'll tell you. Every moment of that exploration was hell. We had to travel by river. Whirlpools, rapids, jagged rocks. Every time we camped at night, the mosquitoes covered us like a blanket. Snakes all over the place, as well. When the natives found out what we were after, they refused us porters; and when we pressed on, they tried to kill us. If we'd been merely exploring, we'd have given in within a month. But we knew what we were looking for, and that made all the difference.'

Gordon's black eyes were wide open with interest. 'Did the seeds grow?'

'Five years ago I was invited to visit India. The Nilgiri Hills, in the south. They showed me a forest of cinchonas, producing their own seeds to grow more trees still. Hundreds of lives being saved every year in the Indian Army. Thousands, perhaps. Now then, the point about all this. My companion and I, we were trained as bota- nists. Knew the likeliest place to find the forests we wanted – right soil, right rainfall, right altitude. We knew how to recognize the trees out of hundreds of others, and when to collect the seeds and how to store and germinate them. And at the same time we could keep our eyes open for new plants.'

'What do you mean by a new plant, sir?'

'A plant that's unknown in England, but might be

worth bringing back to try out. Got a garden at home, have you?'

'Yes. My mother knows quite a lot about flowers, I think.' Gordon had never taken any great interest in the garden. The hard digging was the work of the gardener and his boy, while the planning of the beds and the cutting and arranging of flowers was women's work. Or so he had always assumed.

'Narcissus, lilac, gladiolus, primrose – any of that kind of thing?' The botanist did not wait for an answer, probably guessing that Gordon did not know. 'You might think that common things like that have always grown in England. Not a bit of it. Man called Tradescant found them more than two hundred and fifty years ago – some in Russia, some in Algeria, some in the West Indies. Brought them to England and settled them in.' He paused, laughing at himself. 'Going on a bit, aren't I? Point is this. Explorers need reasons for exploring. Some of them make maps – chart coastlines, trace rivers back to their sources. Your friend Marco Polo was looking for trade. There are as many reasons as there are men – but there ought to be *something*.'

Sir Desmond Langton was, to guess from his appearance, almost fifty years old. Perhaps he had forgotten how it felt simply to see a place for the first time, to arrive somewhere new. What he had said was interesting, but somehow missed the point. When, making enquiries at Southampton, Gordon had first heard that the *Periwinkle* was about to leave on a voyage to the South Seas, his whole body had swelled with excitement and hope and determination, adding conviction to his lies and making no exaggeration of his enthusiasm necessary.

It seemed that Sir Desmond remembered the lies at the same moment as Gordon: he sighed to himself as he

14

considered what to do. 'Well. Take my compliments to Captain Blake and ask if he can spare his boy for an hour to show you what you ought to know already. Cabin shipshape by noon, or you walk the plank.'

Gordon stood up, staggering slightly as the *Periwinkle* rolled. 'Yes, sir. I'm sorry to have been a disappointment to you, sir.'

'My fault for failing to notice that you spoke like a schoolboy and not like a bootboy. But there's no turning back. I can't pick another boy out of the ocean, so you'll have to forget those dreams of exploration and learn to use a swab. If you're not an orphan, what does your father do?'

It was the question which Gordon had feared and was reluctant to answer. Gordon was not ashamed that his father was in trade – but it meant that the name of John Hardie, vintner, was well-known amongst the members of a higher social class than his own. He lived and worked in Oxford, supplying college High Tables as well as those many undergraduates who devoted their university years more sedulously to pleasure than to study. In addition, he owned an establishment in Pall Mall, London – a property surrounded by the clubs of the gentlemen who patronized him. All his customers were wealthy: it was likely that Sir Desmond Langton himself was one of them. Gordon tried to think of a way in which to answer without revealing too much.

'No more lies from now on,' said Sir Desmond. 'Your father?'

'A wine merchant, sir.'

'Where?'

'Oxford.'

'A wine merchant in Oxford.' Sir Desmond thought for a moment and then hooted with laughter for a second

15

time that morning. 'Gordon *Hardie*. You're telling me that you're John Hardie's son? The heir to The House of Hardie!'

Gordon's pale face flushed. Put like that, it sounded ridiculous. Yet it was true. The family business, founded in 1710, had been handed down from father to son through seven generations. One day Gordon would be expected to take his place behind the green bow windows in the High, condemned to a life of orders and accounts, its dullness only occasionally disturbed by visits to the French châteaux from which he would buy his wines.

'No need to fret,' said Sir Desmond. 'It will be five months before we reach the islands, and I can't return you any more than I can replace you. So, Mr Gordon Hardie, of The House of Hardie, will you do me the inestimable favour of swabbing this floor.' His voice rose to the roar with which he had summoned Gordon half an hour earlier. 'NOW!'

Two
1877

'Your own mother won't recognize you,' said Sir Desmond Langton.

Gordon Hardie, standing beside his master at the rail of the *Periwinkle*, grinned his agreement. No one who had seen the slightly-built and white-faced fourteen-year-old sailing out of Southampton thirty-three months earlier would have guessed this healthy young man to be the same person. Sun and wind had tanned his skin; he had grown tall with the passage of time and strong through the performance of his duties.

As his body matured, his face also had been transformed. His black, wavy hair, neatly trimmed when he left home, fell almost to his shoulders. Thick eyebrows added an impression of power to a strong, high forehead, whilst the neat nose of his childhood seemed to have taken on a life of its own as it developed. It was not only large but aquiline, giving him in profile an eager, questing look. During four months of their two-year stay in the Pacific, Sir Desmond had been immobilized by a crushed foot. Gordon, acting as the botanist's legs, had at each landfall listened while the naturalist described what he hoped to find, and then literally followed his nose. It had led him, according to the nature of each island, along beaches and up rivers and through virgin forests, probing ahead of him as though it could sniff out seeds and flowers and berries which its owner had never before seen.

Gordon himself could not have described his own new face, for he had never seen himself in profile, but he could

17

hardly be unaware of the changes in his body. Even at the end of the five-month voyage back to England in the confined spaces of a sailing ship he knew himself to be fit, able to face any challenge and undertake any task.

Much of his confidence came from the certainty that he had found his vocation. The boyhood reading which enticed him away from the comforts of home and the love of his family had proved to be not too far from the truth. Like some of his heroes he had had to stand his ground under attack from angry islanders and to pump and bale for seven hours without pause when the *Periwinkle* holed herself on a coral reef. In a narrow canoe that was little more than a hollowed tree trunk he had found himself approaching white water which proved to be not rapids but a waterfall, and to this day he could not tell how he had survived. More dangerous, although less dramatic, had been the fever induced by a plant whose tiny barbs had infected his blood; on that occasion it was Sir Desmond who probably saved his life by making an infusion from some of his precious plants.

None of these adventures and near-disasters had diminished his enthusiasm for the life of an explorer. He had, however, come to realize the truth of his employer's first lecture to the useless fourteen-year-old who was his cabin boy. Gordon too understood now that any search should have a purpose: there must be something to be found.

Sir Desmond had not only taught him that lesson but had provided the goal. Gordon had been engaged as a personal servant, not as a member of the ship's crew, and so all his time was at his employer's disposal. No doubt it was the prospect of tedium on the long journey out which prompted the naturalist to become a tutor as well as a master. Drawing on the ship's stores for examples, he had taught Gordon how to dissect a botanical specimen and

18

how to describe it scientifically and to categorize it according to the Linnaean classifications. He lectured him on the composition of soils and the properties of light and water. He lent him books to read and a candle by which to read them; and on the following day interrogated the boy on what he had discovered.

Perhaps in the beginning Gordon's eagerness to learn had something to do with the unromantic nature of the tasks for which he had primarily been employed. But he was still expected to scrub and polish and slop out and darn and carry meals and messages, so that the diligence with which he applied himself to his new studies must soon have been fostered by a dislike of idleness and a genuine fascination with what he was learning.

On the voyage home, which was just ending, there had been no pretence that he was merely a cabin boy. Sir Desmond, declaring that he deserved a reward for two years of vigorous and dangerous field work, promoted him to the post of scientific assistant. There was much to do, for thousands of specimens had been collected. Some had to be kept alive, whilst many were to be carefully dried for preservation. Seeds must be sorted and packaged and labelled, and all must be painstakingly catalogued. It was, after all, just as well that Sir Desmond had employed a schoolboy and not a bootboy: for hours at a time Gordon sat at the cabin table, pausing in the task of taking dictation only during some unusually severe battering of the ship.

Today, though, all the records as well as the specimens were roped away in wooden chests. As the *Periwinkle* glided through the calm estuary water, Sir Desmond's eyes were seeking out familiar landmarks whilst Gordon, beside him, wondered how best to broach the subject which had filled his mind for the past few days. In the end it seemed best to come straight out with it.

'Sir Desmond. Should you have any new expedition in mind, I would very much like to serve with you again. If you would have me.'

Sir Desmond sighed. 'I fear this may prove to be my last expedition,' he said. 'I've five years' work here with the seeds we've brought back. Not just germinating them and growing them on true, but doing a little cross-pollinating and grafting to find out whether man can improve on nature. By the time all that's under way, I may well be growing too old to leap in and out of small boats or wade across raging torrents up to my waist. Besides, I promised my wife . . . You'll discover one day for yourself, my boy, that wives don't always take kindly to being left alone for two or three years.'

'Perhaps I could help you with your experiments for a year or two. And then organize an expedition of my own. To China, perhaps,' Gordon added hopefully. His boyhood fascination with that country was as strong as ever.

'China!' Sir Desmond, who had explored so many parts of the world, had never been to China, but his sigh of regret recognized that he was unlikely now ever to make the journey. 'You could look for Merlot's lily in China.'

'Merlot's lily?' For three years Gordon had listened spellbound to his master's stories of exotic places and treasures, but this was a name new to him.

'Merlot was a missionary who travelled in China and tried to get into Tibet – forbidden territory at the beginning of the century. Well, it still is, come to that. He wasn't a botanist, unfortunately. Ten thousand feet up in the mountains he came across a valley filled with lilies. The queen of lilies, he said – the most beautiful sight he'd ever seen. He wrote a letter of description home, with a drawing. Dug up a few of the bulbs to send as well. Presumably he did it while the lilies were still in flower, so it's not surprising that they didn't survive. What with the change from almost freezing conditions to the heat of the plains, and then a six-month journey back to Europe, they were shrivelled and rotten by the time they arrived. Merlot himself was caught by the Tibetans. They chopped off the heads of the villagers who'd shown him the way into the country, as a hint to anyone else who tried to give a foreigner a helping hand. The missionary himself was simply never heard of again.'

'Did he say in his letter where he saw the lilies?'

'No. You've put your finger on it. Something that could be the most beautiful flower in the world, and no one knows where to find it. So there you are. Go to China and bring back the Merlot lily. Except that then it would be the Hardie lily.'

He laughed as he spoke, but he was not joking. For his own part, Gordon was unable even to attempt a smile. His heart swelled to bursting point. It was as though he had suddenly and for the first time realized why he had been born. Falling in love, he thought, must be something like this. Perhaps one day he would meet a girl, whom he did not yet know to exist, and realize that he had been waiting for her all his life. She would give him no choice. There would be a compulsion to love her – just as the lily was now placing him under a compulsion to search for it.

'My God!' exclaimed Sir Desmond. 'What have I done?'

Gordon blinked and looked at the older man, puzzled as to his meaning.

'Irresponsible!' growled the botanist. 'I remember, on the voyage out, telling you that if you wanted to be an explorer you needed a goal, and that was true enough.

Something else I should have emphasized. You need money as well.'

'You mentioned once that the Royal Botanic Gardens at Kew sponsors expeditions of this sort from time to time.'

'I should have kept my mouth shut,' growled Sir Desmond. 'I shall be lucky if the next case of cognac I order from The House of Hardie isn't laced with poison. I can't be blamed for your running away, but I don't intend to be responsible for your failure to return to the bosom of your family.'

'My father may have disowned me by now.'

'That's as may be. There's only one way to find out. And if your mother's still alive, chances are that she'll persuade him to own you again.'

An unexpected surge of emotion flooded Gordon's body; he swallowed the lump in his throat, alarmed by what he saw as a failure of imagination. Very often in the past two and a half years he had remembered with shame how he had waved a farewell to his mother with the casual gesture of a boy going off to school as usual. He had understood, and regretted, the alarm she must have felt when he failed to return at the end of the day, and the grief and anxiety which would persist even after she received his letter. But as time passed, and he knew himself to be healthy, he had forgotten that she would still be worried. And the thought had never occurred to him that she herself might become ill, or even die.

'Any brothers?' asked Sir Desmond.

Gordon shook his head. 'A younger sister, that's all.'

'So you should be all right. Not a woman's business, wine. Your father won't want to break a family tradition if he can help it. A word of advice, then. You've got a natural talent. To be a plant-hunter, I mean. But you're –

how old is it now? Seventeen? So. Take whatever training your father has in mind to give you. Go to France if you can, see the vines growing and all the processes of making the wine. One of these days you may be able to bring two talents together, breed a new variety of grape. But don't turn up your nose at the business of keeping accounts and getting to know your customers. One of these days, when The House of Hardie is yours, and thriving well enough to finance an expedition of your own, you may find you can put a manager in for a few years. But first of all you must have at your own fingertips everything you'll want him to do. Take your training.'

Their conversation was interrupted by a loud, repeated shout. Many times during the past two and a half years Gordon had listened as the orders for the mainsail to be lowered and furled were relayed upwards, and had felt the abrupt change from the wind's full power to a more delicate, gliding propulsion. He had leaned against the rail, as he was leaning now, studying the coastline of a tropical island and wondering what treasures were hidden in the interior. Here the water was grey instead of a bright, clear blue, and instead of palm trees fingering the sunshine he could see only the misty outlines of cranes. After such an absence, the life that lay ahead of him was almost as hard to envisage as the life of the islanders who paddled their canoes out to the *Periwinkle* and led her to safe anchorage. The journey to Oxford would be the beginning of a different kind of exploration; but Sir Desmond had reminded him that this too could have a worthwhile goal.

Twenty-four hours later, on the first Sunday of October 1877, Gordon Hardie strode along Oxford's High Street and came to a halt opposite the bow windows of The

House of Hardie, with their small panes of bottle green glass. The premises would of course be unoccupied at this hour: he could stare at them without any danger of being seen and recognized. He would find his father and mother and sister, he hoped, at their home in Holywell. How would they greet him? As the prodigal son returning, to be welcomed and feasted, or as someone who had behaved heartlessly, disappointing their hopes – someone who could not be forgiven? His guess was that his mother would cry and Midge, his sister, would tease, and his father would be at first severe, but willing to be placated by promises of future good behaviour.

So what promises could reasonably be made? Gordon tried to pierce the thick glass with his imagination, to see himself bending over ledgers, or rising to be polite to the son of a duke, who would one day be a duke – and a profitable customer – himself. It was not a prospect which gave him much pleasure. But any undertakings given to his father would be valueless if they were not performed with whole-hearted diligence. He would make another promise, this time to himself – a promise whose fulfilment would provide a reward for good behaviour. In ten years' time his father would be only fifty years old; still well able to manage the business himself without his son's help. There would be no more running away; on this occasion Gordon would ask with good warning for leave of absence. But as long as he was free to make plans in his head for some new expedition, he would be able to endure the slavery of business without complaint. Until October 1887, he would devote himself to the affairs of The House of Hardie. But only until then.

PART ONE
An Oxford Romance

One
1885

Eight years after Gordon Hardie's return from his escapade in the South Seas, another young man arrived in the
High and gazed at the bow windows of The House of
Hardie. It was the first day of the Michaelmas term in
1885: the first day of Archie Yates's new life as an Oxford
undergraduate. His grandfather, the Marquess of Ross,
had travelled with him from the great house of Castlemere
in order to settle his grandson in. As Archie – tall and
athletic, fair-haired and handsome and self-confident –
waited for the footman to set the steps of the carriage so
that the marquess could dismount outside the vintner's
establishment, he felt no doubts about his reception. His
grandfather's name and wealth would ensure his own
welcome.

If Mr John Hardie had any sense, he would be on the
premises in person today. Although his main business was
done in Pall Mall, in London, it was in Oxford that his
firm had first opened its doors early in the eighteenth
century. More to the point, in this first week of the
university year, a new generation of potential customers
was arriving in the city for the first time, and the nature
of their welcome might well determine where they placed
their patronage for the next fifty years. Archie was only
nineteen, but he was sophisticated enough to know that
he represented a prize for any tradesman. During his
three or four years at Oxford he would be treated
generously in the expectation that he would then be a
customer for life. Within the past hour accounts had been

27

opened for him with a bookseller and a tailor. Now it was time to arrange that a constant flow of wine should be available for the entertainment of his friends. Archie followed his grandfather through the door.

'Morning.' The marquess's greeting was brusque: it was his usual way of speaking. Archie, who had been brought up in his grandfather's house, was able to interpret the tone of his voice, recognizing with interest that the vintner was being addressed not as a mere tradesman, but almost as an intimate. The marquess adopted very much the same tone when he was discussing the season's shooting on the Castlemere estate with his head gamekeeper, a man for whom he had respect. It was a voice which recognized specialized knowledge and acknowledged a long and loyal connection. 'My grandson, Archie. Rachel's boy, don't you know.'

'It's a pleasure to meet you again, Mr Yates.' The vintner's handshake was strong and his voice was equally firm; it was clear that he needed no more adequate introduction. 'I remember seeing you shortly after your mother's tragic death, when you and your sister first went to live at Castlemere.'

'Lucy's here with us today,' said the marquess. 'Sent her off with her governess to look at some of the colleges while Archie and I get down to business. He'll have his own account with you, but you can come down on me for it while he's up.'

'You're at The House, I take it, Mr Yates?' said Mr Hardie, pulling a ledger towards him. Archie was about to answer, but his grandfather spoke first.

'No. That's all very well for the tufts.' The marquess himself, and his three sons, had been to Christ Church, the natural choice for those of noble birth. 'But my son-in-law's a military man, don't you know. Has his own ideas.'

'I shall be reading Modern History.' Archie decided it was time to make his own contribution to the conversation. It was not in fact his intention to devote too much of his time to study. His choice of subject had been influenced only partly by his father's views. History was reputed to be easier than Greats. Besides, almost the whole of his time at Eton had been devoted to the classics, and by now he had had enough of them. 'Dr Mackenzie was recommended to us as a tutor, so I shall be at Magdalen.'

'Dr Mackenzie, indeed.' Mr Hardie's dark eyes brightened with interest, and he seemed about to make some remark, but checked himself. 'A very scholarly gentleman,' he said instead, surprising Archie by his apparent familiarity with the historian's name. 'And now, my lord, Mr Yates, if you'd care to step through to the parlour, I've one or two wines waiting here that I'd like you to taste. A Tokay, for example, which has been very well thought of by my young gentlemen. And I hope, Mr Yates, that when you're planning a party or a special dinner, you'll remember that we're always at your disposal to discuss what would best be suited to it. If I'm in London myself, my son will be happy to advise.'

'Settled down now, has he, after that trouble he gave you?' asked the marquess.

'All forgotten, all forgotten. Just as well, I suppose, that he should get the wanderlust out of his system while he was still a boy.'

This exchange meant nothing to Archie, who allowed his attention to wander. They had been led into a room, more spacious than the small front shop, in which glasses and bottles were set out on a table covered with a plush cloth. A wide door, not completely closed, led to what appeared to be an office, and the sound of voices attracted Archie's attention. He took a chair which would allow him to look through the opening.

It was not precisely a quarrel which was going on in the next room, but certainly an extremely vigorous argument. A single glance was enough to convince Archie that the young man and younger woman who faced each other over a desk must be brother and sister. No married couple, and no pair of office colleagues, would debate with quite this degree of liveliness. In any case, there was a physical resemblance to strengthen his guess. The young man must be John Hardie's son. He had the same curly black hair and black eyes, although in the son's case a strong aquiline nose gave him a more craggy and forceful appearance than his suaver father.

The young woman – she was perhaps a year or two older than Archie – was as dark-haired as her brother, and had some of the same strong features. But what seemed aggressive in Gordon Hardie's profile was merely vivacious in hers. Her bright eyes were flashing with pleasure in the argument – and perhaps she had just won it, for now she threw back her head, laughing. Her mouth was wide, her teeth white and regular. It seemed to Archie that he had never seen such a delightful smile.

He wished that she would glance towards him, so that he might intercept her smile and return it. But instead she straightened herself, pressed a few straying locks of hair into place and turned away towards another door at the further end of the room – not walking in a sedate, ladylike manner, but almost skipping, as though the energy pulsing through her petite body could not be controlled. The far door closed behind her. Gordon Hardie came into the room in which the wines were to be tasted, and was introduced.

Archie's mind was not on the matter in hand. His intention was to float through his Oxford career on a river of champagne, so he hardly bothered to listen as his grandfather, a glass of Madeira in his hand, talked of clarets and burgundies and discussed the prospects for the current year's vintage. He was thinking about the girl.

Archie's idea of beauty had been formed by a portrait of his mother, whom he did not otherwise remember; she had died at the birth of his sister Lucy, when Archie himself was barely three years old. It was because they were motherless, with a father who spent most of his time overseas in the army, that they had been brought up in their grandfather's great house, Castlemere. The portrait of the marquess's only daughter, their mother, held pride of place in the long gallery. It showed a tall, slender young woman – she was only twenty-two at the time of her death – with golden hair, rosy lips and a soft, fair complexion.

Lucy, almost certainly, had inherited all these characteristics. At the age of sixteen she had not yet grown to her full height, but her hair was as golden, her waist as tiny and her skin as delicate as her mother's. Her expression was livelier, but perhaps that only represented the difference between a living person and the calm beauty of a face painted on canvas. It was from his mother and sister that Archie had formed his ideal of perfect female beauty. How extraordinary it was, then, that he should find so attractive the small, dark, slightly dishevelled girl whom he had just glimpsed.

For a moment he felt overwhelmed with a desire to pursue her – or at least to make enquiries and discover how he might see her again. But common sense checked him. He had not come up to Oxford to waste time with girls. His life for the next three or four years would be a masculine one. Both in work and in games his companions would be old school friends or new college friends. He was never likely to see this particular young woman again. Supposing his guess to be accurate, she was the daughter of a wine merchant, moving in a social circle quite different from his own.

There was a moment in which this thought filled him with regret. But the moment did not last long. There were too many other new experiences to be savoured as his Oxford career began. Already his college rooms felt like home, although he had seen them for the first time only two hours earlier. He was anxious to return and take full possession of them. Besides, he had ordered lunch there for one o'clock.

As tactfully as possible he drew the marquess's attention to the time.

'Lucy will be waiting for us, sir,' he said.

Two

'Archie! Archie, do come and look at the deer.'

From the moment of her arrival in Oxford Lucy had been in a state of excitement. Everything was new and strange and wonderful. How could Archie be so calm, appearing to take it all for granted? She tugged at his hand, leading him to the window.

'Hang it all, Lucy,' protested her brother. 'I've seen a deer before. There are six hundred at Castlemere, for a start. Now if you can see a tiger lurking out there, that might be worth looking at.'

'But they're so pretty, the deer, and so close. Look how they hold their heads and how delicate those spots are. To have such lovely creatures moving just under your windows for a whole year – oh Archie, you *are* lucky!'

The Marquess of Ross, who liked his grandson but doted on his granddaughter, smiled indulgently. 'Come and sit down while the scout brings in the meal, Lucy,' he said. 'There's little enough room for him to move as it is, until all these boxes are unpacked and out of the way.'

'Scout?' queried Lucy, puzzled.

'The college servants are called scouts,' Archie told her. 'Look, do sit down.'

Lucy shook her head. 'I want to investigate.' Archie had not allowed her to accompany him when he first moved into his rooms earlier that morning. He must have thought that it would be in some way humiliating to have a sister in tow. Perhaps he was not even sure whether he would be allowed to entertain her. Even Archie must

33

sometimes be unsure of himself, in a new place with undiscovered rules. But already he seemed to have recovered his confidence as the master of his new territory. Unlike Lucy herself, who was still being educated at Castlemere by Miss Jarrold, Archie had spent the past five years at Eton, and so must be used to adapting himself to new circumstances and making new friends.

Her investigation did not take long. There were only two rooms in the set. One was small, and bleakly furnished as a bedroom. The other was large by normal standards, if not by those of Castlemere, and hardly seemed furnished at all.

'You'll need more bookcases,' she said, waving one hand at the boxes of books on the floor. 'And a proper carpet. And a less battered table. And some comfortable chairs for your friends. Though the window seats are nice.' She settled herself on one of them, glancing down once more at the deer in the park below and then studying her own reflection in the mirrored side panels of the window recess.

The marquess had arrived at the same conclusion. 'I'll send you down a load of stuff,' he said. 'Don't go buying anything till then. As for you, Miss, what's put this flush in your cheeks? What have you been doing all morning?'

'Going round Oxford with Miss Jarrold, just as you said.'

'Which colleges did you see?'

'I don't remember. Except for New College, because it had such a lovely garden.'

'If you can't remember, then you've wasted the morning.'

'I've made notes for my diary,' Lucy assured him. 'And it wasn't *what* I saw that was exciting. It was the seeing.' Was it possible, she wondered, to explain what she meant

34

to her grandfather without being rude. The marquess was an old man. He had travelled in his youth, but now left Castlemere only rarely, to visit his house in London or shoot on his son's grouse moor in Scotland. It had probably never occurred to him that Lucy might like to have a holiday, to go somewhere – anywhere. To be honest, it had not occurred to Lucy herself until today. But as though she were a different person from yesterday's child in Miss Jarrold's schoolroom, she had suddenly become aware of a world outside, waiting to be explored. Exploring – that was the right word. Moving on without knowing what was coming next. That, in a sense, was what Archie was doing today.

There was a knock at the door. A young man appeared without waiting for any call, hesitated briefly when he saw the family group, but stayed long enough to introduce himself as another freshman on the same staircase and to offer Archie tea later in the day. A second caller, before the first had left, looked hopefully at Archie's wide shoulders and tall, strong body and enquired whether he was interested in college rugger. Yet another unknown visitor, less tentative than the first two, announced that he had Yates, A. down on his list as a wetbob. College tubs, he said, would start at two o'clock on Friday; university rowing trials were on Saturday.

Lucy sighed with envy. All these young men, and the hundreds more who were still settling into their rooms, were waiting to become Archie's friends, if he wanted them. A whole new life, full of new activities, lay before him, while she would have to return to Castlemere with no one to talk to but Miss Jarrold. How lucky Archie was!

It was not in her brother's nature to show excitement. He liked to appear calm and in control of a situation, as though everything that happened was exactly what he had

35

expected. Lucy herself would have been jumping up and down by now with pleasure at the prospect of so many new experiences. Miss Jarrold was continually telling her that she could not be considered a well-brought-up young lady until she had learned to control her emotions and the expression on her face. But Lucy had no intention of spending the rest of her life looking bored. The whole point of growing up would be to get away from Castlemere, which was beautiful and spacious and comfortingly well-ordered but – well, unexciting.

If all went well, her own escape would come in two years' time, when her grandfather had promised to open up his Mayfair house for the whole of the London Season. Her aunt would present her at Court, and for two months she would dance and dine and ride in the park and leave and receive calling cards and change her clothes six times a day.

There was a sense in which all that would be exciting. But although Lucy was not sophisticated enough to be cynical, she knew perfectly well that the whole point of her Season would be to show her off as a marriageable girl. The mothers of various eligible bachelors would weigh her in the social balance, noting her lack of a title and trying to calculate how generous the Marquess of Ross was likely to be to his favourite grandchild when it came to settling a dowry. The marquess, meanwhile, would be making his own stipulations to ensure that Lucy's future station in life would be worthy of her. Only when all these negotiations had been satisfactorily concluded would some young man be allowed to fall in love with her, and Lucy would be told that she might love him back. She would be chaperoned for every moment of the day, and throughout the whole of this period – even if she were enjoying herself – she would be expected to appear cool and calm and hardly interested in what was happening. That could not be thought of as any kind of exploration.

If only she too could come to Oxford and make free-and-easy new friends and learn about subjects which she could not even imagine in her mind, because she had never heard of them. Lucy sighed longingly to herself. But she knew that she was not well enough educated.

Archie himself was not particularly clever. He had come to Oxford because it was the thing to do, and Lucy guessed that he would not spend too much of his time working. But at least he had been well taught at school: he could write verses in Latin and Greek. At the end of his time here he would get a degree of some kind. Lucy, in contrast, had never taken any kind of examination and certainly would not pass one if she tried. She could speak German and French fluently, play the piano adequately and paint watercolours extremely well. But when it came to facts, Miss Jarrold was too often vague, and Lucy lacked any interest in remembering. It was only for a fleeting second that she wondered whether, if she had been someone quite different – someone brilliantly intelligent but still a girl – she would have been allowed to come to Oxford like Archie.

'Are there,' she asked, 'any young women studying here?'

It was an innocent enough question, so the loudness of her brother's reaction startled her. The marquess merely smiled indulgently at her foolishness, but Archie could not control his mirth, laughing as though he would never be able to stop.

'Really, Lucy!' he exclaimed, when at last he could speak. 'What an extraordinary idea! Women at Oxford, indeed!'

Three

Archie Yates had been right to guess that the young woman he glimpsed in The House of Hardie was related to its owner. John Hardie, brushing aside his wife's objection that no one would ever spell or pronounce the name correctly, had christened his only daughter Margaux out of enthusiasm for the magnificent vintage produced at Château Margaux in the year of her birth. But five-year-old Gordon, gazing down for the first time at his baby sister, had exclaimed at her tininess and rechristened her Midge. She had been known by Gordon's choice of name ever since.

At the age of twenty, Midge Hardie supposed that she was as tall as she was ever likely to be: five foot one in her shoes. She would never appear stately. The low-necked velveteen dresses which were the fashion in Oxford in the autumn of 1885, with their sweeping skirts, looked ridiculous on her. But her waist was tiny. Wearing a skirt of a plain, unfussy material and a nipped-in jacket she looked not merely businesslike but smart.

The smartness did not usually extend to her long black hair. However tightly she might strain it off her face and imprison it in the two long plaits which crossed over the top of her head to provide an extra inch of height, one or two curly strands invariably succeeded in escaping, to bounce against her cheeks. So frequently did she use her fingers to comb them back into place that she had ceased to be conscious of the gesture.

Like her brother, Midge was an enthusiast, although

her passion was not, like Gordon's, for the exploration of new territories, but for the exploration of the past. Often it seemed that her slight body, like a bottle of champagne awaiting disgorgement, housed an excess of energy which was liable at any moment to explode. Her physical energy she released twice a week on the hockey field. Her intellectual energy found a more surprising outlet in study. Midge Hardie was a bluestocking.

Like Archie Yates, many undergraduates did not even know that female students existed at Oxford. Elderly dons, who had fought a losing battle to prevent any concessions being made to them, thought them dangerous. Respectable wives and mothers thought them unladylike, and their conventional daughters thought them odd. Only within the past few weeks had permission been granted for them to take the same examinations as men in a limited number of subjects – and Midge knew that however hard-working or brilliant she might prove to be, she would still not be allowed to take a degree.

Nor, naturally, was there any question of her becoming a member of a college. One of her friends, disguising her gender by the use of initials, had a few years earlier entered for a scholarship examination and was placed at the head of the list; but she was not allowed to accept the scholarship. Within the past five years, Somerville Hall and Lady Margaret Hall had been established to provide residence for a few talented daughters of bishops or statesmen, wishing to pursue a course of study; but their teaching had to be organized by a committee devoted to the cause of women's education.

Midge was not a member of either Hall. Because her home was in Oxford it would have been absurd for her to pay residence fees, so she was isolated from the community spirit which developed amongst the two small groups.

But she didn't care. She found the study of history a pleasure in itself, and there was an additional excitement in the feeling that one by one the barriers against women were falling.

On the first Monday of Full Term in October 1885, for example, yet another door had opened to her. Dr Mackenzie, one of the most respected historians in the university, had agreed to supervise her studies. Her weekly hour with him would be called a coaching and not a tutorial, but Midge was not concerned about names. Her acceptance by such an eminent man was a triumph. She had worked her way through the list of books which he had sent her for vacation reading; but that did not prevent her from feeling nervous as well as excited as she stuck in three last hairpins to control her unruly hair, tied on her bonnet and went downstairs.

Mrs Lindsay, one of the chaperones officially provided for the Oxford home students, was already waiting to accompany her. Midge often wondered what the chaperones thought about as they knitted their way through lectures and coachings which appeared not to interest them in the slightest. It made an amusing fantasy to imagine one of them, after several years of silent attendance, suddenly putting her name down for one of the Final Examinations and proving to have absorbed more information than any of her young charges. But it was unlikely to be Mrs Lindsay, plump and gossipy, who would fulfil that particular fantasy. They set off together from the Holywell house for the short journey to Magdalen College.

Midge had already been warned that she and her chaperone must approach Dr Mackenzie's rooms through a side entrance to the college, because the porter would not admit her at the front. Determined not to be late, but equally anxious neither to arrive too early nor to be seen lurking in the cloisters, she alternately hurried her companion up and held her back. So it was precisely as the hour was struck by the bells of half a dozen clocks that she reached Dr Mackenzie's staircase.

She was still studying the names on the boards, to discover where she should go, when a door above closed and a young man, tall and fair-haired, came down the stone steps two at a time. Instinctively Midge pressed herself back against the wall, out of sight. As an accepted pupil, punctually keeping an appointment, she had no reason to feel ashamed of her presence in the college; but it had been continually impressed on her in the past two years that she must deserve each new privilege without ever flaunting it amongst those who still opposed even the most peripheral presence of women in the university. She was not hiding, but nor did she wish to attract attention.

'Phew!' said the young man to himself. It seemed that an ordeal of some kind had just been successfully survived. He tugged off his short commoner's gown and stuffed it under his arm. Some movement of Mrs Lindsay's must have caught his attention, for he glanced briefly at the two women and his eyes flickered with slight surprise at their presence. Surprise, but not interest. Like a young stallion released from its stable he seemed to sniff the air for a moment, testing its possibilities – and then, seeing another young man on the far side of the cloisters, hailed him with a shout and ran to catch him up.

Midge watched him disappear through an arch. He was the most handsome young man she had ever seen in her life. But she did not voice this thought aloud. In teasing arguments with her brother Gordon, she often professed herself unsure whether her chaperone was intended to protect her from the undergraduates or to protect the

41

undergraduates from the dangerous species of female students. But Mrs Lindsay would be quite clear about her duties. Under no circumstances was her charge ever to be alone with any male other than her father and brother, and even while chaperoned she could visit and be visited by only those gentlemen approved by her after proper introduction or authorized by the association to teach her. Even had Mrs Lindsay possessed a sense of humour, this was not a subject on which she could be expected to joke. Already thirty seconds late, Midge subdued the sparkle in her eyes, composed her expression into one of demure intelligence and walked sedately up the fifteen steps which led to Dr Mackenzie's door, ready for her first coaching.

Four
1886

From the beginning of the Michaelmas term until Christmas, and again throughout the Hilary term which began in the January of 1886, Midge Hardie presented herself punctually at the door of Dr Mackenzie's room in Magdalen for her Monday morning coachings. The rapid pace at which she left her home sometimes enveloped her in an atmosphere of rush and impetuosity. But this superficial impression was misleading, for she had a tidy, well-ordered mind and a determined and businesslike character. When she seemed to be hurrying, it was not because there was any danger of her being late, but merely that she could not bear to waste time by strolling.

To arrive too early for an appointment, of course, was equally a waste of time. This thought had fortunately not occurred to her chaperone, Mrs Lindsay, who showed no surprise when, on each Monday morning, she and her charge arrived at Magdalen College five minutes early for Dr Mackenzie's coaching.

Had anyone ever asked Midge the reason why, for this weekly occasion only, she arrived so early that she was forced to wait, shame would have flushed her cheeks. She had by now discovered from her tutor the name of the young man who bounded down the stairs just before her own coaching every Monday, but knew nothing more about him than that. So she could not pretend to admire the brilliance of his mind, the depth of his scholarship. It was humiliating to admit to herself that she was attracted to a stranger only because he was so good-looking, but this was the simple truth. As she stood in an alcove at the foot of the staircase, with her face additionally shaded by the brim of her bonnet, she could feel reasonably sure that Mr Yates would not look in her direction; whilst she herself could gaze admiringly and wish that their paths might cross in some other way, some way which would enable them to become acquainted.

On this March morning of 1886 – the last Monday before the Easter vacation – the sun was shining brightly, making her place of concealment even darker than usual. Outside, in the meadows, daffodils were nodding their heads in bright clusters, whilst a curtain of weeping willows behind them sparkled with the new growth of their branches; but the gloom of the cloistered quadrangle in which she was waiting seemed not to have been disturbed for four hundred years. She exchanged a few words with her chaperone, commenting on this, and then listened with some surprise as the bells of half a dozen nearby colleges and churches chimed the hour, without any sign that Mr Yates's tutorial had come to an end. It was unusual for Dr Mackenzie to overrun his time.

Midge hesitated for a second or two, and then made up her mind. Had she arrived on the stroke of the hour, she could not have known that she was in danger of interrupting a tutorial. If Mr Yates was still there, he would – to judge from his usual look of relief as he emerged – be grateful to see his tutor reminded of the time; and Dr Mackenzie might perhaps effect an introduction.

No, Midge told herself severely. That was too much to expect. But nevertheless she stepped out on to the stairs. 'We don't want to be late,' she said to Mrs Lindsay, and led the way up.

Dr Mackenzie was alone and waiting for her. Was Mr Yates perhaps ill, Midge wondered. But she could not ask this aloud, since her tutor showed no sign that there was anything unusual about his morning's arrangements. Midge sat down, unfolded the sheets of paper on which she had written her weekly essay, and began to read it aloud.

When she first began her studies at the university, she had been alarmed to discover that instead of handing in written work she would be expected to read it out and defend her theories or assertions of fact against the arguments of her tutors. But by now she was accustomed to the system and enjoyed it. On this occasion she had been asked to discuss the causes of the French Revolution and was just approaching her conclusions as to their relative importance when the door burst open.

It was Mr Yates. His face was flushed and his eyes were bloodshot: it was immediately clear that he was suffering from a hangover. Midge, startled by his appearance, checked herself in mid-sentence; whilst Mrs Lindsay, equally surprised – and flustered into the bargain – dropped her ball of white knitting cotton. Dr Mackenzie rose to his feet and bent to pick it up for her.

'I'm sorry,' began Mr Yates, revealing by his breathlessness the haste with which he must have taken the stairs. Dr Mackenzie silenced him with a look and gestured towards a chair in the corner of the room.

'Wait there, if you please,' he said; and then, to Midge, 'Kindly continue.'

Embarrassed and nervous, Midge read on to the end of her essay. Even after she had reached her conclusion, she continued to look down at the papers on her knee.

'I must congratulate you on the excellence of your French accent,' commented Dr Mackenzie.

Midge flushed at the compliment. While she was scattering her essay with liberal quotations from French philosophers and historians she had félt no doubts about her ability to pronounce them, for – like her brother before her – at the age of seventeen she had spent six months in France, at the château of one of her father's suppliers.

'Excuse me just a moment,' said her tutor, and turned his head enquiringly towards the abashed intruder.

'I'm extremely sorry to be so late, Dr Mackenzie. The college won the rugger cuppers on Saturday, and last night – '

The tutor interrupted him. 'I'm aware that Magdalen has had a small sporting triumph,' he said. 'And no one in the college can possibly be ignorant of the fact that the matter was celebrated last night as well as on Saturday. You are not, if I may say so, the only person who went short of sleep. The question of damage to college property is a matter for the Dean. All *I* have to say is that you are not *late* for your tutorial: you have *missed* it. When you throw away an hour of your life, that hour is lost for ever. My time now belongs to someone else, and your behaviour in interrupting us is inexcusable. Good *morning*, Mr Yates.'

Had Midge ever been addressed in such terms, she would have sunk through the floor in shame. But Mr Yates appeared unperturbed as he rose to his feet, bowed politely to his tutor and departed.

Dr Mackenzie's expression of extreme disapproval relaxed into one of amusement. Seeing the surprise in Midge's eyes, he laughed aloud and explained.

'I understand that Mr Yates has some considerable reputation as a sportsman. As well as playing rugger, he rides to hounds and rows, and no doubt will prove himself to be a cricketer next term into the bargain. In the field of scholarship I have few expectations of him, and he himself has even fewer. He will continue to drink too much during his time in residence because for young men of his kind, unfortunately, it is the thing to do. The most I can hope to teach is an occasional fact and a little elementary philosophy – for example, that actions have consequences and, in this case, that time lost can never be regained. He had no right, of course, to rob you of *your* time. Shall we proceed? I would like to discuss first the argument you drew from Rousseau's theory of the general will.'

Midge returned her attention to the matter in hand. When the hour was over, she folded away her essay, but kept in her hand the new sheet on which were listed all the books which she must read during the vacation. There were a great many titles. Because she was studying them as she walked thoughtfully down the staircase, she was startled when a young man who had been sitting on the low wall of the cloister first of all stood up and then prostrated himself at her feet.

'Mr Yates, please! Really, what *are* you doing?' Flustered, she found that her chaperone was too close behind to allow her to step back.

'I'm grovelling at your feet. Surely this isn't the first time that you've been grovelled at.'

Midge bit her lip in an effort to control her smile. He looked too absurd for words. 'Do please get up. Somebody might come.'

'I shan't get up until you forgive me. Naturally I shall have to write an abject apology to my tutor, and my only hope of *his* forgiveness is if I can tell him that I already have yours. It's remarkably dusty down here. It must be three or four centuries since it was last swept. So I hope you won't take too long. I really am most sincerely sorry for my intrusion this morning. It shows what an arrogant beast I am, to think that I must be the Makker's only pupil.'

Midge laughed aloud, and was surprised by the effect of her laughter.

'But I *know* you,' said the undergraduate, scrambling to his feet. 'You all looked so dashed disapproving when I burst in up there that I didn't recognize you beneath the severe expression. But that smile ... You're Miss Hardie, of course.'

'I really think – ' said Mrs Lindsay, preparing to protest against this breach of etiquette; but she was temporarily silenced by the offender's sunny politeness.

'I'm a friend of Miss Hardie's father,' he said, ignoring Midge's disbelieving look. 'My grandfather, the Marquess of Ross, has naturally known him for far longer, but I've had the pleasure of his acquaintance since my arrival in Oxford. Together, naturally, with other members of his family. Are you returning straight home now, Miss Hardie? Perhaps you'll allow me to escort you both there, and to pay my respects to your mother.'

'I'm going to a lecture at Balliol,' Midge said. 'In Mrs Lindsay's company, naturally.'

'Then we could all go together. I'm attending the same course.'

Midge burst out laughing again, with such merriment that the undergraduate looked puzzled whilst Mrs Lindsay showed signs of alarm.

'If you're going to be at the lecture, no doubt we shall see each other there,' Midge said. 'Until then, I'll wish you good morning. You will be leaving your college by the front gate, while we are required to slip out at the side. Shall we go, Mrs Lindsay? Good day, Mr Yates.'

'He should not have behaved in such a manner,' said

Mrs Lindsay, hurrying to keep up with Midge's rapid pace.

'There was no offence in it.'

'Why did you laugh? When he mentioned the lecture.'

'If Mr Yates does attend the lecture today,' said Midge, 'he will enter the Balliol hall through the main door and sit on a bench at one of the dining tables. But you and I, Mrs Lindsay – how shall *we* be expected to approach?'

'Up the winding stair from the Senior Common Room, to sit behind the lecturer at High Table.' Mrs Lindsay had been acting as an official chaperone for women students for five years already, and was well acquainted with all the rules and restrictions imposed by different colleges; she was puzzled only by the purpose of the question.

'Exactly so. And from our seats at High Table we look down into the hall. I know the face of every undergraduate who attends these lectures, and Mr Yates has never been one of them. He doesn't even know where a woman student is expected to sit, or he would have realized at once that I wouldn't believe him. I very strongly suspect that Mr Yates has not attended a single lecture since he came up to Oxford.'

Too late, she realized that her pleasure in the encounter must be increasing her chaperone's doubts about the situation. But it was impossible to conceal her elation. As they approached Balliol, she stroked her hair into tidiness and tugged at her jacket to smooth its line.

Mr Yates, she noticed as soon as she took her seat, had chosen a place at the furthest end of the hall – presumably so that anyone who entered would be found to sit in front of him, and in his view. When he caught sight of her he looked momentarily surprised, and then deliberately stood up and made his way to a place so near to the dais that Midge was bound to see him every time she looked towards the lecturer.

An hour later, as the hall emptied, Midge looked down at the notebook in which, as a rule, she made a précis of what the lecturer said. The page was empty.

Five

On the last day of Archie's Easter vacation, Lucy rose early in order to ride with her brother. Reaching the brow of the hill at the end of their gallop, they reined in their horses and sat for a moment without speaking, looking down at their grandfather's house. Castlemere had been built in the style of a French château. At this early hour of an April morning, the mist which often lay in the valley was especially thick above the moat, so that the four turrets of the great house, with their elegant pointed roofs of grey slate, seemed to be floating above a cloud, like part of a fairy-tale palace. Within the house, Lucy knew, an army of servants would at this moment be busily polishing and scrubbing and blackleading and carrying coals and hot water, but no sound rose to the ears of the two watchers. Only the occasional stamp of their horses' hooves disturbed the silence.

Lucy gave a sigh of contentment. 'Just look at Castlemere,' she said. 'Like a dream, it's so beautiful. Such a *romantic* house.' She looked indignantly at her brother when his only comment was a laugh. 'Don't you agree?'

'I wouldn't call it romantic. Romantic's a girl's word. Of course I agree that it's beautiful. But it won't do for me to think about it too much.'

Lucy nodded, understanding what he meant. Archie had been brought to Castlemere when he was only three years old. It was his home: it was unlikely that he could remember any other, for the house in which he was born had been sold soon after their mother's death. Their father now kept only a set of rooms in London to use on his infrequent leaves, coming to Castlemere as a visitor, a stranger to his son and daughter.

The three sons of the marquess all possessed properties of their own, so Archie had been brought up in his grandfather's house almost as though he were a son and heir. But he was not. It was sensible of him to bear in mind all the time that when the Marquess of Ross died, Castlemere would pass to his eldest son, the present viscount. It was to be hoped that the marquess would make generous provision in his will for the children of the daughter he had loved so dearly and mourned so bitterly, but neither of them would have any right to remain at Castlemere.

Lucy herself, of course, could expect to move to another home on the occasion of her marriage. It might not be as grand or as beautiful as Castlemere, but it would probably be as comfortable. Her brother's future was less predictable. What would he do, she wondered, after he had taken his degree? Or rather, when he had finished his terms at Oxford – because the comments of his tutors, and of the dean of his college, which Archie had recounted with great amusement, did not suggest to Lucy that he was likely to pass any examinations. When he returned to the university later in the day there would be no need for him to pack the books he had brought home for vacation reading, for they had never been unpacked.

It was not the function of a younger sister to badger him back to the grindstone of study. 'How are you going to spend the summer term?' she asked.

'Trinity Term.' Archie made the correction kindly. 'Well, I shall play cricket, of course. And keep up the rowing. Grandfather has promised to bring you up for Eights Week.'

Lucy's face lit up with the excitement of an expedition away from home. 'What is Eights Week?'

'A kind of regatta. All the college boats race against each other. You and Grandfather can sit on the college barge and cheer us on. Anyone who has a pretty sister is expected to produce her for Eights Week, and you'll be the prettiest of the lot. There's much more to it than rowing, of course. All sorts of things go on. Magdalen will have a ball. Bring your most stunning dress.'

'Shall I be your partner?'

'Well, you've heard me talk of Digby, who rows stroke. His sister will be coming as well. So she'll be my partner and you'll be Digby's. But there'll be a whole crowd of us. You won't be stuck with any chap you don't like.'

'Will all the girls be somebody's sister?' Lucy laughed at the idea.

'Well, of course. I mean to say, dash it all: everyone is.'

'But it seems an odd way of finding a partner. Digby has never met me, and I don't suppose you've set eyes on Digby's sister. Don't you meet any girls at Oxford – girls you can get to *know*?'

There was an odd kind of silence. Lucy had been chatting frivolously, not greatly concerned about the answers to her questions. But now it seemed to her that this was a question that Archie would like to answer, if only he could think what he wanted to say. She waited.

'Not the sort of girl to take to a ball,' Archie said. Lucy, who knew her brother well, didn't believe that he was telling the truth. She looked at him sharply but, to prevent her from pressing him further, he dug in his heels and set his horse at the steepest slope of the hill. Lucy followed him, although he might have expected her to descend into the valley by the more gentle gradient of the

53

ride. She had been lifted on to her first pony at the age of three and had never known what it meant to be afraid in the saddle.

Lucy was approaching her seventeenth birthday, but was not yet quite sure what sort of a person she was. When her grandfather treated her like a child, under the care of her governess, she *felt* like a child. But recently the marquess had begun to invite her to act as his hostess when he entertained guests, despite the fact that she was not yet 'out'. And at the moment when she stepped out of her own room and came down the grand curving staircase which was one of the glories of Castlemere, with her hair up and wearing an elegant low-cut dress, she left the child behind her and took on the behaviour of a woman.

Sometimes she wondered whether her character on any day was determined by her clothes. White muslin and a wide-brimmed hat kept her young; velvet and lace transformed her into a society lady. In her riding habit she was something different again – energetic and adventurous; a taller, stronger version of the tomboy she had been as a girl.

There was an alternative possibility. Lucy was quick to admire anyone who was cleverer, more good-looking, braver or simply more interesting than herself; and her admiration expressed itself in emulation. Admiration of her grandfather helped her – sitting at the far end of the long dinner table – to observe the etiquette of the meal, turning her head from left to right and back again as each new course was served, and ready to discuss franchise reform, the Irish question or the progress of General Gordon's expedition. The marquess had taught her how to converse – to be articulate in expressing an opinion and polite in defending it. Naturally, all her opinions were his own.

She admired Archie as well, because he was so sure of himself: so good-looking and so successful at whatever he chose to do. In his company she became young again, anxious to do him credit by looking her prettiest, or determined to keep up with him on the hunting field. Yet even while warming to his approval, she was aware that in living up to his expectations she was again acting a part, adopting his enthusiasms instead of developing her own.

It was a question which sometimes worried her. Without being vain, she knew that she was beautiful, and so felt none of the insecurity which might have affected a plainer or less well-connected girl. Men would fall in love with her. She would marry one of them, and have children. Would she then become only what they expected her to be – a certain kind of wife, a certain kind of mother? Somehow, before that happened, she must try to become an interesting person, and that meant having interests of her own. But her quiet upbringing at Castlemere had given her little idea of what these might be.

For example, she had never travelled anywhere at all except in her grandfather's carriage. She longed to visit strange places, to see magnificent mountains and beautiful rivers and wild forests in foreign countries – or at least, she thought that was what she wanted. But how was it possible to be sure, when arranging even the simplest railway journey to London for herself was outside her experience?

One interest Lucy did acknowledge. She had a talent for water-colouring. Although lacking the wider artist's imagination which would have inspired her to paint on a larger canvas, she could depict whatever was in front of her eyes with meticulous accuracy and genuine artistry. She loved to paint flowers – and that was a genuine love. This afternoon, she promised herself, after Archie had returned to Oxford, she would take her paints into the garden. By focusing all her concentration on a single flower, she would for an hour or two be herself, Lucy Yates, and not somebody else's idea of her.

Six

While Archie Yates was travelling towards Oxford on that last day of his Easter vacation, Gordon Hardie and his father were moving in the opposite direction. The Marquess of Ross had made it known to Mr John Hardie that he wished to make a generous gift of wine to his eldest grandson, Lord Beverley, on the occasion of his forthcoming twenty-first birthday. Mr Hardie's advice on the subject was solicited, and at the same time it was suggested that he might check the cellar books at Castlemere with a view to making good any deficiencies found in the stocks.

Such a service was a routine matter for Mr Hardie, and it had become equally customary for his son to accompany him. One day Gordon himself would be expected to give advice to the aristocratic patrons of The House of Hardie: this was a practical way in which to become familiar with their tastes. In addition, the work was more rapidly accomplished when his father could keep his hands and eyes free to inspect the bins and check the books whilst dictating his comments for Gordon to write down.

Gordon had a particular reason for welcoming the opportunity to visit Castlemere. He waited until the marquess had come to the end of his instructions and was about to dismiss them.

'If I might make so bold, my lord . . . I've been told that Castlemere possesses the finest medieval herb garden in the whole of England.'

'The only one, I wouldn't be surprised. Can't say that I

know much about it myself. Prefer the fruit of the vine to any foul-smelling tisane when it comes to keeping good health, don't you know. Interested in that sort of thing, are you? Have a word with my head gardener, Curtis. He'll tell you where to find it.'

'I'm very much obliged to you.' Gordon ignored his father's frown. Any disapproval which Mr Hardie felt would be caused not by the thought that his son's request was impertinent, but by the reminder that Gordon had not yet outgrown the enthusiasm for unusual plants which he had picked up, like an infectious disease, during his boyish escapade to the South Seas. But no criticisms would be expressed in the presence of either the marquess or his butler, who was ready now to escort them to the cellars.

At half past three in the afternoon Gordon stepped out of the house for a short break in the fresh air. He blinked for a moment in the bright light, and then set off on his private errand. The herb garden, he was told, could be reached by the family directly from the west terrace of the great house, but Gordon was instructed to approach it from the other direction, by crossing the moat and passing through the walled garden in which soft fruit and vegetables were grown.

Knowing that his time was short, he hurried along a path lined with espaliered pears and apples towards the twelve-foot-high stone wall on the further side, patterned with the fan-trained skeletons of peaches and apricots. He pushed open the arched door in the centre of the wall and then was forced to stop. Although he did his best to bring his hurrying pace to an immediate check, he almost knocked over the young woman who was sitting in the path with her back to him. For her part, she was so startled to feel a stranger brush against her shoulder that

58

she jumped to her feet, clutching a box of paints in one hand and a watercolour pad in the other, but dropping her brush and spilling the jar of water she had been using.

Gordon began to stammer his apologies while he was still bending down to retrieve what she had dropped. Only as he straightened himself did he see her face for the first time. Long corn-coloured hair, loosely tied back with a blue ribbon, framed a small face with the delicate pink and white complexion of a china doll. But there was nothing doll-like about her lively blue eyes, and her lips were curved and full of movement. So perfect was her beauty that for a moment he was struck dumb by it. But to remain silent would be impolite. 'Please forgive me,' he said humbly.

The young woman's startled expression melted into a smile. 'It was foolish of me to sit so near the door and in the middle of the path,' she said. 'But the gardeners never come here except with me, so I was not expecting . . .' She paused for the explanation which she had every right to demand.

'I have a particular interest in old species of plants,' Gordon told her. 'His lordship was kind enough to give me permission to inspect the herb garden. But of course I don't wish to intrude on your privacy. If you'll allow me to fetch some water for you, I'll leave you to continue your work.'

'No need. It's finished already.' Now that he had explained his presence, a new warmth came into her smile and her voice was friendly: she held out her water-colour as though to prove that she was telling the truth.

Gordon accepted the invitation to study it. Instead of the general garden view which he would have expected a young lady to attempt, she had depicted a group of crocuses in the bottom left-hand corner of the page, and above them had painted an enlarged and meticulously detailed representation of a single flower and its leaf.

'But it's not completely finished,' he pointed out. 'You haven't signed it.'

'This is not a painting to hang in an exhibition,' she said, laughing. 'There's no need for a signature.'

'Except that it would allow me to know your name.'

She flushed delightfully. 'I'm Lucy Yates.'

It took Gordon only a second to realize that she must be the sister of Archie Yates, whom he had met at The House of Hardie; so the Marquess of Ross would be her grandfather.

Gordon knew that he ought to withdraw at once – but she was clearly waiting for him to complete the introductions.

'My name is Gordon Hardie.' He was anxious that there should be no misunderstanding about his status. 'My father and I are here to advise your grandfather on his cellar.'

Instead of dismissing him, Lucy held out her hand. She was still young, he realized, as he bent over it: society had not yet been given the opportunity to make her haughty.

'Your subject is an unusual one,' he commented.

'This is the saffron crocus,' Lucy told him. 'You can recognize it by the long stigmas. It's the stigmas which are dried to make saffron. To produce one ounce of saffron, more than four thousand flowers are needed.'

'You know a great deal about it, Miss Yates.' Gordon, as it happened, knew even more, but he was nevertheless sincere in his admiration.

'My grandmother loved this garden. She died three years ago, but when I was quite young she taught me to recognize all the herbs and to know their uses. Nowadays saffron is only used in cooking, to add colour. But in the olden days it was a specific for jaundice, and prescribed in cases of measles to speed up the eruptive state. My grandmother kept a book of old receipts. I thought it would be interesting to interleave it with illustrations.'

'Do you know how this crocus came to England?' Gordon asked her. Almost certainly she – like himself as a boy – would have assumed that it was native to the country. As he had expected, she looked puzzled. 'A pilgrim returning from the Holy Land in the reign of Edward II collected some seeds as he travelled through Asia Minor,' he told her. 'Had they been discovered, he would have been killed. So he hollowed out his pilgrim's stave to make a secret place for them. He carried them to his home in Walden, where they grew and multiplied so successfully that it has been known as Saffron Walden ever since.'

The effect of his story was all he could have wished. Lucy's eyes widened with astonishment and regret.

'How exciting it must have been to live in those times,' she sighed. 'If only such adventures were possible nowadays!'

'They're still waiting for anyone who looks for them,' said Gordon. 'I myself, as a boy, ran away to sea and found myself in the company of a man who had achieved just such a triumph – and he is still alive today.'

'You ran away to sea!' Lucy clapped her hands in excitement. 'I thought such things only happened in Mudie's novels. Do tell me how you were able to do it, and where you went.'

Gordon would willingly have recounted the complete day-by-day history of his voyage in order to remain in her company. But the sound of the stable clock striking the hour made him pause. His father would be seriously displeased if he returned to the cellars and found no one waiting to assist him. Reluctantly, he excused himself.

'Like Scheherazade!' exclaimed Lucy. 'You leave me just when I long to hear more. You must promise to return and continue your story.'

'I hope . . . I wish . . .' But Gordon, who a moment earlier had been made boastful by his wish to impress, was suddenly aware that he ought not to be talking to any young lady alone in this way, and especially not to the granddaughter of his patron. Fumbling for words, he apologized both for disturbing her and for leaving her, and backed away.

'Was it interesting?' asked his father, as he relit their lantern.

'Was what interesting?'

Mr Hardie looked at him sharply. 'The herb garden. Wasn't that what you were so anxious to see?'

'Oh yes. Yes. Most unusual.' Only then did Gordon realize that he had not noticed a single flower, with the exception of the saffron crocus which had provided such a perfect introduction to Lucy Yates's interest. 'I'd very much like the chance to inspect it in greater detail. At leisure. Perhaps, when you've prepared your suggestions for the coming-of-age gift, I could carry them here in person instead of entrusting them to the post, and then – ' The enthusiasm in his voice faded away, and he did not finish the suggestion. If he returned to Castlemere without warning, he could not expect a repetition of today's encounter. Lucy Yates would be riding in the park, or paying a call, or playing the piano in the music room. And even were she once again to be found in the herb garden, she was not for him. Gordon shook his head vigorously, like a dog throwing off water, as he tried to free himself from the memory of that young, beautiful face. He opened his book and prepared to set down his father's comments. For the remainder of his time in Castlemere, and during the journey back to Oxford, he did not allow himself to think of Lucy Yates again.

Every night for almost nine years Gordon Hardie had set aside an hour before he went to sleep in which to further his dream of a future in which he was an explorer and not a vintner: this was in addition to the time he spent, whenever he could spare it, assisting in the Oxford Botanic Garden. By now, his knowledge of botany – which neither his school nor his father had thought important – was scholarly as well as practical. He had acquired a shelf of second-hand books on the subject, and every night he committed to memory a page of text and illustration so that later, lying in bed, he could summon the information before his mind's eye.

Tonight's subject was *Abelia chinensis*, of special interest to Gordon because it had been discovered in China, the country which he was determined to visit one day. As he studied its characteristics, he tried to imagine the feeling of Clarke Abel when he first set eyes on the delicate pink and white flowers, as pale and perfect as Lucy Yates's complexion. If Gordon ever met her again, he could recount the story of Abel, who collected thousands of seeds and plants, only to lose almost all of them to shipwreck, fire or pirates; but who nevertheless saved enough to make his journey worth while. Then Gordon would say that he himself hoped to make such a journey one day. Her blue eyes would open wide and she would clasp her hands together with anxiety and excitement.

Gordon closed the book and prepared himself for bed. As he lay in the darkness he set in motion the waking dream with which he brought every day to a close. He was in China, leading the way along a mountain path. Mules and coolies plodded behind him, whilst far ahead the snow-capped peaks of the Himalayas soared above the clouds. In a moment – but he was always asleep before the moment arrived – he would round a bend and see in front of him some flower or shrub or climbing plant that no Englishman had ever seen before. Or even – ever since Sir Desmond had first mentioned it to him, this had become his greatest ambition – the lily which had been glimpsed once, many years ago, by a French missionary in a valley ten thousand feet high, and never found again.

Tonight there was a difference in his waking dream. He was not alone at the head of the column. A woman was walking beside him, as adventurous and resolute as himself: the long blonde hair which blew around her shoulders identified his companion as Lucy Yates. Gordon closed his eyes and dismissed tne dream from his mind. It was, of course, impossible.

Seven

Even Archie Yates, who had little interest in architecture, acknowledged the beauty of Magdalen Tower. Its solid stone walls, pierced parapet and delicate pinnacles stood sentinel at the end of the bridge – not so much guarding the city as welcoming any traveller from the east to the university. The tower was part of his own college: he both took it for granted and felt a possessive pride in it. Once every year, however, it ceased to be merely a landmark. For it was an old Oxford tradition that on May Morning the choristers who more usually provided the music in Magdalen chapel should greet the rising sun by carolling from the top of the college tower. Perhaps equally ancient was the custom that the Magdalen undergraduates should listen to the ceremony from the river at the foot of the tower, first stocking up their punts with picnic breakfasts of a largely liquid variety.

Not often did Archie fail to take advantage of an opportunity to become drunk, but for once he had joined the sober minority. This was to be a respectable social occasion. He had invited Midge Hardie to listen to the singing with him.

Naturally, her mother had to be invited as well, to act as chaperone; but as the last faint, pure notes of the choristers died away and Archie stood up in the punt and prepared to move it away from the congested area of the river, he noticed with satisfaction that Mrs Hardie – no doubt unused to five o'clock awakenings – had fallen asleep.

Smoothly and gracefully Archie pressed the long wooden pole down into the river bed, using it both to propel and to steer the punt. Then, hand over hand, he tossed it neatly up into the air, ready for the next thrust. Not a single drop of water was allowed to splash his white flannels or trickle down towards the cuff of his striped blazer. He was showing off. Midge, sitting on cushions in the shallow boat, knew that as well as he did. She grinned at him teasingly; and Archie, delighted that she should prove as reluctant as himself to awaken her mother by speaking, grinned back.

There was no need to travel far to find a peaceful spot for the picnic, for none of the other May Day revellers had moved away from the foot of the tower. Archie stuck his pole down into the mud near the bank of the Botanic Garden to act as a mooring post and, for safety's sake, tied the other end of the punt to a weeping willow.

'We could walk a little,' he suggested to Midge, standing on the bank after he had made all secure and speaking quietly in order that Mrs Hardie should not be disturbed. 'You must be cold, sitting still on the river for so long.'

'We mustn't go out of my mother's sight.' But even as she spoke, Midge was rising to her feet and holding out both hands towards his own so that he could help her on to the bank. Her spring was light and athletic and she needed no help in regaining her balance. Archie, nevertheless, continued to hold her hands for a few seconds until, with her mouth twitching in a smile, she disengaged them.

Side by side they walked to and fro along a short section of the river bank, glancing towards Mrs Hardie each time they passed the punt, so that she should not be alarmed for long if she woke to find herself alone. The grass was wet with the early-morning dew, so Midge lifted the skirts of her Liberty gown an inch or two off the ground to keep it dry. The movement enabled Archie to see and approve of the smallness of her feet and ankles. But he knew better than to remark on them.

'What made you choose to become a student here?' he asked. 'Since I first made your acquaintance, I've enquired amongst my friends and learned that there are more young women studying for examinations at Oxford than I'd realized. But most of them seem to be the daughters of clergymen, and – '

'And you think that a vintner's daughter shouldn't presume to be of such company?'

'Of course not. Nothing of the sort. Only perhaps that in your case it mightn't be your father who pressed you to extend your studies. It must have been your own choice.'

'Indeed it was.'

'Then I repeat my question. Why?'

'Wouldn't it be enough for me to say, when speaking to a scholar such as yourself, that the fascination of exploring history – '

'You mustn't tease me, Miss Hardie,' protested Archie. 'It's unfair, when chivalry prevents me from teasing you back – even if I could find any ground on which to attack. I'm sure Dr Mackenzie has made my lack of scholarship very clear to you. And in any case, you might more pleasantly have explored the subject without the stress of submitting yourself to examinations.'

'The examinations are the important ingredient,' Midge told him. 'The only way in which I shall be able to prove that my education must be held in as much respect as yours.'

'Prove it to whom? No gentleman is likely to pause before choosing a wife in order to enquire as to her marks in the Final Examinations.'

'Not every young woman, Mr Yates, has the good fortune to be "chosen".'

The emphasis which his companion placed on this last word was puzzling to Archie, suggesting that she in some way disapproved of the normal system by which marriage was proposed and accepted. 'Someone so attractive,' he began, but was forced to bring both speech and perambulation to a halt when Midge stopped and turned to face him. Her dark eyes were still bright, but now it was with earnestness rather than teasing.

'You didn't think I was fishing for your compliments, I hope,' she exclaimed. 'I wasn't thinking solely of myself then, but of all the young women . . . A gentleman as fortunate as yourself, Mr Yates, can have little idea how many girls sacrifice the years of their youth and beauty to take care of a parent and find themselves penniless and alone in the world when they are past the age to be attractive to anyone. I'm not talking of the rich or the poor, but of women who have enjoyed a comfortable upbringing and believed themselves secure. Almost the only position open to them is that of governess – and although they may succeed in finding employment, all too often they're incapable of carrying out their duties satisfactorily, because their own education has been so inadequate.'

'Dash it all, you're surely not suggesting that the lecture halls of Oxford should be overrun by governesses.'

Midge laughed, her momentary seriousness forgotten. 'Indeed no. For a single spoiled child in some wealthy family to receive the benefit of so much learning – but only in a single subject – would be a waste of resources and the cause of a most unbalanced education. What the future governesses need is an all-round education – the same kind of education that you yourself must have enjoyed at school.'

'So you've answered my question at last!' exclaimed Archie. 'You propose to be a schoolmistress! You will educate governesses, who will educate more governesses, who – '

'Now you're teasing me.' Midge's eyes sparkled with merriment. 'Let me ask you this. You have a sister, perhaps. Or let us come closer to home and say that one day you may have a daughter, for whose education you will be responsible. Will you think it right to place your daughter in the hands of someone more ignorant than yourself?'

'We won't discuss the question of whether it's possible for anyone to be more ignorant than myself.' Archie matched Midge's grin with his own. 'And we won't talk about my non-existent daughter. I have an actual sister, who has indeed been educated by a governess. She has lived comfortably at home while I have been imprisoned at Eton – and treated caringly while I went in fear of beatings. While I have had my face pressed into the mud of a playing field by the weight of bodies on top of me, she has been taken for delightful country walks in order to appreciate the beauty of the countryside. She has been able to ride every morning of her life, instead of only during the vacations. And she has been allowed to sit and paint to her heart's content, whilst I have been forced to waste the best years of my life on the study of Latin and Greek. She is a most fortunate young woman, and if I ever have a daughter, I trust that I shall be able to offer her as happy a childhood.' This, for Archie, was a long speech. He laughed at himself deprecatingly as he brought it to an end.

His companion was smiling as well, and yet not surrendering her argument. 'But suppose that your sister's passion had been not for painting but for Greek. Would her governess have been able to complete her education in such a subject?'

'You stretch the imagination too far, Miss Hardie.' The thought of Lucy requesting an opportunity to compose Greek verse was so far-fetched as to be laughable. 'You're coming dangerously near to the suggestion that girls should be educated in the same manner as boys!'

'But why – ?' The argument might well have continued vigorously for some time, had not a slight disturbance of the backwater's calm surface suggested that Mrs Hardie was stirring. Archie, noticing this, put a hand up to his companion's elbow to turn her back towards the punt before her absence was noticed.

It was astonishing that such a light touch could have so violent an effect on him. He had enjoyed looking at Midge as she sat in the punt, and the clasp of her hand as she jumped from it had briefly disturbed him. It had given him pleasure to elicit her flashing smile, and the earnestness of her conversation amused him. But this simple gesture of caution and convention seemed to move the two of them out of mere acquaintanceship and into some more intense relationship. He was, after all, touching only the sleeve of her dress, and yet that was enough to flood his body with the desire to take her into his arms. Convention controlled his behaviour; but as he followed her back towards the punt, assuring Mrs Hardie that she had slept for only a few seconds and handing the ingredients of the picnic breakfast for Midge to lay out, his imagination was exploring the social possibilities of the term.

He would like to see her in a ball dress. How slim and white her bare arms would be! How straight she would hold herself, allowing a *décolleté* bodice to show her neck and shoulders to advantage. If she were to be his partner, he could legitimately take her hand, turn her into his arms, place his own hand lightly on her back, hold her closer as they spun round the floor in a waltz or a reel. If only . . .

But there was no point in thinking along such lines. He had already promised his sister that he would take her to Magdalen's Eights Week Ball. Sternly he dismissed his imaginings. It must be enough to enjoy the pleasures of the day. With a practised hand, he sent the first champagne cork flying into the air.

Eight

Nothing like Eights Week in Oxford had ever happened to Lucy before. Suddenly grown up, she floated round the city on a cloud of delight. It was not merely her own self-confidence which told her that she had emerged at last from the schoolroom, but the manner in which everyone treated her. True, she was still required to be accompanied everywhere by Miss Jarrold, but that was only because she had no mother. Miss Jarrold herself instinctively recognized a difference in her role, transforming herself from a governess into a companion during the course of the journey from Castlemere.

Magdalen was to hold its ball on the Thursday of Eights Week, and Lucy had not allowed Archie to forget his promise to invite her. Her grandfather, who proposed to go with her to Oxford, had in good time given her a generous present of money to be spent on new clothes, telling her gruffly that she was to be a credit to her brother and hang the expense. So on this calm, warm June night of the ball she had put up her golden hair and worn her golden dress and had been the prettiest girl at the dance. All her partners had told her so – and even if they had not, Lucy, without being vain, knew it to be true. Archie had made sure in advance that his friends would fill her programme, but there was no need for his solicitude; from the moment of her first appearance she had been surrounded by young men begging for a dance.

The next morning, even before she was awake, flowers began to arrive at the hotel, with messages begging her to visit one or other of her partners for morning coffee, luncheon, afternoon tea, a walk, dinner – anything for which she could spare the time.

'Turn 'em all down,' growled the marquess. 'Archie's got everything fixed.'

Lucy accepted his instructions, secretly glad that her new-found social confidence was not to be tested by private conversation. It was almost excitement enough to be staying in an hotel for the first time in her life. And in any case she had already discovered that she would meet most of her new swains again down by the river. For while the ball had provided the high point of Lucy's week, Archie's enthusiasm was concentrated on the rowing which provided the *raison d'être* of the whole week's social activity.

He had taken pains to explain the system to his sister, so that she should not embarrass him by asking the wrong questions out of ignorance. The river, he told her, was not wide enough for the boats manned by the various colleges to race side by side. So instead they were split up into Divisions, racing at intervals, and within each Division the starting point of each boat was a fixed distance behind the one in front. If it succeeded in overtaking before the finishing line was reached, then the next day it would start the race in the higher position.

'It's called bumping,' he told her. 'But of course there's no need actually to bump. Just to catch up.'

'Has Magdalen bumped?' asked Lucy. It was a tactful question.

'Every day so far this week. If we can keep it up, we shall go Head of the River on Saturday. You'll come and watch, of course. The college has a barge. Not what you'd think of as a barge. A kind of floating grandstand. You can watch the races from the top and then go down for tea and ices.'

It was something else to which Lucy could look forward. On Saturday afternoon, wearing another new dress – this time of white muslin embroidered with yellow buttercups – and carrying a matching parasol, she saw with pleasure that the top viewing deck of the barge was already crowded with the young men who had danced with her at the ball, today wearing blazers and boaters. They pressed around her, delighted when she remembered their names, and repeated all the explanations of the day's events which Archie had already given her.

The marquess, leaving her in her brother's care, went off to the Christ Church barge to meet his own friends and cheer on his own Eight. Miss Jarrold hovered unobtrusively in the background, not needed until it was time for Archie to change into his rowing clothes. Lucy tried to take an interest in the racing, but found that there was little to see. Most of the bumps, if there were any, took place out of sight, long before the boats rounded the bend and approached the finishing line. The intervals between the races were long, and it was too early yet for tea.

It was while she was staring across the river, waiting for something to happen, that her eye was caught by a face amongst the crowds thronging the towpath. So loudly did her heart start to beat that she felt sure her brother must hear it. From the first moment of her arrival in Oxford, she had been hoping for some chance encounter with the young man who had intruded on her in the herb garden at Castlemere two months earlier. He had returned three days after that to continue their conversation, as though he had been aware of the invitation which she knew she must not put into words; but then had taken his leave in a manner suggesting that they could not expect to meet again.

During the past two days, as she loitered along Oxford's High Street on the excuse of looking at the shops, she had lingered as long as she dared near the bow windows of The House of Hardie, hoping that at any moment Gordon Hardie might emerge on some errand and catch sight of her. She wanted him to know that she was in the same city; nothing more. But she had not succeeded in glimpsing him – until now. 'Could we walk for a little?' she asked her brother, disguising her eagerness with a pretence of nonchalance. 'Over there, on the other bank?'

Archie looked briefly doubtful. 'They're mostly town people there,' he said. 'But if you like.' He helped her down the steps and offered his arm. Together they crossed Folly Bridge and began to stroll along the towpath.

Strolling, rather than brisk walking, was the general activity on this hot summer day, so Lucy had been right to suppose that the couple she had seen walking away would before too long retrace their steps towards the bridge. She felt her cheeks flushing as she straightened her back and twirled her parasol and chatted to her brother with even more than her usual animation. She was not precisely flirting – indeed, she could not have explained to herself what her true motive was. She merely wanted – yes, that was it: she wanted Mr Gordon Hardie to reflect as he passed her that although his companion was good-looking in her way, Miss Lucy Yates was prettier.

No sooner had Lucy formulated the thought than she was ashamed of it. There was still time to turn back. Although she could identify the approaching couple by the thin red stripes on the dress which she had noted from the opposite bank, neither of them would be expecting to see her here and only one of them would recognize her. But even as she turned to Archie, ready to suggest a return, he came to a halt of his own accord. Not, however, in order to retreat. Instead, to Lucy's amazement, he was smiling, raising his boater, holding out a hand.

'Miss Hardie! How frightfully delightful to see you. You've come to cheer Magdalen on, I hope. For the sake of your weekly coachings.' His acknowledgement of Gordon Hardie's presence was less effusive, suggesting to Lucy that the two men had come across each other only in the way of business; but he performed all the necessary introductions politely and seemed not to notice that his sister and Mr Hardie, while not admitting that they were already acquainted, were careful to avoid any form of words which might make this appear to be a first meeting. The radiance of Lucy's smile must have prompted Archie towards his next remark.

'You must come on to the barge and watch the First Division,' he said to the brother and sister. 'Keep Lucy company while I'm rowing.'

'You're in the first boat in your freshman year!' Midge's voice was admiring, as no doubt Archie had hoped it would be; but the twinkle in her dark eyes suggested to Lucy that she was amused by his wish to impress her. Now that Midge's relationship to Gordon had been revealed, Lucy was prepared to like her immensely and to recognize the attractiveness of her vivacious features.

As propriety demanded, Lucy conversed chiefly with Midge during the half hour in which the four of them took tea together. But as the time approached for the last race, Archie disappeared to change and row down to the stake post from which the Magdalen boat would start, while Midge laughingly accepted the suggestion that she should

76

find a place against the railing, since her lack of inches would make it impossible for her to see over the heads of the other Magdalen supporters. Miss Jarrold, not wishing to push herself forward, remained at the back of the barge. In the middle of the crush Lucy and Gordon, although enjoying no privacy, were able to hold a private conversation.

'I've thought so much about what you told me,' Lucy confessed. 'About your wish to travel in China and Tibet, and your hopes of finding new plants to bring to England.'

'I was rash to do so. My own family has no idea yet of my hopes. You'll be discreet, I trust.'

'Oh, of course. And I've been trying to learn . . . I told my governess that we should study more geography together, because I'm so very ignorant of the countries of the world. I can recite their capitals and climates and principal rivers, but really I know nothing of importance about foreign parts. We began our studies with China. Well, not studies as Archie would think of it, because I'm too old to sit with a governess now. But Miss Jarrold has found books for me to read, and we talk about them together. And in history I have been learning about Marco Polo, because you made his life sound so interesting. Are you laughing at me, Mr Hardie?'

'I'm overwhelmed with delight at your interest. I'm wondering whether anyone would notice if I were to kiss your hand in homage. And I'm observing that you are, if possible, more beautiful when you blush than when you are pale.'

Lucy's flush deepened with the observation, and she was glad when the sound of a starting pistol allowed her the opportunity to free her hand. 'We must see what happens!' she exclaimed. 'Archie would never forgive us if we had to ask.'

There was a long pause before the first slim boat

appeared round the bend, closely followed by a second. The rowers strained, the coxes shouted, and the cheers of the spectators rose to form a single roar. As though Archie had arranged the matter especially to impress his sister – and Midge Hardie – the Magdalen boat caught up with the leader immediately in front of the barge, and only a few feet away from the finishing line.

From the upper deck of the Magdalen barge came an explosion of cheering and flying straw hats. Lucy, jumping up and down in delight, found that for some reason she was holding both Mr Gordon Hardie's hands. Luckily no one could possibly notice – least of all Midge, who was staring down at the victorious crew. After a moment in which the rowers had slumped over their oars in exhaustion, they were now joining in the general jubilation before paddling gently towards the boathouse.

In order to free herself unobtrusively, Lucy used the excuse of joining Midge at the rail, but her feelings were still very near the surface. In a curious way she found herself looking at Archie through the other woman's eyes. How strong he was, and how handsome! Now, when she thought that nobody was noticing, the teasing amusement had disappeared from Midge's expression. Lucy was able to interpret the look which had replaced it, because she knew that very much the same light must be shining in her own eyes – although with a different object. She assured herself that it reflected merely a natural admiration; nothing more. But in her heart she recognized that both for Midge and for herself, the emotion was something deeper than that.

Nine

Two days after her chance encounter with Archie Yates on the towpath, Midge received a letter from him. To celebrate its success during Eights Week, Magdalen was to hold a second dance – a Head of the River Ball – on the last night of term. Archie would esteem it an honour if Miss Hardie would consent to be his partner for the occasion.

Midge made no immediate comment on the letter, but as she passed it across the breakfast table for her mother to read, the corners of her mouth twitched with pleasure. Naturally she had known for some weeks before it took place that Magdalen – like many other colleges – would have an Eights Week Ball: and after the pleasant May Morning picnic she had enjoyed with Archie had secretly hoped that he might invite her to it. It had come as some consolation to discover that it was his sister whom he had taken instead, but a trace of her disappointment still lingered.

This second event, although necessarily arranged at short notice, was likely to be a far more memorable occasion. Every college in Oxford held a ball during Eights Week, but only one college each year was in addition entitled to celebrate success in winning the regatta and going Head of the River.

'Mr Yates,' Midge reminded her mother, 'is a member of the winning crew. As his partner I shall shine in reflected glory.' She laughed at herself, but took it for granted that she would go. If her brother had been present he would have teased, and her father would have frowned doubtfully. But Gordon had already left for work, and Mr Hardie was spending the month at his London establishment. Midge herself saw no problem in consorting socially with one of her father's customers. She was not being invited as John Hardie's daughter, but as a fellow-student of Archie Yates: a friend in her own right.

Mrs Hardie read the invitation carefully. She had, of course, met Archie on May Day: but this second invitation – and such an important one – prompted her to ask further questions about him. Midge answered willingly, knowing that her mother would neither jump to instant – and erroneous – conclusions about a possible romance, nor express doubts about a friendship with the grandson of a marquess solely on the grounds of any class barrier.

Mrs Hardie was a practical, sensible woman. She dressed smartly without being ostentatiously fashionable and still wore her hair in the neat bun which had been in vogue twenty years earlier. Like her daughter she was small and trim in figure, but her nature was calm where Midge's was impulsive.

She ran her household efficiently and might well have proved herself as successful in business as her husband had the need ever arisen. Her daughter's wish to study as an undergraduate naturally startled her at first; but, accepting it, she had ever since loyally defended Midge against the whisperings of more conventional mothers and daughters.

She accepted without argument now Midge's explanation of her first acquaintance and developing friendship with Archie: that they were both pupils of Dr Mackenzie. It was not to be expected that she should completely understand a relationship between two undergraduates, when the entry of young women into this society was so recent. 'Have you something suitable to wear?' she asked.

'The red silk?' suggested Midge.

'White would be more suitable.'

'But I look insipid in white.' Although Midge's hair was so dark, her complexion was milky white. From the moment when she was first allowed to choose her own clothes, she had picked colours which were either striking or severe; mere prettiness was not her style. The discussion became one of dressmakers and dates – for there was very little time. Midge interrupted it by laughing aloud.

'I was trying to imagine myself dancing with Mr Yates,' she explained. 'What a ludicrous couple we shall make. He must be six foot at the very least. He will look so immensely elegant in his tails – and I shall be this tiny creature at his knees. He'll look right over my head and hardly know that I'm there at all. Really, it's not of the slightest importance how I dress – and if I talk about it any longer, I shall be late for my coaching.' She had never mentioned to her mother – and did not do so now – that one reward for her Monday morning punctuality was a brief meeting with Archie Yates each week.

The night of the ball arrived, and Midge, chaperoned by her mother, stepped into a different world. She had lived in Oxford all her life and knew every street and the outside of every building in the city. It was probably the delight she took in walking between high medieval walls – and on cobblestones which through the centuries had been trodden by so many students before her – that had first aroused her interest in history. During the past two years, allowed for the first time into some of the colleges, she had obtained her first glimpse of the academic world of the university. But the privileged life of the undergraduates remained a closed book to her. She often heard from her father of the damage they did in the course of their drunken revels, but was never on the streets to witness these herself.

Now, suddenly, she found herself part of this other life – even though it might be only for a single night – and the beauty of it snatched her breath away. The paths through Magdalen's old cloisters and gardens were lined with coloured lanterns, whilst torches flared on the river banks and in the deer park, and candles flickered on stone parapets. There was one marquee for dancing and another for supper, but the night was so warm that it was as pleasant to stroll in the grounds as to dance. All the chaperones seemed sensibly to have decided that they could not be continually jumping up to pace behind their charges, and remained clustered in the main marquee. So as Midge and her partner danced or walked, she felt no restriction on her conversation – except what was imposed by Archie's choice of topics.

He had no true interest in history, although he disguised this by laughing off the subject as one for working hours and not for relaxation. He did not read novels or poetry or even biography, and so could volunteer no opinion on the latest publications. When she enquired about his plans for the future, he supposed briefly that he would follow his father into the army – assuming that his grandfather would settle an allowance on him, since a fellow could not be expected to live on his pay. The prospect was still too remote for him to give it much attention. Instead of discussing it further, he asked Midge so many questions about her family, her years at the Oxford High School, and her way of life now, that she felt almost as though she were the native of some newly-discovered country under interrogation by the explorer who had stumbled upon her habitat.

'I like to hear you talk,' said Archie when she tried

once more to escape from the subject of herself. His own enthusiasms were for games and horses, rowing and shooting – subjects about which Midge knew nothing. He lacked the fluency needed to describe what it was about these activities which made them so engrossing, and recognized this by merely stating his recreations and then brushing them aside as unworthy of further discussion. There was a moment, as they strolled in silence along the river walk, enjoying the rippled reflection of the moon, when Midge felt uneasy at the thought that they had so little in common. She was not well acquainted with many young men. Only with her brother was she accustomed to converse easily, and his enthusiasms, although different from her own, were as intense as articulately expressed – but perhaps, she told herself, brothers were always less inhibited.

Certainly Archie appeared not to be embarrassed by the silence – and when he broke it, it was with a suggestion which illogically banished Midge's doubts.

'Although the Long Vacation begins tomorrow, there's no need for me to return to Castlemere immediately,' he said. 'I could stay up for a few days – a week or two. If I could hope for your company, I'd certainly do that. You'll be tired tomorrow, after the ball, I expect. But the next day, if the weather holds, we could take a picnic to Nuneham in one of the college boats.'

'That would be delightful. I'll ask my mother, and – '

'Dash it all, you don't need to trouble her again, do you?'

'I'm afraid – ' Midge paused doubtfully. The chaperones paid by the Association which supervised the Oxford home students were provided for academic purposes only. Once the vacation began, she would have to rely on her family.

'I mean that you don't need to be chaperoned at all,' Archie suggested. 'Your mother, I take it, doesn't accompany you every time you walk to the shops in Oxford. The river is a very public place – and a small boat enforces decorous behaviour if it's not to capsize.'

There are backwaters, thought Midge to herself, but to say that aloud would suggest that she did not trust Archie. 'The rules of the Association are very strict,' she reminded him instead.

'But presumably apply only during the term. Still, if the idea doesn't appeal – '

'Oh, but it does!' The thought that he might withdraw his invitation was unbearable. Midge realized that she would be risking her reputation if she were to accept. But she reminded herself at the same time that in choosing to become a student she had turned her back on the over-protected life that most of her friends, moving from a father's house to that of a husband, would lead. She had determined that when she completed her own education she would use it to help other girls towards independence. Why should she not start now by taking responsibility for her own behaviour? She would come to no harm in Archie's company – and if all she had to evade was gossip, a good deal could be accomplished by wearing a wide-brimmed hat and keeping her head down until the boat was out of sight of Magdalen Bridge. 'I should love to picnic with you,' she said.

The days which followed were full of delights and deceptions. Midge and Archie did not stray far from the two rivers by which Oxford was almost surrounded. Sometimes they went out in a punt or rowing boat, sometimes they walked along the towpaths, and sometimes, as the July air became heavy with heat, they sat side by side in the shade of a weeping willow on the bank, cooled by the movement of the swirling water.

It was the River Cherwell which was in the end Midge's undoing. At the end of a long walk across the water meadows, she was standing with Archie in the centre of a small bridge, looking down at the ducks, when a large punt, laden with a family party, slid silently out from below. Midge was still looking down when one of the occupants looked up. It was the president of the Association whose rules governed Midge's life as a student.

Realizing at once that she had been recognized, Midge kept her head. Instead of attempting to dart out of sight, she smiled down with a calmness that she certainly did not feel. Only when the punt had disappeared round a bend in the river did she explain rapidly to Archie what had happened.

'It's very likely that she'll make a call on my mother,' she said. 'Making some other excuse for it, no doubt, but intending to find out whose company I was in.'

'What business is it of hers, interfering old hen?' growled Archie.

It was too complicated to explain to him the strictness of the rules by which she was bound. No doubt Magdalen had its own code which its members were supposed to obey, but when an undergraduate was caught climbing over the college wall long after the gate was closed, or behaving rowdily or drunkenly in the street, the penalty was nothing more serious than a fine. Midge, by contrast, knew that she could be prevented from completing her studies if her behaviour was known to be open to criticism. She set off at a brisk pace along the towpath which led towards the city.

Archie's long legs made it easy for him to catch up with her. He took hold of a hand to tug her to a halt. 'My grandfather has written to summon me back to Castle-mere,' he said. 'I'm afraid we shan't see each other until next term. Shall you miss me?'

'Of course I shall. You won't forget me, will you?'

'How could I?' Without warning, Archie pulled her closer and kissed her, almost lifting her off her feet. It was a clumsy kiss, the gesture of an inexperienced young man – but Midge was even less experienced, for she had never been kissed before. There was a moment in which she was dazed with delight: Archie had time to embrace her again. Only then did she look around anxiously to reassure herself that they had not been observed.

'Until October then,' she said. Using all the speed that she was accustomed to show on the hockey field, she picked up her skirts and ran.

Ten

Midge went straight to The House of Hardie, relieved to remember that her father would still be in London. 'Will you walk with me for a few moments?' she asked her brother breathlessly.

Gordon looked surprised, but proved willing to stretch his legs after a long spell at his desk. 'What are you looking so flustered about?' he asked.

'If Mrs Johnson should happen to call on Mother at home and should ask what I was doing this afternoon, may I say that I was with you?'

Gordon stood still and looked seriously at his sister. 'And where *were* you?'

Half defiant and half ashamed, Midge told him, confessing the name of her companion and the circumstances of her discovery.

'And suppose that Mrs Johnson were to catch a glimpse of me as she leaves the house – or even to study the family photographs on the piano? She would soon realize that the blond Mr Yates was not your black-haired brother.'

'But you could have been with us. Standing a foot or two away, by the other balustrade of the bridge. She wouldn't have been able to see from the river whether there was anyone there. And there could be no harm in my being with Mr Yates as long as some third person was with us.'

'It's not like you to tell lies, Midge.'

Midge flushed at the well-deserved reproof. She had learned her lesson already and had no intention of misleading her mother again. But that resolve was for the future. Her need now was more immediate.

'As for your choice of companion – ' Gordon, it seemed, was in a preaching mood. 'What can you possibly see in someone like Mr Yates?'

'He's very good-looking.'

'You've never been the fluttery sort of girl to be swept off your feet by that sort of thing, thank goodness. You've got brains. You must realize that he's stupid.'

Midge's flush deepened. Gordon might be her elder brother, but that did not entitle him to take such an advantage of her need for help. 'Even the least fluttery kind of girl likes to be admired,' she said with spirit. 'And an ability to pass examinations is not one which inspires much admiration amongst young men. When someone like Mr Yates . . . He's not just handsome, Gordon. He's so *good* at everything. Playing games, and rowing, that kind of thing. He'll be captain of rowing next year. Everyone in his college has such respect for him. Any girl in England would have felt honoured to be invited by him to a ball, and – '

'And he chose you. So you are flattered, and you've let the flattery go to your head.'

Midge stamped her foot with the exasperation of not being able to quarrel with her brother lest he should refuse her request. 'Haven't you ever been in love?' she cried.

Gordon's expressive eyes looked at first surprised by what her question revealed, and then interested as he searched his mind for an answer to it. 'No,' he said at last.

It was Midge's turn now to be surprised. 'But you must have met beautiful girls, fascinating girls.'

'Beautiful girls, yes, one or two.' He allowed himself a

moment to think about them. 'And naturally they arouse my admiration. A wish to be in their company. But – ' He was paying her the compliment of talking seriously, Midge realized, and she listened with interest. 'I've no intention of marrying for a good many years yet. To fall in love now, when nothing could come of it, would be a waste of emotion. When the time comes, I shall choose someone who would make a good wife and then fall in love with her.'

Midge looked suspiciously at her brother – wondering whether, as usual, he was teasing her. But for once he appeared to be speaking seriously. 'That's not how things happen,' she said. 'People fall in love because they find someone attractive – beautiful or handsome or kind. There's a feeling – you *must* know it, Gordon – that someone is special. The person you've been waiting for. The one person in the world that you want to spend your life with. And if that one person feels the same about you . . . *That's* the way things happen.'

'You may be right to some extent. About the feelings, I mean. Perhaps a first reaction can't be completely controlled. But you can check your emotions before they become too deep. To allow an infatuation to rule your life can't be right. It's only in books – the sort of books that I thought you despised – that two people who've been swept off their feet by outward appearances can spend the rest of their lives together without becoming bored. Just imagine yourself facing Archie Yates over the breakfast table every day for the next fifty years. What would you ever find to talk about?'

'There's more to marriage than just conversation.'

'Of course there is,' Gordon agreed. 'But it's through conversation that you can discover shared interests. What have you and Mr Yates got in common, Midge? You're worth a dozen of him, and you ought to know it. Besides, I don't think that my attitude to choosing a wife is as unusual as all that. Take the young gentleman we've just been discussing.' The two of them had been standing still outside the University Church for the past few moments, but now walked on at a slow pace towards Carfax. 'Mr Archie Yates will have no thought of marriage in his head now, at the age of twenty. When he does begin to entertain such thoughts, he'll look for a wife amongst the families of his grandfather's friends. That's not to belittle any feelings which he may have for you. It's a statement of fact – of what is certain to happen.'

'I don't – '

Gordon waved aside her attempt to interrupt and continued with his argument. 'The aristocracy brings its children up to study form and pedigree before they buy or back a horse,' he pointed out. 'And having discovered the system to be successful in the equine field, they apply it to human relationships as well. Mr Yates may not be an aristocrat in the sense of owning a title or a fortune or great estates, but his grandfather will have brought him up to pay attention to breeding.'

'Breeding has nothing to do with worth,' said Midge, a trace of defiance in her voice.

'Of course it hasn't, any more than what we may deserve has anything to do with the rewards we earn. But that won't make any difference. I deal with these people all the time, Midge. They're affable to me, and some of them genuinely regard Father as a friend. But they live in a different world from us, and when it comes to marriage, they close the gates. Don't fall in love with him, Midge. Nothing can come of it.'

There was a long silence as Midge considered what he had said. Until that afternoon the thought of marriage to

Archie had not entered her head. She had mapped out for herself two years earlier the kind of life that she hoped and expected to lead. It was to be a useful life – a life of service to her fellow-women. Even the admiration she felt for Archie's good looks and – for Gordon was right about this – the flattery of being picked out by an undergraduate so eminent in his year, even this had not affected the way she saw her future. But he had kissed her, and now everything was different.

The memory of that kiss was enough to make her body flush with heat and at the same time shiver with cold, as though she had a fever. It had told her that she was in love with Archie. And at the same time it had signified that he was in love with her – inexperienced though she might be in her relationships with young men, she was sure of that.

Equally important was the fact that she had accepted his kiss without any reaction of displeasure. Midge's pedigree might not seem impressive to someone like the Marquess of Ross, but her upbringing had been strict. Her mother had made it clear that she should never allow herself to be kissed until she was engaged to be married – indeed, that a kiss was in itself almost a token of such an engagement. It would be ridiculous to suppose that Archie had meant the gesture to hold such importance, but that was the only way in which Midge herself had been able to accept it.

Even had she been sure of her own feelings, she would not have confessed them to Gordon. It was a deeply confused young woman who held her head and chin high as she tried to defend a position which her own mind had already deserted. 'Can't you believe that a young man and a young woman may enjoy a friendship which has nothing to do with the possibility of marriage?'

'To tell you the truth, no, I can't believe it,' said Gordon. 'But because you are such an unusual young woman – and because I for one take such pleasure in your conversation – I'll stretch my imagination to allow that you may have the talent for such a friendship. Only, though, with a man intelligent enough to appreciate *your* intelligence. Mr Yates is not that man. And although you're talking of friendship, I suspect you're still thinking of love. You're bringing certain disappointment on yourself, Midge.'

'You're talking to me as though you were Father.'

Gordon grinned, laughing away the seriousness of their conversation. 'That's because I'm agreeing to be your fellow-conspirator, so that Father will never have the opportunity to say it all himself. I see now why you brought me out here to walk, instead of sitting down to talk in the office. Well, if you stretch the distance and direction and time of our walk when you describe it, I won't say anything to discredit you. As long as you can promise me that there was no impropriety.'

For a second time Midge remembered the moment when Archie had kissed her. Nothing could have been less proper. But she had confessed enough to Gordon already, and was in no mood to provoke another lecture. 'Of course,' she said.

Eleven

More than she expected or thought wise, Midge missed Archie's company during the long summer vacation when he was at home in Castlemere and she remained in Oxford. So when the new university year began in October, she resolved to restrain her feelings. Whilst still looking forward to their weekly encounters outside Dr Mackenzie's door, and accepting Archie's invitations to any social event at which other people would be present, she took care not to await his notes too anxiously to feel disconsolate if a week passed without a meeting. It was important, she realized, that she should continue to maintain her own interests in her own active life. As the autumn of 1886 turned to winter and the new year began, she flung herself into her work and games with even more energy than usual.

In the third month of 1887 winter tightened its grip on Oxford just as the first daffodils of spring were lowering their heads in readiness to flower. A snowy January and a wet February had swollen the rivers and flooded the water meadows, so that when March was blown in by a freezing north-east wind, the city woke up one morning to find itself almost surrounded by ice. Working citizens grumbled as they picked their way cautiously over frozen snow, or felt their horses slipping into potholes. But Midge's eyes sparkled with pleasure as she hunted for her skates in the box room at the top of the house and gave them to the gardener to be sharpened and screwed on to her boots. Her usual exercise during the winter took place on the hockey field, where a team of home students played energetically against the two ladies' halls. With the ground unfit for play, it took only a few messages to bring the team to a new assembly point in Port Meadow. The Meadow flooded and froze regularly enough for most of the girls who had been brought up in Oxford to be accomplished skaters. Midge was the fastest of them all, pausing only occasionally to help someone regain her feet, or to laugh at the contortions of young children trying to keep their balance. She returned home glowing with pleasure and the warmth of exercise.

'We've all arranged to meet again tomorrow,' she told her mother. 'To take advantage of the ice as long as it lasts.'

The next afternoon she was ready and waiting when three of her friends arrived to call for her. A fur-trimmed bonnet which framed her face snugly was warm as well as becoming, and she wore fur mittens and her heaviest cloak and warmest petticoats. Her skirt was the one in which she normally played hockey: it was a little shorter than her other clothes and so less likely to trip her as she skated.

'Are you going to Port Meadow again?' asked her mother, as Midge put her head into the boudoir to say goodbye.

'No, not today. We decided – ' Midge only with a considerable effort prevented herself from flushing, since the suggestion and the decision had both been her own – 'We decided to meet on Magdalen Bridge instead.'

'Why go there?' Although the Hardies' home was not too far from the bridge, Mrs Hardie knew that most of Midge's friends lived in North Oxford. 'Port Meadow is so much more convenient – and so large.'

'But the flooding was only shallow there. So there are

tufts of grass sticking up through the ice. It's impossible to get up a good speed without the danger of running into a hummock and falling. The grass in the water meadows besides Magdalen is completely covered, and the ice is smooth and perfect. Or so we've been told, at least.'

'It must be more dangerous, though, if the water is deeper.'

'It's the difference only between three inches and six. We're unlikely to drown in either.'

'But if you should skate from the water meadow on to the river bed without noticing it . . .' Her mother's anxiety was genuine, but she was perhaps reluctant to fuss over Midge like a child in front of her friends, for she did not press the point.

Mrs Hardie found it as difficult as anyone else to know precisely how this new kind of young woman, the female student, should be treated. Midge had made it clear from the beginning that she would be too busy with her studies to join in all the social activities – the leaving of cards and the taking of tea – normally expected of an unmarried daughter living at home. Sensible and busy herself, Mrs Hardie was prepared to give her daughter credit for being sensible as well, and treated her almost as though she were a young married woman. When Midge needed or asked to be escorted, the matter was arranged; but at other times she was not expected to account for her movements during every moment of the day. 'You'll all stay together, won't you?' was all her mother asked now to indicate that she was still concerned about the danger of an accident.

'Of course.' Midge kissed her mother goodbye and hurried away before any further questions could be asked.

Her conscience was not completely easy. Although she had given her friends no inkling of it, she had to admit to herself the reason why she had suggested the new venue. Any Magdalen undergraduate who might feel in the mood for skating was hardly likely to make the long journey to Port Meadow when he had a natural rink on his own doorstep. Midge had no way of knowing whether Archie Yates could skate. But the ground was too hard for rugger and there was too much ice on the Isis for rowing. It was likely that he would try his skill, if only for the sake of exercise and fresh air. Midge was ashamed of herself for hoping for such an encounter – and, indeed, for plotting so actively to make it possible – but she seemed unable to help herself. She was in love with Archie.

She had been in love with him ever since he kissed her. She had been in love with him ever since he danced with her at the ball. She had been in love with him ever since she listened in his company to the choristers singing from Magdalen Tower. She had been in love with him from the moment she first set eyes on him. She forced herself to think back in such a way, because this was the only means of persuading herself that it was ridiculous. To fall in love with a handsome face before knowing anything at all about its owner's character – only a fool would behave in such a way, and Midge knew that in most respects she was not a fool. But on this one subject reason seemed to have deserted her.

It was not a completely hopeless passion. Midge was as certain as she well could be that Archie's feelings for her were equally strong. But the conventions of society and the routines of their lives made it impossible for them to enjoy any private meeting. She could look forward only to exchanges of meaningless conversation on public social occasions or, even more rarely, to a touch which would be either formal or apparently accidental. If Archie were to declare himself, he could be received at the house as an accepted suitor and a new pattern of behaviour would be allowed to develop. Yet how could he be expected to come to the point of declaration when there was no natural opportunity for their relationship to develop? What was required was a background of social intercourse between two families, and nothing of the kind had existed in the past, or ever would exist.

Although it was in the hope of glimpsing Archie that she had chosen the assembly point on Magdalen Bridge, she soon forgot about him in the excitement of meeting the rest of her friends. As they carried their skates down to the water meadow, Midge lingered behind for a moment, her breath taken away by the beauty of the scene. Behind Magdalen's lonely tower the sky was a deep blue, as cloudless as it had been on May Morning. Beneath it stretched a landscape which could have come from any century. As far as her eye could see the ice was covered with laughing, shouting, moving people. In just such a way must the first wandering scholars who came to rest in Oxford have disported themselves on winter days.

Very often, when her work seemed dull and her eyes ached from all the reading she had to do, Midge drew strength from the thought that she had a place – if only a barely-acknowledged place – in a tradition which was already six centuries old. Now she found an equal pleasure in thinking of her recreation as part of the unchanging pattern of the seasons. The huge elms, their gaunt outlines pointed by frost, would many times in their long lives have looked down on such a swirling scene. Even the younger and more slender willow trees – which alone now indicated the course of the river – must often before this year have felt themselves clutched for support or used as a braking point by a skater who had not yet learned how to stop.

Midge had no problem of this kind. She had promised her mother that she would stay with the group, but her skill and speed inevitably separated them from time to time. Exploring the boundaries of the area on which the ice was safe, she had only one companion at her side as she crossed the frozen river and passed in a graceful glide in front of the iron gates which separated the gardens of Magdalen College from its meadows. A group of undergraduates was clustered there, jeering at those of their friends who had taken to the ice and now appeared determined to crack it by the heaviness of their falls. Archie was one of the group.

So swiftly did Midge pass on that first occasion that he had no chance to notice her. But ten minutes later, outdistancing her companion, she returned on the same circuit. This time she slowed as she passed the group, as though she needed to be cautious in passing the rowdy beginners. She turned her head; her fur-lined face lit up in surprised recognition. She smiled and waved her hand lightly. Then she sped away.

Within only a few seconds her face was red with shame and anger. She had hoped and planned for precisely such an encounter, but now she could hardly bear to think that she could have behaved in such a cheap manner. To be in love was no excuse; it was no excuse for anything at all.

She could almost have cried with vexation. To sit at home and wait meekly until a young man should call to court her would be shaming to her pride in her own independence – but to go out and look for him was even more shaming to her self-respect. Would she really be content, as she had always persuaded herself, to be a schoolteacher, unloved and unmarried? Her love of study was genuine enough, and so was her wish to live a useful life, but why should that mean that she must cut herself off from the usual pleasures of being young? She had as much right to happiness as anyone else, but how was she supposed to find it?

There was no easy answer as to what she should do – but it was clear enough what she ought *not* to do. For the rest of the afternoon she stayed close to her friends and at the furthest point from the college, practising figure skating and refusing to race. Archie, she had noticed, was not wearing skates; he was not likely to take more than a few steps on to the ice. If the frost continued, she suggested to her companions when at last they were all tired, it would perhaps after all be more convenient to meet at Port Meadow the next day.

So for the three afternoons which followed she kept well away from Magdalen. On the fourth day, however, the temperature began to rise. As she walked home from her morning lecture she noticed that the sun was shining not only brightly but warmly. This might well be the last opportunity of the winter to use her skates.

Her friends called for her as usual, but brought with them warning news. The Thames had flooded its banks for a second time, so that the ice on Port Meadow was now covered with water. 'We should go back to the Cherwell water meadows,' they said. 'We've told the others. They'll meet us on Magdalen Bridge again.'

Midge said nothing. This time the decision was not hers; there was no shame in merely accepting it. It would be easy enough to keep away from the college gates. Why should she deny herself a last afternoon of pleasant exercise merely as a kind of self-mortification?

She tucked her straying hair inside her bonnet. 'To Magdalen, then,' she said.

Twelve

For four afternoons running Archie had jerkily circled the water meadows on his borrowed skates. On the first two occasions he was glad that Midge did not appear to be in the vicinity; accustomed to appearing accomplished at everything he tried, he did not take kindly to his first clumsiness at this new skill. But once he had got the hang of it, he started to look out for her. The River Cherwell divided into three as it enclosed and crossed the water meadows, and so hard was the frost at first that even these channels had frozen over, making it possible to skate as far north as the Parks. So the area to be searched was a large one – and half the city, it seemed, was playing truant from school or business or study to take advantage of the weather.

Archie found it hard to understand his eagerness for Midge's company. She was too clever for him. His own education had left him able to translate verses into or out of Latin and Greek, but not to argue logically on abstract subjects, nor to follow allusions plucked from the history or literature of several countries: he had learned to read a little French, but could not understand a word when Midge rattled it off at the speed of an express train. But then, girls were not meant for talking to. What he liked about Midge was the physical pleasure of dancing with her, or walking with her, or looking at her as he rowed or punted. In her company his pulse quickened as though to keep pace with her own vivacious energy.

If he were to meet her on the ice, there would be no

need to talk. They could move together, perhaps even holding crossed hands as they skated. Archie could – truthfully enough – describe himself as a tyro and ask for help and instruction and support. But first he must find her.

Soon it would be too late. A sunny morning had begun to melt the thinnest ice near the banks of the Cherwell, although the meadow was still firm enough. Archie might have been expected to take pleasure in the thought that the river would soon be fit once again for rowing. Instead, a new urgency of spirit added power to the thrust of his feet as he moved from one group to another, scanning every face he passed. Twice he thought from a distance that he could see Midge; but every young woman who possessed a fur-trimmed bonnet was wearing it today, and each time he found himself mistaken.

He stood still in the centre of the most popular area. When everyone else was moving, perhaps it made better sense to remain in the same place. Almost at once he was rewarded. Midge was skating backwards, her arms stretched out to pull along a friend whose first lesson it seemed to be. The cold had brought roses to her cheeks and her eyes sparkled with pleasure and encouragement. Archie watched for a moment without moving. Then he positioned himself so that Midge could not help but crash into him.

Naturally he was alert to ensure that she did not fall – and quick, too, to catch her friend and help her towards a tree which she could hold. In the flurry of mutual apologies Archie saw mischief in Midge's smile. She had recognized that the accident was no accident – and she was pleased.

'I must help my friend back to the others,' said Midge. Archie bowed his head in agreement and waited to see

101

whether she would return. Two minutes later she sped past him without stopping, outdistancing those of her companions who had started level with her in a race.

Amidst all the activity of circling, zigzagging skaters, no one could notice that Archie was following Midge's track. It took him a little while to catch up with her. Although his legs were stronger, and far longer, than hers, he had not mastered the gliding movement which propelled her speedily forward, making her skates sing a high, sharp song as they cut through the ice; instead, he came almost to a halt after each thrust of the blade. Only when they were far from the bridge and from most of the other skaters did she check herself and turn to wait for him.

'I'm delighted to see that you can be frivolous, Miss Hardie.' Archie staggered slightly as he came to a halt; stopping, he found, required even more skill than progressing forward. 'I'd imagined you hard at your books during every moment of the term.'

'I've adopted the custom of the university,' Midge said lightly. 'A little exercise in the afternoon, and back to work after tea.'

'Won't you practise your future profession on me?' he asked. 'I'm in need of a teacher. Will you show me how to skate backwards?'

Midge gave a demonstration. Archie attempted and failed to copy her. She stood beside him and called out instructions, which he was unable to follow. With her back to him, and from a little distance, she began to swerve gracefully and slowly towards him, telling him to move back in time with her own movements. Archie waited until she was so close that he could put his hands on her waist and move as though they were dancing.

'Really, Mr Yates!' exclaimed Midge, twisting herself free.

'Dash it all, a chap needs a bit of support,' Archie said plaintively. 'Darned slippery stuff, this ice. Now, if you were to hold my hands and sort of push me backwards in front of you – '

Midge pursed her lips and shook her head just as though she were a schoolteacher already but nevertheless did as he suggested. It seemed to Archie, though, that there was no profit to be taken from success. It was easy enough to lose his balance and fall, bringing his teacher down on top of him.

So tiny was Midge, and so light, that as Archie lay on the ice he felt as though he were covered only with a confusion of clothes. She looked down at him with laughing eyes which recognized that Archie was becoming an expert in non-accidental accidents.

By the time she regained her feet, snow had begun to fall again. The white flakes rested and glistened in the black fur which framed her face, and on her eyebrows and eyelashes. They softened her features, so that Archie, standing less steadily beside her, wondered how he could ever have thought of her merely as handsome. She was beautiful: a snow princess. His look must have spoken for him, for she lowered her gaze for a moment. Then, with her usual energy, she shook her skirts free of snow.

'I must go back to my friends,' she said, and made off without waiting for him. Archie, lost in admiration of her swift gliding movement, was slow to start in pursuit. Once he had pushed off, he did his best to catch her up, cursing the ungainly stiffness of his own movements which slowed him down and kept him at a distance.

Midge was skating down the centre of the river channel, where the ice was smoothest. It was only near the banks

103

that the ice had become thin; in the middle, even a well-built rowing man like Archie could hear no sound of cracking beneath his skates. But his eyes narrowed with anxiety as he saw the direction she was taking.

Late on the previous evening a rowdy group of non-skaters had taken to the ice, each pushing a wooden chair for support in front of him. Their friends – of whom Archie was one – had entered with spirit into the horse-play, and before the evening was out the chairs were blazing in a huge bonfire which burned a hole in the ice near the river bank. During the night the area had frozen over again, but so thinly that for safety's sake it had been broken up with sticks. For most of the day it had been obvious enough that the place was unsafe; but it was beginning to grow dark and the snow, which by now was falling heavily, might well have made the danger invisible. Midge would notice that no one was skating there, but might not guess why.

'Miss Hardie!' he shouted, doing his best to increase his speed. But she had too great a start; he could not hope to catch her up in time. Instead, he came to a halt and cupped his hands round his mouth, bellowing as though he were a towpath coach admonishing a rowing eight. 'Miss Hardie! Come back!'

Thirteen

Midge knew very well that she was behaving in an unladylike manner. Properly brought-up young ladies skated demurely in pairs, their hands tucked inside muffs, their backs straight, their feet moving gracefully but not too fast. They did not hold their skirts off the ground and lean forward, biting their skates into the ice as though they were racing some unseen competitor. But there was a reason for her present speed. She was hurrying back to rejoin the companions whom she should never have left, and if her head was thrusting forward, and turned down instead of being erect, it was not only because the position gave more power to her legs, but because by now the snow was falling thickly enough almost to blind her if she looked straight ahead.

She followed the river's curving course: it was less crowded than the meadow, because most of the merrymakers were nervous of the deep water below the ice. Faintly, from a distance, she heard Archie call her name: but he would not seriously expect her to stop. She sped on, past the Grove in which deer huddled round bales of hay, past Magdalen's eighteenth-century New Building, and on towards the bridge.

'Miss Hardie! Come back!'

Half of Oxford must have heard the shout. Was Archie trying to embarrass her? She would have to wait for him, if only to remonstrate. It was another of Midge's unladylike talents that she knew how to turn her feet and body sideways to make her skates judder to a halt within a few inches, however fast she might be going. She was just about to make the turn – but was still moving at speed – when she felt the ice give way beneath her. There was not even the sound of cracking to give her warning. One moment she was on thick ice and a minute later she was in the water.

At the moment when she fell, her ankle was turning in one direction while the weight of her body moved in another. But she hardly had time to register the pain, for the chill of the water numbed her lower limbs. There was little danger of drowning, because it was near the river bank that the ice had given way. The water here was no more than two or three feet deep, and by flinging herself quickly forward she was able to grasp the exposed root of a tree. But the weight of her wet clothes pulled her down and the task of hauling herself on to the bank with her fingerless mittens seemed beyond her. Gasping with cold, she turned her head to see if anyone was near enough to help. The snow was falling in straight thick lines, forming a screen around her and deadening all sound. Less than half an hour earlier the whole area had seemed over-crowded, but now it was as though she were alone in the world.

Through the screen Archie appeared, his face anxious and his movements awkward. It seemed as though he knew where he should look for her, and what he might find, for he leapt from the ice to the bank. Midge felt his hands beneath her shoulders, drawing her out of the water to lie for a few seconds on dry land.

'Are you hurt?'

'My right ankle, perhaps.' Midge struggled into a sitting position. 'Nothing serious, I'm sure.'

'Hang on a second.' It took him very little longer to find his ordinary boots and pull them on. Returning, he bent down and picked her up as though she weighed nothing at all before striding through the tall gates which led into his college.

'Where are you taking me?'

'To a fire,' said Archie briefly. 'You could catch pneumonia unless we can get you warm again quickly.'

Shivering uncontrollably, Midge lacked the strength to protest. Once or twice in the past she had indulged in daydreams of being carried away by this strong, handsome young man, but had always been able to laugh herself out of them. She was not that kind of weak, helpless girl. She could stand on her own feet and look after herself. So, at least, she had always believed. But now it was indeed welcome to feel that she was being looked after. Nevertheless, anxiety pricked at her mind when she realized that Archie was taking her towards the building in which he had his set of rooms. To be alone with an undergraduate on college premises was the most heinous crime which could be imagined by the Association for the Education of Women. She turned her head anxiously from side to side to see whether anyone in authority was watching. But the snow which had cut her off from help now served to make her invisible in a more useful manner. It was through a white, silent, uninhabited world that Archie was carrying her.

He kicked open the door of his room and very carefully set her down, supporting her while he took off her cloak and then helping her to a chair. He threw more coals on to the smouldering fire and used the bellows to encourage it into flame. Then he crossed the room again and, before closing the door, pulled at a much heavier outer door and latched it shut.

'What are you doing?' Midge asked with chattering teeth.

'Sporting my oak. Means I'm not to be disturbed. So that I won't be interrupted while I'm working! It'll be a surprise for my scout if he comes – the first time I've ever sported it.' His smile of amusement changed to one of earnest explanation as he realized that his guest was anxious. 'The thing is, it can't be opened from the other side. But *you* can walk out whenever you choose, just by lifting the latch. Let me take your boot off before the ankle swells up. Which one is hurt?'

Still shivering violently, Midge indicated her right foot. Archie held it firmly in position while easing off the boot; then, more swiftly, he removed the left one as well. Springing briskly to his feet, he considered what to do next.

'You should take off that heavy skirt,' he said. 'Hang it over the fireguard to dry. You'll never get warm while your clothes are soaking. I'm pretty wet myself.' He took off his coat as he spoke. 'Why don't I change my clothes in my bedroom while you see what you can do in here to make yourself more comfortable?'

'You're very thoughtful, Mr Yates.' Midge spoke sincerely. The heat of the fire was bringing her numbed legs back to life and her shivering had stopped. In a moment or two she would be warm again. Her skirts, which had begun to steam, would no doubt be uncomfortable for walking but she had gone into the water only up to her knees. 'I ought to rejoin my friends as soon as possible, though. They'll be expecting to walk home with me, and they're bound to be anxious if I don't appear.' In such heavy snow, all skating would have come to an end by now.

'You can't walk on that ankle.'

'It's only turned, not broken. If I rub it . . .'

'I can do that.' Archie went down on his knees beside

108

her chair. 'This sort of thing happens all the time on the rugger field.' But on their way towards her ankle his hands gripped the hem of her skirt and squeezed the water out of a small section of it. 'Hang it all,' he said. 'You can't sit in this. Take it off and let me wring it out. Ten minutes' drying it over the fireguard will make all the difference.'

Midge swallowed the lump which was choking her throat and, without speaking, undid the fastenings of her skirt. She justified this to herself with the reminder that she was wearing a flannel petticoat which was just as thick and decent as her overskirt. And yet she knew that by her action she was allowing a situation which was already a breach of rules to change into something far more danger-ous. She knew – but seemed unable to stop herself.

'That's better.' Archie dealt briskly with the skirt before returning his attention to her ankle. She felt his thumbs pressing in, searching for the strained muscle and massag-ing it. His hands moved upward underneath the wet petticoat, rubbing her chilled calf back to life as well. He might even have explored further still had Midge not checked him with a breathless assurance.

'I can stand now, I'm sure. Let me try.'

She needed his support as she rose to her feet and tested the strength of her ankle. Archie kept his hands under her elbows and leaned forward and down towards her. In a moment he would be kissing her. Midge wanted him to do so, but at the same time knew that she must stop him, if only because she felt herself to be a prisoner.

'Mr Yates! You're taking advantage . . .'

'I'm sorry.' Archie straightened himself at once. 'But dash it all, you've let me kiss you before,' he said soulfully.

'I oughtn't to have done. That sort of behaviour is only

permissible if – if there is some kind of understanding.'

'You mean, that we shall marry one day? Well, may we not share such an understanding? I'm not my own master yet, worse luck. But when I'm twenty-one, when I've finished at Oxford, when my grandfather has set me up – oh, I'm so much in love with you. You must know how I feel. And I hoped you might care for me just a bit.'

'I do, but – '

'Well then.' He took her into his arms, kissing her with such force that Midge felt her lips bruising against her teeth. So much taller was he than herself that he almost lifted her off the ground. When, after a few moments, he relaxed his grip and her feet touched the carpet again, her injured ankle buckled under her weight. She staggered and fell sideways on to the silky rug which Archie had brought with him from Castlemere. Before she had time to pick herself up, Archie was lying on the floor beside her.

'No!' she said, but Archie's kiss closed her lips. She felt his hands moving over her body, tugging at her clothes. She tried to struggle against the weight of his body, but her own movements excited her and became a part of his. Now he was kissing her neck, murmuring over and over again that he loved her. Midge knew that she must stop him, and knew that she could not.

When at last he was still again she opened her eyes and saw Archie's face still close to hers. His skin was flushed and, in the second before his eyes evaded her glance, she recognized that he was feeling now the same kind of anxiety that she had experienced a few moments earlier.

Her own feelings were no longer complicated. She was ashamed. Shame kept her silent as Archie collected her clothes and helped her into his tiny bedroom to dress. Shame held back her tears. Had she been attacked by a stranger she could have cried with anger or regret. But although it was true that Archie was too strong for her to resist, she knew that she could have stopped him if she had been resolute enough before it was too late.

How could she face him again? She was frightened of what might be the consequences of his own shame. Would he turn his back on her, without reason, just because she had done what he wanted her to do? Half an hour earlier he had talked tenderly – hadn't he? – of marriage. She was too proud to ask for his reassurance now, but frightened lest he should fail to offer it. The pale face and collected demeanour with which she opened the bedroom door when she was ready concealed a terror which made her unable to move.

Archie, smiling again in his usual good-natured and light-hearted way, ascribed her stillness only to the injured ankle. He had nothing on his mind, it seemed, except the best course of action to pursue.

'Why don't I carry you to The House of Hardie?' he suggested. 'It's only a short distance, and your father can make sure that you have transport home. Then I'll go back to find your friends. I'll tell them that you've had a slight accident and have asked me to carry a message. They won't know when you had the accident – nor how long you've been with your father. They won't even need to know that I'm a friend of yours. In an emergency, any stranger would have helped you in the same way.'

Midge nodded her head. Archie picked up her skates and gave them to her to carry. Once again he lifted her up in his arms.

'I'd better be only an accidental passer-by when I deliver you to your father as well,' he said. 'So now, before we go . . . I've never known anyone like you, you know. I can hardly believe that you love me.' He kissed

111

her once more before arranging her cloak in such a way that it covered her completely. They both pretended that this was only to protect her from the snow, but it served its purpose in smuggling her unchallenged out of the college.

The chief clerk jumped to his feet in alarm as Midge was carried into The House of Hardie and made comfortable on a chair. A messenger was sent off at once to find Mr Hardie, who was doing business in one of the colleges: Midge guessed that Archie would leave the premises before his return. She listened in silence as her rescuer gave the impression that he had found her by chance after her fall through the ice and had brought her straight there. He did not in so many words tell a lie, but his story was far from being the truth. Had Gordon been in the shop, he would have seen through it at once – but Gordon was in Portugal, negotiating with the suppliers of the firm's port. Midge herself thanked Archie and told him where her friends would be waiting for her, but said nothing else.

That night, unable to sleep, she passed the events of the afternoon over and over again through her memory. Ashamed and afraid, she searched for excuses for her own behaviour and for Archie's, and could find none. She had committed the worst sin imaginable for a young woman. That fact was inescapable; all she could hope to escape were the consequences.

Archie had said that he loved her, and it had been the truth; she was sure of that. He had said, too, that they should have an understanding to marry one day. Could she feel the same certainty there? Even at the time he had hedged the promise around with doubts. Had she believed him? Had he seduced her with an offer of marriage, or had it been solely the strength of her own desires which kept her in his arms?

Midge, who never cried, began to cry now. She had been a fool – in the way that hundreds of girls every day, no doubt, were fools. Of course Archie would not marry her. Whatever the practical objections to an immediate engagement, there was no law which said that a young man must have reached his majority and graduated before asking his future wife to wait for him. Archie had chosen his words as carefully to her as he had later in the parlour of The House of Hardie. He was not by nature a deceitful young man. But no doubt he had managed to persuade himself that lies were to be found only in words spoken and not those left unsaid.

But no, she told herself, she must not make Archie out to be a villain. He was good-natured and affectionate, and he loved her. There was no obstacle to their marriage. When he thought about it, he would realize what he must do – and because he did love her, it would be no hardship.

It did not occur to Midge at this moment of crisis in her life to ask herself seriously whether she wanted to be Archie's wife. Gordon had once tried to persuade her that Archie was the wrong man for her, and when she was thinking sensibly she had recognized that this might be true. It was the touch of Archie's fingers, the passion of Archie's kisses, which had thrown common sense out of the window, banishing her doubts and convincing her that she could expect no greater joy than to spend the rest of her life in his company. It was too late now to call common sense back. She had allowed herself to be ruined by Archie, and Archie must see that there was, in honour, only one course open to him. He must marry her. He must.

Fourteen

Using the injury to her ankle as an excuse, Midge sent a note to Dr Mackenzie to say that she would be unable to attend the last Monday coaching of the term, enclosing the essay which she would have read aloud to him. In return she received his comments on it and a reading list for the Easter vacation, when in preparation for her Finals she must begin to revise all the work of the past three years. The icy weather had brought colds or broken bones to so many people that there was nothing in the least remarkable about this exchange of correspondence. Only Midge knew its real meaning.

She was frightened of meeting Archie again. Or rather, she did not want to encounter him in the presence of Mrs Lindsay, as he came away from his tutorial. Part of the pleasure of their weekly exchange of bows had been the pretence – for the chaperone's sake – that they hardly knew each other. But if he were to treat her now as a mere acquaintance, it would be hard to bear the uncertainty of wondering whether this still was, as it had been previously, a joke between two people whose friendship went far deeper.

The prospect of a casual encounter might frighten her, yet she became alarmed as the days passed without any word from Archie. It would be perfectly proper for her rescuer to call at the house and enquire after her health – indeed, it was the expected thing to do, so that Mrs Hardie might have the opportunity of thanking him. Was he feeling guilty? Did he despise her? When, oh when would she see him again? Anxious and heartsick, she lost her appetite. Black shadows ringed her eyes with tiredness but, when her mother warned her not to sit at her books so late into the night, Midge did not dare to confess that her sleeplessness had another cause. As though to fuel the fire of her shame, her body ached with love for Archie. She longed for him to hold her in his arms again.

For five days Midge allowed herself to be ruled by unhappiness. Then, with the determination which was more characteristic of her, she pulled herself together. If one thing was certain, it was that a man who married only out of a sense of obligation was unlikely to make his wife happy. Archie's silence might be hurtful, but a forced marriage would be worse. Because Midge was sure that he loved her, she found it possible to accept this thought without pain, as suggesting only the most unlikely contingency. She must put him out of her mind until he chose to make contact with her again.

This was not as easily done as decided, since suddenly reminders of him seemed to assail her at every turn. Gordon was still in Portugal, and the maids, airing his bedroom one morning, left the door open. Midge glanced through it as she passed by, and found her eye caught by a picture of Castlemere.

She went into the room to study the painting more closely. It was an original water-colour, with the name of the house in neat lettering at the top and the artist's signature at the foot. L. Yates. Midge smiled to herself. She had noticed the expression almost of hero-worship with which Archie's sister conversed with Gordon during their Eights Week meeting; the child must have sent this as a gift to keep herself in Gordon's mind.

Midge did no more than glance at the picture, because she was already late for breakfast. But when she arrived at the table, it was to find that she could not escape from Castlemere, because the name was on her father's lips.

'Young Mr Yates is a grandson of the Marquess of Ross,' he explained to Midge, repeating what he had just been telling Mrs Hardie without realizing that the statement would hardly come as news to his daughter. 'Due to have his coming-of-age ball in the vacation. His lordship isn't inclined to waste his best wines on such an occasion, and Mr Yates himself favours only champagne, so we're to take a big extra order down. Gordon usually deals with that kind of thing, but he won't be back in time. I'd better set it in hand myself.'

He continued to talk to his wife while Midge toyed with her food. Would her father travel with the wagon himself, she wondered. Could she ask to accompany him – just as a vacation treat, a trip to the country? But no; if she should come face to face with Archie in his own home, it would be humiliating to feel that she only had the right to cross the threshold as the daughter of one of his tradesmen. She excused herself from the table and went back to Gordon's room.

The painting of Castlemere was an accomplished one for such a young girl. Lucy Yates had delineated her home with a mastery of perspective and a precision of detail worthy of an architect's drawing; then she had softened the picture with mist and cloud and pale washes of colour. But it was not in admiration of the painting that Midge considered it so carefully.

Naturally, Archie had often talked of his home, but he took it too much for granted to describe it in detail. He had never made it clear that Castlemere was not so much a house as a palace. Midge found herself counting the turrets, estimating the number of rooms and courtyards, wondering how many servants were needed to run it.

There was a moment in which her confidence faltered. She had not been brought up to be a châtelaine. She would have neither the confidence nor the experience to run such an establishment – nor, indeed, the wish to devote her time to such a task.

She shook her head, laughing at herself, although with little humour. What conceit, to object to a role which could not be offered to her! Castlemere would never belong to Archie. He had made it clear enough that he had little money of his own, but must rely on his grandfather to set him up in whatever profession he chose to follow. In fact, if he were to turn his back now on Midge, it was likely not to be because she was unqualified to run a grand house, but because she would lack the kind of marriage settlement to provide him with a comfortable life.

What kind of life would that be? Midge tried to imagine Archie in three or four years' time. Would he go into the army, as he had once suggested, condemning his wife to the gypsy life of any officer's family? Midge could hardly imagine him as a clergyman, and he was certainly not clever enough for any profession requiring brains and academic qualifications. A gentleman farmer was perhaps the only other possibility, offering his wife a place in county society, but almost certainly cutting her off from any kind of intellectual pursuits. And whatever he chose to do, he would never allow his wife to take paid employment. The time might come when Midge would have to ask herself whether her decision to be a teacher was a true vocation or merely an idea which would seem second-best when set against an offer of marriage.

Ruefully she remembered the advice that Gordon had given her the previous summer. The way to find happiness was first of all to choose a way of life and only then to search for a companion with whom it could be shared. Did that apply only to men, or could a woman claim the same right?

Midge felt her back straightening and her resolve stiffening as she put the question to herself. She was still too much in love to follow the answer right through at this moment. If Archie were to appear now – to tell her again that he loved her, to ask her to marry him – she could not with her hand on her heart promise herself that she would pause to consider the future in detail before accepting him. But if he did not come . . .

There would be no need to wait long before the situation became clear, for there was an easy test of his intentions. If his feeling for her was sincere, he would surely take the opportunity of his coming-of-age to let her meet his family, allowing the grandfather of whom he stood in awe a chance to appraise the girl he professed to love. Not that he would necessarily be forced to make the relationship obvious. In a large party, Midge would be only one amongst scores of his friends. An invitation to the occasion would not necessarily be significant. But if he chose *not* to invite her – why then, Midge told herself, a student of history at the University of Oxford – a woman who was being trained to read documents and understand their significance – ought to be able to interpret silence and draw the only sensible conclusion from it.

And in that case she must put the past behind her. She had behaved foolishly, sinfully, but she ought not to allow the events of half an hour to determine the whole future course of her life. Instead of guilt, she must summon up pride. She had her own ambitions, her own plans for the future. They had been enough for her before, and they would be again.

The decision was easy to take, but did not prevent her

from listening for each postal delivery. News of her skating accident brought several notes of enquiry and good wishes from her friends; but not until three days after term had ended did she arrive at the breakfast table to find the letter she was hoping for waiting beside her place.

A letter, to describe it more accurately, which came from the right place. A coat of arms stamped into the thick red seal, told her that and made her spirits jump with hope. But the feel of the epistle between her fingers brought doubts. An invitation would have been printed on thick card. The contents of this, all too obviously, were handwritten on paper. But then, a letter might prove to be a special way of inviting a special guest . . .

Midge forced herself to laugh at these ridiculous imaginings which could so easily be resolved by the breaking of the seal. But a growing fear in her heart made her reluctant to risk the discovery in front of the rest of the family. At the sound of her father's firm footsteps coming down the stairs, she tucked the letter into the waistband of her skirt. Only later, when she was alone, did she find out what Archie had to say.

'Dear Miss Hardie.' Archie's handwriting, unspoilt by any efforts to scribble lecture notes at speed, was round and clear: almost that of a schoolboy still. The purpose of his letter, alas, was equally clear.

'I'd meant to write to you sooner to enquire after your injured ankle and hope that you took no harm from your ducking and by now are fully restored to health. But since my return to Castlemere I've been kept almost a prisoner in my room, with no company but the vacation reading list. My tutors, it seems, are displeased with my progress over the past five terms; and the Dean, reading their reports, has written a most ungentlemanly letter to my grandfather. As though a chap should be expected to spend the whole of his life in libraries! I'm sure my grandfather had a high old time when he was up at Oxford himself, but now there are frowns of disapproval and lectures about too many distractions, and altogether it seems that my nose is to be forced to the grindstone. I've tried to persuade my grandfather that friendships are more important than books, but he'll have none of it.

'So I fear that all the happy hours that you and I spent on the river last year, and which I'd hoped to repeat this summer, must remain a thing of the past. You can guess how much I shall regret this, because you're such a good sport and my admiration for you knows no bounds – but what can a fellow do when the whole world conspires to squash him flat?'

There were two further paragraphs to the letter, fulsome with compliments about her looks and intelligence and almost maudlin with regrets that some other chap would one day enjoy the benefit of them, but Midge hardly troubled to read the words. He had made his meaning plain enough. The shame which would have driven Midge herself into marriage, had it been offered, was driving Archie away from it. She was not good enough for him: the marquess must have made that clear. In a moment of anger she even wondered whether the wording of the letter had been dictated to its writer, so subtly did it avoid any phrase which might have justified a suit for breach of promise, had Midge been of a spiteful disposition.

For a second time within a few days she felt tears pricking at her eyes but this time, straightening her back and holding her head high, she forced them back. She must not, would not cry. An impulsive young man had

had second thoughts and, in doing so, had given her the opportunity to think sensibly herself. That she should feel unhappy for a moment was natural enough. But it was not the end of the world: only the end of a romance.

PART TWO

A Proposal of Marriage

One

'Haven't you ever been in love?'

Midge had hurled that question – almost an accusation – at Gordon on the summer afternoon when he agreed to provide her with a pretence of respectability. His answer had been an honest one. No, he had never been in love.

So passionate was his determination to travel to China one day that the only love affair he could allow himself was with his own ambition. Any entanglement with a young woman would be a distraction. Besides, how could it end except in the heartache of parting – for the idea that a female could endure the certain hardship of his expedition was unthinkable. It would be heartless to enter an engagement before his departure and to expect his betrothed to wait alone for three years, without any of the usual pleasures of courtship. And if – even worse – he were to marry, how could he possibly desert a young bride? So it was that during his early twenties he had kept a tight rein on his emotions, enjoying the company of young women, but careful never to encourage any intimacy.

'You must have met beautiful girls!' That had been another of Midge's challenges. It was true; but only once had his breath been snatched away by such an intense physical attraction that he needed to curb his feelings immediately if he were not to be swept off his feet. Lucy Yates, painting in the herb garden at Castlemere or clapping her hands with excitement on the Magdalen barge, was the loveliest creature he had ever seen. Only a child, of course, but beauty in bud was the purest of all.

Common sense had come to his rescue. Lucy Yates would never be allowed to marry into trade. The Marquess of Ross would have far more ambitious plans for such a beauty. So there was no point in considering even for a second what might happen if Gordon were to fall in love with her. Any such inclination was to be stifled at birth.

The fact that it was Archie Yates's sister who had so greatly attracted him helped his understanding of Midge's infatuation – but also his discouragement of it. Miss Hardie would not be considered good enough for the grandson of a marquess. And because Gordon himself had successfully resisted the temptation to fall in love, he believed his sister could and should do the same.

During the nine months following their conversation, though, he gave little thought to Midge's problems, for his own affairs needed all his attention. Before he could embark on his great adventure, there were plans which must be put into effect. And time was passing. He had fixed on October 1887 for the start of his expedition. Now it was April. Only six months more!

Almost ten years had passed since he returned to Oxford from his voyage to the South Seas: ten years in which he had devoted himself to the affairs of The House of Hardie. He had served his father well, working on each side of the business in turn. The danger was that he might come to be thought of as indispensable. That was one reason why he began to speak of his plans earlier than he had originally intended, in order that his replacement might be found and trained in good time.

Mr Hardie was at first astonished by Gordon's request for a three-year leave of absence, and then disapproving. But although Gordon put the request forward politely, as though permission were being asked, he made the true situation clear. Mr Hardie could either cast his only son off in disgust or else let him return eventually to his place in The House of Hardie. There was no real choice.

So by April 1887, although Mrs Hardie was still attempting to dissuade her son from a journey which seemed fraught with danger, her husband had sufficiently conceded defeat to make a practical suggestion.

'We could bring Will here from London,' he said, as they discussed the future over Sunday afternoon tea. 'He knows the selling side of the business as well as anyone, and it would be a promotion for him. He's no family to hold him back, now that his mother's dead – and he could lodge with us, couldn't he, my dear, until he finds somewhere that suits him in Oxford?'

'Just remind me, which one is Will?' Mrs Hardie rarely visited London and was not as familiar with the staff there as with those who worked in Oxford.

'Will Witney, my dear. The boy who fell into the cellar.'

Ten years earlier, Mr Hardie had told his family the story of a guttersnipe's dramatic entry into The House of Hardie. Not so much running as propelling himself like a bullet along the pavement of Pall Mall, the twelve-year-old had failed to notice the trapdoor which was just being opened. The Hardie cellars extended under the street, and barrels brought by the cartload were delivered via the opening. Will might easily have been killed by his fall.

'Oh yes,' recalled Mrs Hardie. 'Does he still limp?'

'He always will, I'm afraid. That was the main reason why we felt an obligation to offer him work. As an errand-boy, the only talent he had to offer until then was speed. Naturally, he lost his job – and it was all due to our cellarman's negligence.'

'Shouldn't he have been at school?' asked Mrs Hardie.

'I expect so. He'd been playing truant for years in order to support his mother. Not exactly promising material, you might have thought when we took him on. Illiterate, innumerate, shabby, and none too clean.'

'And yet you're going to put him in charge at Oxford?'

Gordon laughed, guessing that his mother was alarmed by such a picture of her proposed lodger. 'That was all ten years ago, Mother.' Will had proved to have a natural intelligence, unspoiled by any interference from school-teachers. He was a boy who had never been bored by lessons, because he so rarely attended them. As soon as he saw the point of learning something, he had picked it up at the speed of greased lightning. 'Father sent him off to night school at the firm's expense.'

'Never known a boy learn to read so fast,' said Mr Hardie. 'Remarkable! Whenever Will saw a chance of promotion, he made sure that he was qualified to apply for it. By the time he was seventeen he could keep a ledger in a copperplate hand – and draw up accounts and keep a balance. Before he was twenty-one, he'd learned to understand business letters in both French and German, and to write straightforward answers. What's more, he started taking an interest in the goods he was selling. It's not often that I have the chance to educate a completely unspoiled palate. He's almost as good a judge of wine as Gordon is, though he doesn't find it as easy to put his opinions into words.'

'I suspect that he simply marks everything out of ten,' suggested Gordon, grinning. 'He's a good fellow though.'

'Certainly there's a lot to be said for bringing him here.' Mr Hardie was thinking aloud. 'We gave him a rise in wages to celebrate his twenty-first birthday – the end of his apprenticeship, you might say – but we couldn't promote him any further.' The staff of The House of

Hardie were loyal for life, and only death or extreme old age freed a place for any newer arrival. 'Yes, we'll move him here in June.'

'You'll like him, Mother.' Gordon did his best to be reassuring. 'And so will Midge. He's got a sense of humour. Where is Midge?'

'Working. Always working at those books of hers. She's making herself ill. It can't be right.'

Should he go and look for her, and persuade her to come for a walk? No, she would not want to be disturbed. So at least Gordon persuaded himself – but he had a stronger reason for choosing instead to retire to his own room. Now that his father had accepted the situation, he could start to gather the sponsorship needed to finance his expedition. He began to draw up three lists of possible patrons: commercial plant nurseries, scholarly institutions, and private gentlemen. At the head of the third list he wrote the name of the Marquess of Ross.

Lucy was reading a book of sermons when the message came. No one had forbidden her to paint or to play the piano or to read a novel, but these activities – simply because she enjoyed them – were surely unsuitable for someone in mourning for a dead father. The sermons, though, were ponderously dull, so she accepted the interruption with pleasure. The marquess's request, brought by a footman, was that she should meet the head gardener in the orangery, to discuss a proposal being made by Mr Gordon Hardie.

Mr Hardie! Lucy's eyes sparkled with a pleasure which she concealed behind a decorous nod of the head. How many times had she sighed over the rules of etiquette which made it impossible for her to arrange another meeting! The chance encounter during the Eights Week festivities – and Archie's unexpected alacrity in inviting Mr Hardie and his sister on to the Magdalen barge – had been a delightful surprise. But during the month since then, Lucy had known she had no hope of seeing Mr Hardie again unless he chose to come to Castlemere.

And now he had come! Lucy sent for her maid to bring her cloak and bonnet, and they went together to the meeting place. Mr Hardie's eyes, as he greeted her, showed that he had not been prepared to see her in black; but perhaps he thought it would be impertinent to enquire the reason.

'My grandfather tells me you have a proposal to make in respect of the garden,' she said.

'Yes, I have. He's been gracious enough to approve it in principle. But he tells me that you are the member of the family who has inherited your grandmother's love of plants. The work is only to go ahead if you agree.'

There was little chance that Lucy would not, but she waited calmly to hear what he had in mind.

'The suggestion is that Castlemere should have a rock garden.'

'A rockery, do you mean?'

'No. More than that. A miniature Alpine landscape, with peaks and valleys, all in proportion.'

'I've never seen such a thing.'

'I'm not surprised. I know of only one, and although the rocks are dramatically arranged, it lacks appropriate planting.'

'I'm afraid my support will be of little use,' said Lucy. 'I'm not familiar with any plants which would be suitable.'

'Ah, but that's the point!' exclaimed Gordon earnestly. 'If your garden staff will undertake the task of construction while I'm away in China, I'll bring back with me a collection of alpines. Of alpine primulas in particular – there are known to be so many in the mountains between China and Tibet that I can hope to provide a selection of plants which have never been seen in England before.'

'You're going to China?'

'As soon as I've found enough patrons,' Gordon told her. 'I've been commissioned to look for new varieties of rhododendron by a nursery which intends to propagate and sell them. I shall supply material to the herbarium in the Oxford Botanic Garden; to others as well, I trust. But my expenses will be high. I need to interest private gentlemen in the venture, promising them something unique in return.'

'I'm surprised by my grandfather's interest.'

131

'I reminded him that the medieval herb garden here is of historic importance. I'm sure botanists come from all over the country to see it. It serves as a memorial to your ancestors who created it.'

'So you've invited him to create his own memorial!' Lucy laughed aloud at the unexpectedness of the thought.

'No. The name attached to it is to be yours. If you authorize it.'

Lucy clapped her hands with pleasure. 'Of course I agree.' She turned to the head gardener who had been listening with a resigned lack of enthusiasm. 'Can you procure rock, Curtis? What colour should it be, Mr Hardie? And what aspect is most suitable? Have you found a place already, or shall we explore?' She set off even as she spoke, at such a brisk pace that the maid and gardener were soon left behind.

'When I broached the subject to his lordship, he said that it might serve to cheer you up. I didn't know what he meant but I see that you're in mourning. I hope . . .'

'My father has died,' Lucy told him. 'Of cholera, while he was serving on the North-West Frontier.'

'You must be very upset.'

'I hardly knew him,' Lucy admitted. 'On three occasions in my life he spent a few weeks at Castlemere as a visitor. I'd hoped that perhaps when I was eighteen I might be allowed to travel out to India. To get to know him and – and to see a little of the world at the same time. Now the opportunity – of his acquaintance, I mean – has been lost for ever. There's a sadness, yes.'

'So now you're alone in the world?'

Pausing so that the maid and gardener might catch up with them, Lucy shook her head. 'My grandfather will continue to care for me. And Archie, now that he's twenty-one, has become my official guardian. Not that I shall allow him to bully me, of course.' She laughed again, this time with a trace of shame. 'One hardly likes to confess these things. The news of my father's death reached us here only two days before Archie was to celebrate his coming-of-age with a great fair for the tenants and a dinner and ball for all his friends. All the invitations had been sent out and answered, all the food and wine ordered, and musicians engaged. Even the flowers, many of them, had been picked. We had to send a message to every guest who was expected. Yet of course my father had been dead for some time already when the news reached us at last. It was tempting to wish that the message could have taken three days longer to arrive. So that there would have been fewer disappointments.'

She hoped he might reassure her that such a thought was natural, and not an indication of heartlessness on her part. But Gordon was staring at her in a curious way – so intently that she felt herself flush. What she had first liked about him was the sparkle in his dark eyes even when he was at his most earnest. But she was startled now by a flash of grimness in them. Did he despise her for allowing a small social problem to intrude into her mourning?

'The celebrations will only have been postponed, I imagine,' he said, walking on again.

'Oh yes. They're to be held as soon as possible after Archie's term ends – before his friends have had time to scatter too widely for the Long Vacation. It's hard on the tenants, because it will all come too near to the fair which is planned to celebrate the Queen's Jubilee, but . . .' She shrugged her shoulders. 'Would this be a suitable place, Mr Hardie?'

'For what?'

Had he forgotten the purpose of his visit? If so, he was quick to collect himself and study the area to which she had brought him – a small gorge cut out in the past by a stream later diverted to flow through the moat. Stepping aside, she watched as he took a note pad from his pocket and began to draw quick sketches. With vigorous movements of his hands he indicated to the gardener the height of a 'mountain' or the zigzag of a path. 'I'll send you a plan,' he said. 'And order the rock, if his lordship approves.' Still scribbling, he paced out the area in rough measurement, before rejoining Lucy with an expression of apology on his face.

'I'm taking too much on myself,' he said. 'What do I know of landscape design? You, with your artist's eye, will be able to create a picture in stone. Will you support my application to your grandfather, Miss Yates?'

'You ask more than you realize,' Lucy answered, laughing. 'The consequence of my support will be that I can't hope to see you again for at least three years. Kindness to you is cruelty to myself.'

She spoke with the tone of voice that she learned at her grandfather's dinner table. The form of badinage in which she had been taught to pay or to parry compliments was not coquetry but a superficial conversational skill, useful in society. Even as she spoke the words though, it came to her that she was telling the truth, and for a moment she could not continue. Only with a determined effort did she maintain the sparkle in her eyes.

'I shall tell him that he must be the most generous of all your patrons,' she said. 'So that he may have the best of your discoveries. But I shall say this only on one condition – that before you go you will take tea with me in the library, and show me on the globe where you are going. How you will travel there, how long it will take. I demand to hear it all – and you can't refuse me, while I hold my grandfather's purse in my hand.'

134

'Can you believe that I would refuse you in any case, Miss Yates? Even empty-handed, your beauty would command me.' He bowed low over her hand, entering into the flirtatious extravagance of what he doubtless took to be only a game in words. Lucy was not sophisticated enough to make him understand that she wanted him to mean what he said. She had to be content with the fact that his visit to Castlemere extended itself by more than an hour as he pointed out his route, telling her what he hoped to find and what dangers he must expect to meet.

'Oh!' exclaimed Lucy when at last he rose to go. 'How I envy you! If only I could make such a journey with you!'

The air between them was charged with silence. Gordon could have laughed the remark off as foolish; he could have detailed the objections which made such a wish impossible in practical terms; he could have murmured some polite formality which, meaning nothing itself, would have reduced her own remark to nothingness. He did none of these things. Instead, he backed towards the door without speaking, his dark eyes meeting her gaze steadily. Lucy felt the blood drain from her face. He was reading her mind, and understanding that what she said was quite literally what she meant. It was true that more than almost anything else in the world she longed for the adventure of travel in strange places. But without any qualification at all, what her heart and mind and body yearned for was the company and love of Gordon Hardie.

135

Three

Did Midge know? As Gordon made his way back to Oxford, the question repeated itself in his mind. He should have been exulting in the marquess's generosity. Alternatively, he might have examined his own emotions, and those of Lucy Yates. There were questions to be asked in that area as well, but he pushed them to the back of his mind while he considered this other: had Midge known that Archie Yates had invited all his friends to a coming-of-age ball in the Easter vacation? Had she received an invitation herself?

By the time he arrived home, his sister had already retired to bed. Or so their mother told him – but when Gordon himself went upstairs an hour later he could see under her door the candle glow which meant that she was still reading. He decided not to disturb her. It would be unkind to throw his information at her like a challenge. It must be dropped casually into a conversation, so that she could ignore it or enquire further as she chose.

Gordon lay awake for a long time that night, but it was not any longer of Midge that he thought, but Lucy Yates. Over and over again he passed through his memory the last few moments of his conversation with her. Could he possibly have misinterpreted her feelings?

No, he could not. She was in love with him. To admit that was not to be guilty of immodesty. Lucy was young and had not yet been introduced into society – her excitement during the previous year's Eights Week celebrations had been that of a girl glimpsing for the first time the pleasures of the life that might lie ahead. She was ready to fall in love; ready to be attracted to the first man who came along, just because he represented the wider world outside Castlemere.

If she had chosen Gordon rather than one of her brother's friends it might be only because he was twenty-seven rather than twenty. Or, more probably, she had fallen in love with the freedom which he seemed to represent. Herself yearning for wider horizons, she would see no possibility of attaining them. How natural it was that she should be stirred by the company of someone who could not only tell her about countries on the other side of the world, but who proposed to visit them. She had fallen in love with a plan, a way of life.

So Gordon tried to persuade himself, and all the time he knew that it was only part of the truth. He could recognize that Lucy Yates was in love with him because he had already fallen in love with her.

It had been easy to conceal that, even from himself, as long as she was hardly aware of his existence. But she had revealed her feelings, and so the emotion which each of them had tried to hide had stretched out through their silence to spark a flame into life. The flame, like that of a candle, could be starved of oxygen until it guttered or died, or it could be snuffed out at once, but it would be hypocritical to pretend that there had never been a moment in which it burned.

What of it, Gordon asked himself. Nothing must be allowed to change his plans. If he abandoned his expedition in order to court Lucy Yates, he would hold the loss against her for the rest of his life. And it would all be for nothing. Even her own wishes, if she were brave enough to express them, would not succeed in securing his admission to Castlemere as a suitor. The greatest kindness he could do her would be never to see her again – and that would also be a kindness to himself. For a little while longer Gordon tossed restlessly in his bed. But he was a young man with a strong will as well as a blazing ambition. Before he fell asleep that night he had made his decision to block all thought of Lucy out of his mind.

The next morning, before church, he went in search of Midge. He found her working in her own room, her head bent low over a table spread with books and notebooks. So intense was her concentration on the new notes she was making that she did not appear to hear him come into the room; and when he spoke to interrupt her scribbling, her eyes as she looked up did not at first seem able to focus on him.

Gordon was shocked by his sister's appearance – and by his own failure to take note earlier of what must have been apparent for some time. To say that she was pale would not signify very much, for her complexion was naturally white; but there was a new look of strain about her expression. Her face seemed to have become thinner, tightening the skin over her cheekbones; there were dark circles beneath her eyes. It would not, he supposed, be tactful to tell her that she looked like a ghost. Instead, he smiled in what he hoped was an easy manner.

'It's a glorious day,' he said. 'You should be out in the garden, enjoying the air.'

'The wind blows my notes about,' Midge said. Her hand held the pen poised over the inkwell, to show that she was allowing herself only the briefest of interruptions.

'Then stop working for a little while. Sunday should be a day of rest. Come out and talk with me for a few moments.'

Midge shook her head. 'I can't, Gordon. I've got so much to do.'

'A walk round the garden will refresh your mind and ease your eyes.'

'You don't understand,' she said. 'The Final Examinations are so close now. I have to revise everything I've learned in the past three years. And when I re-read the essays I wrote in my first year, I'm appalled to find how immature they are. The work of a schoolgirl still. I must work through all those subjects again and try to improve my reasoning. The only way I can hope to cover all the ground before the examination is by keeping strictly to a timetable of what must be done each day. And there are not enough hours in the day as it is. If I were to take time away from the work just to chatter, I should feel so worried at the thought of all the minutes slipping past that I shouldn't enjoy our conversation anyway.'

Gordon nodded, abandoning the attempt to persuade her. He could sympathize with the efficient way she had planned her work and the determination with which she followed the plan, because exactly the same determination had carried him through his own secret botanical studies. But there was more to his silence than that. He had forgotten that her examinations were so near. And if she were worried about them – as clearly she was – it would be an unkindness to add to her troubles by introducing the subject of Archie Yates.

'But you mustn't make yourself ill,' he said. 'A few moments in the sunshine each day, walking briskly, will send you back to your books with new energy. Won't you try to make a place for that in your timetable?'

Midge smiled at him. It was the smile of someone who recognized the friendly spirit in which advice was given but had no intention of accepting it. Gordon grinned ruefully back as he realized this, and retreated. He was still anxious to know what had happened to her friendship with Archie; but he would have to wait.

Four

Midge had refused to spare any of her working time for Gordon, but there was one social encounter which she could not, in politeness, ignore. When William Witney arrived from London to take up his new duties in Oxford, and to lodge with the Hardies, she was waiting with her mother to greet him.

Even before he arrived, he gave the impression of being two quite different people. To Midge, who had never met him, he would naturally be Mr Witney, and he would be addressed in the same way by all members of the staff on the business premises of The House of Hardie. But to Mr Hardie and Gordon, who had known him since he was twelve, the new manager had always been simply Will. It was amusing to hear them reminding themselves that they must change to a more formal manner as soon as they stepped out of the house.

The sense of Mr Witney's dual character was more dramatically suggested to Midge when he first raised his hat to acknowledge his introduction to her. He was a well-built man and his correct business clothes provided all the *gravitas* appropriate to his new appointment. But beneath the high hat his reddish hair grew straight upwards, like a bottle brush. He was clean-shaven, and the effect of the short, bristly hair was to change the whole aspect of his body. Now his broad shoulders and upright bearing gave an impression of athleticism rather than dignity. Only when he moved to follow Mrs Hardie upstairs did Midge notice his limp – a reminder of his first plunging introduction to The House of Hardie.

A third contradiction in his personality was not revealed at once. On the day of his arrival, Mr Witney spoke in the formal voice of a man accustomed to conversing with the aristocracy. Although he did not imitate their accent, he used the same cadences and grammatical constructions as his customers. But as Midge came to know him better, she discovered that he had another way of speaking – an easy and unaffected manner, hinting at a sense of humour that he was always ready to turn against himself, and liable at any moment to explode into vigorous Cockney; not so much reverting to the natural speech of his childhood as parodying it. The grin which accompanied this lighter style of conversation transformed his face into that of a young man: he was only a year or two older than Midge herself.

This free and easy manner, though, was to be a later discovery. When he moved into the house as a lodger, it was inevitable that he should at first be treated with an excess of politeness, and should reply in kind. On the one hand, enquiries were made as to his tastes; on the other, he was anxious to discover how the life of the family proceeded as a rule, so that he could fit in without disturbing its routines.

It was Midge herself who broke the ice of this over-elaborate consideration. On what seemed set to be the hottest day of June, she appeared at breakfast wearing a high-necked white blouse and a severe black skirt instead of the bright colours and light materials which were her usual summer choice. Rising to his feet as she entered the dining room, Mr Witney was so amazed by her appearance that he remained frozen in an awkwardly bent position, staring at her.

141

Midge burst out laughing. During the past two months she had been working so hard and worrying so much that her normal merriment had deserted her. But now the strain of revision was over and the new stress of putting her views and knowledge on to paper had not yet begun. She was able to smile as she explained to their lodger.

'This is a day of doom for me,' she said, although the brightness of her eyes seemed to contradict the words. 'The first day of the Final Schools Examination. A lamb would be decked for the slaughter with garlands, but we sacrificial victims are expected to dress ourselves appropriately for our own funerals. I shall be apparelled in this hideous fashion for twelve days, and I shall expect your undivided sympathy for the whole of that period.'

'Of course you shall have it, Miss Hardie.' Mr Witney bowed, and spoke in his dignified voice. 'Although surely you should be triumphant rather than downcast. I understand that for a good many years now women have been demanding the right to take the same examinations as men, so that their abilities can be truly measured. This is also a day of privilege for you, is it not?'

It could almost have been her brother Gordon speaking, so well did the gravity of his voice conceal the teasing choice of words. It was difficult not to compare the speed of his understanding with Archie Yates's plodding attempt to understand the importance of the examinations to her.

Midge reminded herself that she was trying not to think about Archie, and gave Mr Witney a light-hearted grin.

'You're quite right,' she agreed. 'I must regard it as an opportunity to demonstrate my brilliance rather than as an ordeal in which all my weaknesses will be probed. It will become a disaster only if I prove not to be brilliant after all.'

There were moments during the next few days when

142

she was forced to recognize that she did indeed lack brilliance. She had worked hard at her studies, and possessed a retentive memory and a well-ordered mind. But it was not, in the Oxford sense, a first-class mind. In conversation she was able to develop an argument in ways which were sometimes wild but often imaginatively effective. But in writing, when she became anxious to stay close to fact and eschew fantasy, her theories were expressed more cautiously and, although accurate, were dull. Reading through her answers at the end of each examination, she was clear-minded enough to recognize that they would earn her a place only in the Second Class.

Well, that would be respectable enough, if not exactly what she had hoped for in the beginning. To someone like Archie, a Second would represent an unattainable height; more probably he would have to be content, when the time came, with a mere pass degree. Once again Midge reminded herself that she was not to think about Archie.

For as long as her Finals were in progress, she refused to allow herself any feeling of tiredness. But as the last word was written, the last paper handed in, she was overcome by a combination of exhaustion and depression. Outside the Examination Schools, exuberant groups of undergraduates would be waiting to welcome the prisoners released from their ordeal. All the male examinees would be swept off to celebrate; and even amongst the very much smaller number of women, those who lived in a hall could expect to be met by their fellow-residents. Only Midge herself would emerge alone to a day which no longer had any purpose. Lonely and weary, she dragged herself outside.

'Cor blimey, Miss Hardie,' said a Cockney voice in her ear. 'You look proper done in, and that's a fact.' Mr

Witney raised his hat to reveal that ludicrous bristle of ginger hair. His mouth was grinning, but his eyes were concerned as he offered her his arm.

'Where are you taking me?' Midge was sufficiently pleased by his unexpected appearance to shake off some of her apathy.

'All over Oxford,' said Mr Witney, his Cockney accent fading away into earnestness, 'the young toffs are celebrating the end of their examinations with an orgy of the champagne which they've obtained from The House of Hardie but almost certainly haven't paid for. Is the daughter of the House, I asked myself, to be the only one of the lot of them who goes home sober?' He was steering her gently in the direction of The House of Hardie, which was not far from the Examination Schools, on the other side of the High. In the parlour, set out as though for a wine tasting, a bottle of champagne in a silver bucket of ice stood between two glasses.

Mr Witney pulled out a chair for her. He had left the door of the parlour open, Midge noticed. Perhaps so that he could keep an eye on the staff working in the shop; perhaps also so that they should not suspect him of planning a tête-à-tête with their employer's daughter.

'Your father's in London and your brother's in Cambridge,' he told her, opening the bottle. 'I had a word with Mrs Hardie after breakfast. The chaise will be here for you in half an hour. I hope I'm not presuming. But I didn't like to think of you going home as though it were an ordinary day.'

'It was very thoughtful of you.' Midge never allowed herself to feel tired for more than a moment or two and, as the bubbles touched her lips for the first sip at this unaccustomed time of day, she forced herself into good spirits again. Her smile of appreciation, in fact, was even

144

warmer than it would normally have been, just because of the effort needed to shake off the feeling of anticlimax.

'Good,' said Mr Witney, noticing this. 'You really did look a picture of misery when you came out on to the steps there. I was afraid something must have gone wrong. There was a nightmare I used to have before the tests I took with my night study classes – that I'd turn over the paper and find I'd prepared quite the wrong subject – French when it should have been Chinese, or something like that.' He was chattering to spare her the effort of talking. 'Here's to your First.' He raised his glass.

Midge shook her head. 'No chance of that, I'm afraid. And what would it signify, in any case? Although I'm allowed to take the examinations, I shan't be awarded a degree.'

'Do I hear a trace of resentment in your voice there?'

'Yes,' she admitted. 'It rankles that women are allowed to do only what men permit. A married woman may own her own property if a wholly male parliament graciously gives her permission to do so. If women are ever allowed to vote, it will be because that same group of men has reluctantly conceded the right to them.'

Mr Witney's voice changed as he considered her view seriously. 'Do you propose to raise your banner in that cause?'

'No,' said Midge. 'It's too early. So many of the arguments used by bigoted men are true, in fact. The first battle must be fought on the field of education. Only when there's a generation of women who are able to manage their own affairs and understand the affairs of the nation shall we be justified in talking about rights.'

'Yet you yourself – '

'I was more fortunate than most girls. My father, as I'm

145

sure you know, is generous and fair-minded. He was willing to allow me the same chance of education as my brother, if I seemed able to profit by it. I've done better, indeed, because I was never expected to work in the family business. But there was an element of luck about it. The Oxford High School for Girls opened its doors just in time to help me qualify for university education – and the greatest good fortune is that of living in Oxford, so that I've been able to study without leaving home.'

'And so – ?'

'And so I hope to become a schoolteacher. An assistant teacher to start with, of course, but as soon as I have sufficient experience I shall do my best to find a post as headmistress, so that I can choose my own pupils – and, indeed, go out to find them. Drag them away from their embroidery and their piano lessons, and educate them as thoroughly as their brothers.'

Fleetingly, as she spoke, she remembered the conversation she had had with Archie on this subject a year earlier. Her views, imperceptibly, had changed. Then she had expected to train future governesses in order that girls from good families might in future be better taught at home. Now she planned to bring such girls directly under her own influence and help them qualify to study at Oxford or Cambridge. Perhaps in time the present barriers of masculine prejudice would crumble beneath the weight of numbers.

Comparing this conversation with the earlier one, she recognized that a second ingredient was also different. Archie had been offered the best education that money could buy, and Midge suspected that it had left him with a feeling of contempt for the 'beaks' who were so obviously his social inferiors. Her ambitions must have seemed second-rate to him, so that he could discuss them only as a joke. Mr Witney, in contrast, had wasted his own chance of elementary schooling, such as it was. But he had made up for it since then, discovering what he needed to know and applying himself in his limited free time to making good the deficiencies in his knowledge. He, like herself, must recognize that it was education which could offer an escape from the handicaps of birth. He would understand, with such a background, why she thought her work could be important. As he refilled her glass, she felt her spirits bubbling as lightly as the champagne.

'I hope you'll choose to work in Oxford,' he said. 'The High School – '

Midge interrupted the suggestion with a shake of her head. 'I wouldn't want to work as a colleague with teachers who still think of me as a pupil,' she said. 'I shall apply to the Ladies' College at Cheltenham as soon as I hear my examination results. But, of course, I'm not the one who will do the choosing.'

'You'll be at home at least for the vacation, I hope. These past few weeks – you've been working so hard – I've been looking forward to the chance to get better acquainted now that you have more time to relax.'

'I hope to be in Oxford in three weeks' time for the *viva voce* examination,' Midge told him. 'Until then, I'm going to stay with a friend of mine. Her family owns a holiday home in the Lake District. We shall be able to walk the fells. After all this time at my books, I need to take some exercise.'

She smiled with all the pleasure of anticipation at the thought of striding out freely in the mountain air. But there was a different expression in the eyes of Mr Witney, who made no attempt to conceal his disappointment. As though . . . Once before, in the middle of a conversation

147

with a young man, she had seen such a look. Archie Yates, grovelling on the ground in mock apology, had acted a part, laughing; and then without warning had looked at her as though for the first time – and seemed to like what he saw.

Was she allowing her imagination to be ruled by conceit in believing that Mr Witney was making the same kind of silent appeal? If so, she must pretend, for his sake, not to notice. She drained her glass and stood up, thanking him for the kindness of his thought in meeting and cheering her. The words were sincere, but meant no more than she said. She had burned her fingers once by allowing a young man's entreaties to melt her heart. The consequences, fortunately, had been no more than a short period of extreme anxiety lest she should find herself pregnant, followed by the humiliation and unhappiness which Archie's letter had inflicted on her. It had been a lesson to teach her how quickly an infatuation could rage out of hand like a forest fire. She did not propose to make the same mistake again.

148

Five

'Congratulations!' exclaimed Gordon. The examination results were out: Midge had been placed in the Second Class. Her smile of pleasure seemed genuine enough; it was impossible for him to tell whether she had secretly expected a First.

'We should celebrate,' he decided. 'A day on the river. We'll take a picnic and I'll row you to Godstow.' Now that all the undergraduates had gone down for the Long Vacation there would be no difficulty in hiring a boat.

'I may not have to work, but surely *you* must,' said Midge.

Gordon laughed. 'Business is always slow in August,' he reminded her. 'And I can't persuade Will – Mr Witney – to let me do a full day's work. He's been so quick to pick up his new responsibilities that I've been able to leave him in charge while I searched for patrons; and now that I'm back in Oxford and prepared to pull my weight for a few more weeks, I find that there's no room for me. He's a sound chap, to be sure. I shall be able to travel with an easy conscience, knowing that the Oxford shop is in good hands. So, the river?'

Midge smiled in agreement and went off to discuss a picnic hamper with the cook, leaving Gordon to wonder how best to introduce the subject which had nagged at his mind for several weeks. Now that Midge need neither work nor worry, his questions would not distract her – but they might be hurtful unless he could express them tactfully.

While he was rowing, he wasted no breath on conversation, for the distance was a long one with no one to share the work against the current. Only when he had moored the boat and helped his sister to spread out a cloth in a low-lying meadow, did he open the conversation with a casual comment.

'This is something you've missed this summer. Last year, I remember, you spent a good deal of time on the river.'

'Last year I was a second-year student. Quite a different person from the harassed third-year approaching Finals.'

'And has it been the same with dances?'

'Even less possible,' said Midge briefly. 'A ball may last for only five or six hours. But there's all the distraction of choosing clothes. And resting beforehand and recovering afterwards. A whole week's work can disappear into the programme of a single ball. I told myself at the beginning of the year that there would be other summers, other chances of social distraction. It's been no great sacrifice to devote just these few months to my studies. Shall I cut you a piece of pie, or will you serve yourself?'

'A small piece, thank you.' But Gordon did not allow himself to be distracted by the change of subject. 'I would have thought, though, that you might have allowed yourself an occasional short break. To celebrate Mr Yates's coming-of-age, for example, since you and he are friends.'

'We *were* friends.' Midge's colour rose as she made the correction. 'The friendship has come to an end. If that's what you were trying to discover, you could have asked more directly.'

'I've no right to intrude into your private affairs. Though I must say, I think you've been wise – '

'Oh, it wasn't I who was wise. If we're going to discuss this tedious subject, you might as well hear the truth of it.

150

I was the fool you always thought me. And Mr Yates behaved precisely as you anticipated. I award you a First Class for intelligent prophecy.'

'How did it come about?' It was easy to tell that Midge was angry, but her anger seemed to be with herself rather than with Gordon's prying.

'He wrote to me at the beginning of the Easter vacation. His tutors' report on his work had been unfavourable. The Dean himself had opinions to be expressed on the subject. There was a strong suggestion that Mr Yates was allowing himself too many distractions. The Marquess of Ross, I gather, expressed some displeasure on reading these opinions. Since it was not to be expected that Mr Yates should abandon his rowing or his games or his dining companions, it was clear that I was the distraction most easily surrendered.'

'Did the marquess know of your friendship?'

'I gathered that he knew and disapproved. Not necessarily of myself as an individual. My impression was that any entanglement with a female person would be frowned on at least until Mr Yates had taken his degree. But an exception might, I suppose, have been made for an heiress. It's of no consequence.'

'I think it's of great consequence.' Gordon, thoroughly indignant on his sister's behalf, would have continued, but she put up a hand to stop him.

'I've had time to think about it, Gordon. I was upset for a day or two, certainly, but since then . . . I asked myself why I'd decided to study at the university. It wasn't because I propose to spend the rest of my life trying to discover something that no one has ever known before. I'm not a true scholar in that sense. The reason I chose to take a degree – or, at least, to pass the examinations – was because there was a job I wanted to do, and still want to. Now then; if I get married, my husband will not allow me to work.'

She paused for her brother's agreement to this statement, and he nodded his head. No husband could allow it to be thought that he was unable to support his wife.

'So I must choose between work and marriage. I've always known this. It's just that because neither a post nor a husband has been immediately on offer in the past, it proved too tempting when the first one came along – or seemed to. I was swept off my feet. Now that I can think about it reasonably, I see that Mr Yates has done me a very good turn. If my first suitor had been a gentleman who was in all respects suitable, someone I loved and continued to love, someone who was steadfast in his wish to marry me – well, I might still have been swept off my feet, but this time with no safety barrier to hold me back while I considered deeply what was best for me.'

'You can't be sure that marriage isn't the right thing. A loving husband, children, your own establishment – are you wise to turn your back on all this without having sampled it?'

'Once I move into that world, there's no turning back,' Midge pointed out. 'It's only if I start work and find it unsatisfying that I might perhaps hope for a second chance. You're going to explore an unknown country, Gordon, and you're excited about it even though you have little idea what you'll find there. You could look at it this way: that I shall be exploring too. The life of the spinster-by-choice is an uncharted one. Like you, I shall be taking a risk. But you must allow that I too can be excited.'

Gordon hardly knew what to say. Was Midge simply making the best of a bad job? Did she realize that in her sort of exploration, as in his own, there were bound to be moments of fear and loneliness, as well as the excitement she hoped for? He found it hard to decide whether to admire or to feel sorry for her. She seemed to sense his doubts, because the carefree merriment which until recently he had always been accustomed to see in her eyes returned as she laughed.

'First love is a notoriously dangerous condition, Gordon. I've learned from my experience, and it will save me from making the same mistake again. If I'm ever tempted in the future, I shall remember what I've just said – and what you said to me a year ago – and pause to consider more seriously where my affections may be leading me. I ought to be grateful to Mr Yates for taking this practical side of my education in hand.'

'Mr Yates is a bounder.' Gordon could read through his sister's apparently careless tone of voice to guess that she had been hurt. But there seemed no pretence as she shook her head to disagree with his comment.

'Mr Yates is a year younger than myself, and perhaps in some respects just as unsophisticated. You mustn't think of him as some wicked schemer, Gordon. I'm sure that his affection for me was genuine enough. It was foolish of him to put it into words, perhaps, just as it was foolish of me to allow him to become too familiar. But – '

'What do you mean by that?'

'Oh heavens, Gordon, don't jump down my throat. I mean nothing at all by it. I may have been a little humiliated, but I haven't been disgraced. A lack of decorum, perhaps, nothing more.'

'Those words of Mr Yates that you referred to – ' At the beginning of the conversation Gordon had been curious, and prepared to feel some indignation on his sister's account. But now it was his own anger which rose to thicken his voice and rob him of appetite. 'Did he

153

speak of marriage? Were there other occasions, after the one I know of, when you were alone together? Did he lead you into that lack of decorum you mentioned by allowing you to think of him as a fiancé – on the basis of some understanding, perhaps, which would be confirmed when he came of age and was his own master?'

For a second time in their conversation Midge flushed, making the answers to his questions clear enough. But then she took a grip of herself. Picking up a knife, she brandished it threateningly in his direction, while the familiar twinkle returned to her eyes.

'I understood that I'd been invited for a light-hearted picnic,' she said. 'To mark the end of my student slavery and a return to normal social life. I'm not prepared to spoil the day by devoting any more time and attention to a young gentleman whose part in my life is over. He and I won't meet again, and there's no point at all in discussing the past. The only business on our agenda is that of Mrs Tavory's closed apple tart. Can you eat half of it?'

'I've no appetite,' said Gordon.

'Then the ducks are in luck.' Midge began to break off small pieces of the crust and toss them into the water. A flotilla of mallards made towards them like an arrowhead from the far side of the river. 'Mrs Tavory would never forgive us if we returned it to her unappreciated.'

'Oh well,' said Gordon. 'I suppose I need to keep up my strength if I'm to row you back to Oxford. Yes, I could manage half.'

Just for one moment longer Midge looked at him seriously.

'If you should happen to meet Mr Yates in the course of business before you leave for China,' she said, 'I should take it very poorly if you were to mention my name. I accepted my *congé* with dignity, I hope, and for the sake

154

of my self-respect the matter is to be regarded as closed. Agreed?'

Gordon bit into the crumbling pastry and did not care that he was speaking with his mouth full. 'Agreed,' he said.

Six

At the moment when Gordon promised his sister not to interfere in her affairs, he had no intention of breaking his word. It was unfortunate that when he paid a visit to Castlemere only a few days after the river picnic – in order to assure himself that the stone he had chosen for the rock garden had been correctly cut and delivered – the first person he saw was Archie Yates.

Archie was returning from his morning ride at the time of the encounter in the stable courtyard. There was a moment in which Gordon, standing on the ground, felt himself to be small and inferior in comparison with the straight-backed rider who literally looked down on him from the saddle of his horse. Angry first with himself at succumbing to such a feeling, he was quick to turn his indignation against the confident young man as he tossed the reins to one of the grooms. Archie no doubt simply took it for granted that other men would unsaddle and cover and walk and groom the steaming chestnut at the end of his gallop – just as Gordon himself took it for granted that Mrs Tavory, the Hardies' cook, would produce food for him to eat at every meal. But Gordon, recovering his own sense of dignity, saw arrogance both in that careless gesture and in Archie's failure to recognize him. He placed himself under the wide arch of the courtyard entrance.

'Can you spare me a minute, Mr Yates?'

Gordon was tall, but Archie was taller – and a very much more solid figure. His tight riding boots and breeches emphasized the length and muscle of his legs, so that even standing on the ground he appeared to be looking down on Gordon – puzzled at first, but then nodding with a recognition which contained elements of surprise and annoyance.

'You'll get your money,' he said. 'My grandfather's in Scotland for the shooting. He'll deal with all this sort of thing when he gets back.'

Gordon's lips tightened with irritation. It was, as a matter of fact, the policy of The House of Hardie not to pester undergraduates for payment. Experience showed that most bills were settled in the end, and a curious sense of honour amongst the younger members of the aristocracy persuaded them to patronize most loyally those tradesmen to whom they owed the most. But that was a minor matter compared with the annoyance of being taken to be a mere debt-collector. Gordon had a better opinion of himself than that, and Archie's mistake stung him into intemperance.

'I'm not concerned with money,' he said. 'Only with a different kind of obligation. To my sister.'

'I trust Miss Hardie is well. And I hope in addition that she was successful in her examinations.'

'If she was, it's no thanks to you, Mr Yates. It could hardly have given her confidence to feel herself disdained.'

'I don't know what you mean,' said Archie. 'I have the greatest respect for your sister.'

'Then I wonder what your feelings would be towards anyone who treated your own sister in such a cavalier manner.'

The colour rose in Archie's cheeks, suggesting that he might feel some shame in respect of the past as well as irritation at Gordon's attitude.

'What are you trying to imply?' he asked. 'I'm sure such a phrase would never be used by your sister, from whom I parted on good terms – both of us acknowledging the need to concentrate on our studies.'

'If she said that, it was her pride speaking.'

'Then it was a proper pride,' exclaimed Archie with some spirit. 'And I doubt if she will thank you for suggesting that it was not the truth.'

Uneasily, Gordon recognized that this was so; but he had gone too far to drop the subject and walk away. 'It's humiliating for a young woman to admit that she was misled, Mr Yates,' he said stiffly. 'By promises which you ought not to have made, knowing that they could not be kept.'

'I made no promises. If she thought . . .' Archie's eyes flickered with something that looked very much like guilt, but he attempted to defuse the situation by smiling. 'Until I made your sister's acquaintance, I'd never met a young woman student. Her way of life and her ambitions are very different from those of, say, my sister and her friends. I may not always have interpreted her behaviour correctly. But as I saw it, for a little while we were both interested to develop a relationship which was a novel one to each of us. And, equally, we both recognized the moment when such an exploration came to a natural halt.'

'It may suit you to say so.' Gordon did not attempt to hide his disbelief. 'It seems to me that you took advantage of an unsophisticated young woman and encouraged her affection for you in an inexcusable manner. If the expression of your own feelings was not genuine, then your behaviour has not been that of a gentleman. If at the time you were sincere, then some explanation is required for your change of heart.'

Even as he spoke, he knew that he was behaving like a

158

fool. He had broken his promise to Midge in a way which could do her no good. If she ever discovered his meddling, she would be justified in quarrelling with him. And what, after all, had Archie done? Kissed her once or twice, perhaps. Midge had spoken only of a lack of decorum, so it was unthinkable that they should have gone further than that. A frank admission and apology would suffice to close the matter.

But Gordon himself had gone too far. The grandson of the Marquess of Ross could hardly be expected to take lightly the suggestion that he was not a gentleman. As Archie drew himself up in indignation there was a curious moment in which Gordon was able to understand why his clever, petite, dark-haired sister might feel attracted to a man who was in every way her opposite. There was no doubt that Archie Yates was a good-looking young man – and even now, when he was angry, there was a kind of healthy youthfulness about him which any woman might well find appealing. But Gordon was not allowed long to consider this.

'I owe you no kind of explanation,' Archie said, 'and I am not prepared to discuss my personal affairs with the son of my wine merchant. Kindly stand aside.'

Gordon stood his ground, blocking the way through the arch, although common sense told him that there was nothing to be gained by prolonging a confrontation which he had been unwise to begin. It was perhaps because he was looking into Archie's eyes that he failed to notice in time the fist which swung up to hit him under the chin. The force of the blow lifted him into the air before leaving him sprawling on the ground. A well-polished riding boot set itself firmly down a few inches from his face, and for a moment Gordon thought that he was about to be kicked. But, instead, Archie's toe scuffed into the dirt and tossed a scattering of dust over Gordon's hair. Then he was gone.

Gordon pulled himself up into a sitting position and touched his chin cautiously, deciding that his jaw was not – as at first he had thought – broken. Pain and fury struggled for dominance. It was fury which won – but it must already be too late for him to catch up with Archie and wrestle him to the ground. He stood up, staggering slightly, and was forced to lean against the courtyard wall for a moment. Only when his head ceased to swim and his eyes began to focus again did he become aware that he was not alone.

'Mr Hardie, are you hurt? Did you fall?' Lucy Yates spoke breathlessly, as though she had been running. Her blue eyes were anxious, and the hand she held out towards him trembled slightly, as though she would have liked to touch and help him rather than merely express a greeting. 'The servants told me you were here. I wanted to discuss the placing of the rocks with you, to be sure that we should agree. But first you must come to the house and let me bathe your hand.'

Gordon glanced down. He must have cut himself when he fell, but the wound, although bleeding, was not deep. Nothing would induce him to enter Castlemere now. He touched her fingers and bowed over them. Then he used his undamaged hand to brush the dirt from his clothes, rejecting her invitation with a shake of the head.

'I'll wash it in the stream as we pass,' he said. 'By all means let us talk of the rock garden together.' He tried to smile as he spoke, but was unable to force the muscles of his mouth into any pretence of cheerfulness, because the whole of his body was still seething with fury. Even as he followed Lucy through the grounds, there was a tightness in his mood which he could not control. He had inadvert-

160

ently humiliated Midge in her absence, and at the same time had allowed Archie to humiliate him. If only there were some way in which he could get even.

Within a matter of moments that way presented itself. Gordon stooped to dip his hand into the narrow stream which lower in its course would provide the projected rock garden with its waterfalls and miniature river. But Lucy, stepping across the water, went down on her knees and pulled him down to the same level so that she could hold the cut under water. She pressed it open with her fingers to wash away the grains of dirt.

'And now it should be disinfected,' she told him, still holding his hand so that she might study it. As he shrugged the necessity away, she looked at him, her bright blue eyes at first troubled by his lack of care, and then sparkling with a teasing merriment. 'How can you be trusted to venture on dangerous journeys, Mr Hardie, if you are not prepared to take proper precautions in small matters?'

'I see that I need to be looked after.' Was he joking? Gordon himself did not know. Even while he at last forced himself to smile, he felt his hand trembling in her grip.

'It would certainly be wise of you to take a companion. And no one you invited would be likely to refuse you.'

The whole world around Gordon became silent and still. Even the stream, it seemed, was arrested in its course – or else it was time itself which was standing still. Gordon stared into Lucy's eyes. How young she was – and how brave, to expose herself in such a way to a rebuff.

But why should she be rebuffed? What an exquisite revenge it would be if Archie Yates should be forced to endure the thought of his sister marrying into the family which had not been good enough for himself. There would be no reason for Gordon to feel guilt about such an outcome. He had not led Lucy on – the wishes she was revealing to him were her own. Nor would he be acting against his own inclinations, for he had recognized very early in their acquaintance how easy it would be to fall in love with this beautiful young woman. It would require only the very slightest relaxation of his self-control.

He did not relax it now. Although there was a smile on his face, it was his anger, not his love, which spoke.

'Will you marry me?' he asked.

Seven

Had Lucy Yates been the heroine of one of the novels which she was so fond of reading, she would have swooned with delight at the sound of the words she had longed to hear. But she was a healthy and practical girl, and to faint now would put her in danger of falling into the stream. Instead, she rose to her feet so that Gordon could kiss her if he wished. He would do so, she was sure, as soon as he heard her answer. A more sophisticated girl might have pretended to be surprised, or even hesitant; but Lucy allowed her happiness to reveal itself in honesty.

'Indeed I will marry you, Mr Hardie – as long as I may be the companion of whom I spoke. I can face any hardship except that of being a deserted bride. Will you promise that I may come with you to China?'

Gordon too stood up, staring at her with serious eyes. 'The hardships would be greater than you imagine,' he said. 'The climate near the Tibetan frontier is very harsh, and for weeks at a time a tent will provide the only shelter. Mountain tracks will be rough, and dangerous rivers must be crossed. Nor are the people in the remoter villages always friendly. I've read the experiences of other travellers in the region.'

Lucy met his gaze with her head held high. In pointing out the dangers, Gordon was behaving as honourably as she would have expected, but she was not to be daunted.

'I may appear to you to be pampered, and able to live only in the luxury of a house like Castlemere,' she said. 'But I can spend all day in the saddle, and I will outrun you over rough ground if you care to put me to the test. You will take suitable clothes to protect you from the weather, I imagine, and I could do the same. I even have some skills to offer. You will have to collect your plants while they are dormant – but I could paint them while they are still in flower, so that their new owners can see how they will appear.'

'Capital!' exclaimed Gordon. 'Then I hereby appoint you the official artist to the expedition.'

Lucy clapped with pleasure, and then held out her hands to be helped across the stream. Now, surely, he would kiss her, for they were engaged to be married. She stepped forward into his arms; but instead of embracing her, he held her at a distance and his expression clouded. Only a moment earlier he had seemed to share her delight and excitement. What could have caused this change of mood?

'Your family will not consent,' Gordon said. 'And without their permission you won't be able to marry until you're twenty-one. We mustn't behave . . . I ought not . . . I should have approached your grandfather before speaking to you. It would be better, perhaps, if you were to forget . . .'

'Better!' exclaimed Lucy. His sudden reversal surprised but did not offend her. It meant, she was sure, not that he regretted his proposal, but merely that he ought to have approached it in a different manner. It was with genuine gaiety that she teased him. 'I must warn you, Mr Hardie, that if you attempt to withdraw your invitation – *both* your invitations – I shall sue you for breach of promise of marriage. You will be held back in England by the need to defend court proceedings and all your plans will be wrecked. So you may think it after all simpler to follow your inclinations, and pander to mine.'

164

Gordon's smile seemed a little forced, but it *was* a smile.

'Nevertheless,' he said, 'it's not to be expected that your grandfather will approve.'

'My grandfather will allow me whatever I ask,' said Lucy confidently. She had always been able to twist him round her little finger. 'It will be better, I think, if I approach him first, rather than you. I believe that since my father's death it is Archie whose permission will be required. But Archie will obey my grandfather's commands, so there will be no difficulty. Why do you look so doubtful?'

'I hope you're right,' said Gordon.

'I'm sure I am. I shall be able to write to you within a week to say that we may be married as soon as you can procure a licence.'

'It will necessarily be a very hasty and simple affair,' Gordon pointed out. 'You would have expected, I'm sure, to marry in a cathedral, with a beautiful dress and bridesmaids and wedding presents.'

'I think you have quite a wrong idea of me,' Lucy told him spiritedly. 'I've been brought up at Castlemere and so I've accepted the way of life that Castlemere imposes. But I'm not old and set in my ways. The time must come when I shall leave here and make a life for myself – a life which is bound to be of a different kind. I would like it to be with you, Mr Hardie – Gordon.' She moved closer to him, sure that he would not stand aloof any longer. How strong he was as he clasped her fiercely in his arms – how different from the polite young men who had danced with her at Oxford and from the distinguished old men who dined at her grandfather's table. There was no one like him in the world; and he loved her.

As they made their way to the site of the rock garden a

little while later, Lucy felt as though she was floating on a cloud of happiness. She agreed with every suggestion Gordon made, for she admired him and respected his judgement so much that in everything he must know best. He wrote down the date on which he planned to sail, and the name of the ship, and she tucked the paper into her bodice as though it were the most valuable of keepsakes. When the time came for him to go she said goodbye while they were still in that secluded part of the garden, so that she could lose herself in his embrace. She could not have endured the formal parting which would have been necessary within sight of Castlemere.

How could she bear to wait the four days which must pass before her grandfather came back from Scotland? She was almost tempted to approach Archie directly – but Archie for some reason was in a foul temper that day, and Lucy was realistic enough to keep away from him.

The marquess, in contrast, was in a good mood when at last he returned to Castlemere. His son's grouse moor had proved to be well stocked, and he himself had been able to boast the largest bag when the first day's shooting ended. As a rule, Lucy could hardly bear to think of so many birds being terrified into the air merely so that they could be blasted down again. But on this occasion she listened patiently to her grandfather's account, asking tactful questions and offering congratulations.

'And you, young lady. How have you been amusing yourself while I was gone?'

Lucy took a deep breath. She had practised many different ways of approaching her request, but now she could not remember any of them.

'I've been thinking about the future, Granda. I am eighteen now. I would like – I would very much like – to get married.'

The marquess laughed affectionately. 'Plenty of time for that yet. I wouldn't say you were on the shelf at only just eighteen. By the time you finish your London Season next year you'll have proposals of marriage coming at you from all directions.'

'I've received one proposal already, Granda. I'd like to accept it.'

The smile faded from the marquess's face. 'Don't talk nonsense, Lucy. You're far too young. Put it out of your mind. We won't discuss it again.'

'But Granda, don't you even want to know who – ?'

'Makes no difference,' said her grandfather. 'Could be the Duke of Clarence offering to make you Queen of England one day and I'd still say the same. Look here, Lucy, you've finished with your books, and I don't doubt you think you know everything. But you've still to learn how to move in society, how to judge a man, how to choose the kind of life for yourself that will make you happy now and still keep you happy when you're forty. Your Season will be part of your education. A pleasant part, I hope, but with a purpose. Wait.'

'But I *have* chosen the kind of life I want. And I *have* found a man who is brave and clever and loving. London will have no one better to offer.'

'You can judge that when you come to it. When you're twenty-one, you'll be free to do whatever you want. If you think you love this man, and he loves you, put it to the test of time.' His offhand manner made it clear that he expected her fancy to be a passing one.

'It's far too long!' cried Lucy. 'Three years! You can't possibly expect . . . Besides – ' She paused, wondering whether it was wise to mention a fact which might increase her grandfather's disapproval. But what could be stronger than his present opposition? She had nothing to lose. 'He's about to leave on a long journey. As his wife I could

167

accompany him. But if you make me wait so long, I should have to miss what could be the greatest experience of my life.'

'Sounds to me as though you're more in love with the journey than with the man,' grunted the marquess. Then he frowned to himself and looked at her sharply. 'You'd better tell me after all. Who is it?'

'Mr Gordon Hardie.'

'Hardie! How does he come to be on proposing terms with you? And what does he mean by going behind my back?'

'You weren't here when he came, Granda. And I told him that I would ask your permission at once. He will call on you as soon as you will allow.'

'I don't allow. Don't allow anything. In particular I don't allow you to waltz off to heathen parts with a man you scarcely know. I'd have thought *he* had more sense than to lumber himself, even if you haven't. Can't say I blame anyone for falling in love with you, if that's what he's done. You're a pretty child. But a child still, all the same. He ought not to have taken advantage.'

'You allowed my mother to marry when she was only a few months older than I am now.' Lucy waited anxiously for her grandfather's reaction, not knowing whether the mention of his beloved only daughter would soften or upset him.

'Different kettle of fish entirely.' His voice might be thick with emotion, but there was no lack of firmness in it. 'I'd known your father since he was a boy. A younger son; not much money, but a good county family. School friend of your Uncle Edward, and then a fellow-officer in the same regiment. Your mother had known him as well – since she was ten and he was eighteen. Not a hole-in-the-corner rush like this affair of yours. She'd had time to

168

understand the man – and the kind of life she'd be leading if she married him. You have no idea, Lucy. No idea at all. Not your fault. Means I must do the thinking for you, though. The answer's No, and there's an end to it. Don't trouble me with the subject again.'

Lucy could hardly believe what she was hearing. Her grandfather had never before refused her anything on which she had set her heart. Even when, for her fifteenth birthday, she had pleaded to be given her own hunter and chose a horse which he felt was too strong and spirited for her to control, he had given way in the end. She left the room now in silence, feeling an anger that was perhaps childish, but at the same time a disappointment wholly adult – that of a woman in love and determined not to be thwarted.

During all the eighteen years of her life Lucy had accepted her grandfather's authority, even though she might try to wheedle her way out of his decisions. She owed him her duty for the way he had brought her up; there was no doubt about that. But if it were to be considered on a legal basis, his authority had been exercised on behalf of her absent father. And now that her father was dead, it was strictly speaking Archie whose permission was required. Moving quickly, so that she should reach him first, Lucy went to find her brother.

Eight

Archie was inspecting his guns when Lucy came in search of him. He had been presented with a pair of Purdeys for his twenty-first birthday, and they were about to be given their first test.

'Grandfather brought back an invitation for me to go to Scotland next week,' he told his sister. 'For the shooting, of course – but there's more to it than that. There's to be a ball at Lochander Castle, and Aunt Anna has been asked to make up a dinner party. I'm needed to partner cousin Marian.'

'Just for the ball?' asked Lucy with a flash of mischief in her eyes. 'Or has Aunt Anna a more permanent partnership in mind?'

'She may well have.' Archie smiled as readily as his sister at the idea. 'With the three eldest off her hands, she only has Marian to dispose of. But if she's cast me for *that* role, she's in for a disappointment.'

'Because Marian's too young, do you mean?'

'Not that in particular. Marian's – what? Eighteen, it must be by now. There's something to be said, I don't doubt, for packing a girl off from her father's house to a husband's before she's had time to get into any mischief. But it don't suit *me* to marry so young. A man's a fool to tie himself down before twenty-five or twenty-six, at the earliest.'

'So how do you see the ideal marriage?' enquired Lucy in an offhand manner. 'Between a girl of eighteen and a young man of, say, twenty-seven?'

'Something of the sort, I suppose. It's not a matter to which I've given much thought.'

'I'm eighteen,' said Lucy. There was an unusual firmness – almost defiance – in her voice which made Archie look up from the engravings he had been studying on his guns. The bright flush on her face held his full attention. 'And I would like to marry – a gentleman who, as it happens, is exactly twenty-seven years of age. I take it that you would approve such an alliance.'

'There's more to a marriage than the ages of the husband and wife, dash it all.' As Archie spoke, he did his best to think who the man could be. He had not known that she had any young men amongst her close acquaintance – but then, he was so much away from Castlemere that he could not expect to be aware of all her friendships. 'As a rule, though, it's only ill-favoured girls who need to be in haste to catch a husband. Someone as pretty as yourself is in no danger of being left on the shelf. Why not wait a little until you've seen a wider world and have a wider choice?'

'Because I've already made my choice.'

Archie shrugged his shoulders. He had no strong views on whether his sister should marry young. The only important consideration was that she should choose someone suitable. 'And who is the fortunate chap?' he asked.

'Mr Gordon Hardie.'

Archie set the guns back in their case and rose slowly to his feet. 'A gentleman, you said!' he exclaimed. 'You call Hardie a *gentleman*! You must be out of your mind. The man's a bounder. And a tradesman.'

Lucy, still flushed, defended herself with a tenacity which alarmed him. 'I've often heard Granda say how much he respects the opinion of Mr John Hardie,' she said.

'On his own subject, perhaps. He knows about wine. And in the pecking order of tradespeople I'll allow that a vintner stands high, just because he serves only the higher class of customer. But can you see yourself coming to that, Lucy – having to take comfort from the fact that you can at least look down on a grocer's or a butcher's wife?'

'I don't look down on anyone. Or up.'

'I'm being a realist.' He had been drawn into the conversation casually, but by now he was dismayed. To find himself attached by marriage to a man who had so impertinently attacked Archie's own behaviour was unthinkable.

In addition, Archie was well aware that the attack had been justified, although naturally he had no intention of admitting that. He had behaved disgracefully towards Midge Hardie. Part of what he had said to her brother was true; he had genuinely not known how to treat someone who claimed more freedom in her life than most young women. But he could not carry that excuse very far. Midge had made it clear that only a promise of marriage, or at least an understanding, could justify her remaining alone with him. He had not given such a promise, but he could understand that she might have thought he had.

Archie did not feel too much guilt about seducing her. She must surely have realized that he could not help himself, and she had seemed willing. It was in his behaviour afterwards that he had been chiefly to blame – for he had treated her rather like the girl in the nearby tobacconist's shop who was unofficially regarded as being Magdalen property. He knew perfectly well that he ought to have gone to see Midge the next day – but how could he, when he had nothing to say that she would want to hear?

She would expect marriage; girls from that kind of

family always did. But although Archie was not clever, he had a fair share of common sense. Any promises of such a sort which he might make would lead only to disappointment. The liking and desire that he felt for Midge were genuine enough, but he knew that she would not make a suitable wife for him – nor, as his wife, would she be happy. Had he tried to introduce her into his own circle, Lucy would have been kind, because that was her nature; but the rest of his family would have disapproved, the servants would have been scornful and his friends incredulous – whilst Midge herself would have been bored. Since Archie had no estate of his own, he needed a wife who would bring him land as part of her dowry if he was not to live the life of a dependant. To think along those lines was not calculating but practical – for the sake of his future wife as well as himself.

So it was for Midge's sake, he told himself, that he had done his best to save her from a disappointment which would have been greater had it been longer delayed. Although he would have liked to continue in the enjoyment of her company – her conversation, her kisses, and more – without obligations on either side, he recognized that this was impossible. So he had changed the time of his weekly tutorial to avoid the danger of any accidental encounter. He had also invented an order from his grandfather – who was wholly ignorant of Midge's existence – to provide an excuse for his own sudden withdrawal. Only, though, because he thought that such an explanation would prove less hurtful than a blunt statement of his own decision.

One anxiety had remained after the ending of their relationship. If Midge should have a baby . . . His first thought when Gordon Hardie had confronted him five days earlier was that his worst fear was about to be realized. It was relief which helped him to control his anger at the beginning of their conversation – and a different kind of relief which left him in command at the end. Midge had been discreet, he realized. Her brother obviously had his suspicions, but had been given no firm information about what had happened. That meant that she intended to protect her reputation even within her own family. So Archie could consider himself safe from both marriage and paternity.

The pleasure of knocking Gordon Hardie to the ground for impudence had provided a neat end to the episode. Archie would remember Midge with pleasure as well as guilt, but he did not expect ever to see her again. If she were to enter the family by a different door, as Lucy's sister-in-law, how could he face her? There were a good many reasons for opposing Lucy's plans, but this was the one which most strongly prompted him to persuade her that she must be reasonable.

'I'm not like Aunt Anna, Lucy,' he said. 'You needn't fear that I'll ever act as a matchmaker. And Grandfather, I'm sure, looks for nothing but your happiness. You'll never be pushed against your will into an alliance with some great family just because it may suit someone else's interests. But it's a matter of common sense that you should choose a husband of equal rank in society to yourself. Someone who moves in the same world as yourself – whose friends are your friends.'

'I have no *world*, as you call it.' It was hard for Archie to tell whether Lucy was angry or upset. 'And very few friends. I meet no one here but Granda's acquaintances and the daughters of ladies who come to call for half an hour or so. Castlemere may have provided me with a comfortable world, but it's a narrow one. And if I were to do as you say and think only of "suitability" I should find myself trapped for the rest of my life in some other great house – Castlemere under another name.'

'And that's a far better prospect than being trapped in some poky little town house with half a dozen children perhaps and only a maid of all work to help you with them.' Archie spoke as emphatically as his sister. 'Have some sense, Lucy. Unless Grandfather chooses to make you a marriage settlement, you've no money with which to run a household. You haven't been brought up to be a tradesman's wife. You don't know how to cook or clean a house or nurse a sick child.'

'I could learn!' exclaimed Lucy spiritedly. 'And you talk as though the Hardies were paupers. Mr Hardie – Mr *John* Hardie – has a cook, and housemaids, and gardeners. Not as many as there are here, naturally, but a number appropriate to the house. I shouldn't find myself suddenly doing the work of a scullery maid. In any case, as soon as we're married I shall have the chance to explore the real world – the world outside England. I shall be able to accompany Mr Hardie to China.'

'You'll do no such thing!' Until this moment Archie had been arguing with Lucy in the tone of the wrangles which had regularly punctuated their childhood. But her startling announcement reminded him that within the past few months he had inherited the authority with which he could impose common sense on her. 'If you want to marry before you're twenty-one, you'll have to have my permission. And if you think I'd give it to such a marriage as this, you can think again. The idea is preposterous, Lucy. And – ' But Archie checked himself abruptly. He had been about to voice the opinion that Gordon Hardie might have proposed to Lucy only out of spite, to get his own back on the family for what he saw as a slight to Midge. But, setting aside the fact that Archie was not anxious to talk about his relationship with Midge, he saw that this would be to carry the argument too far. Lucy was beautiful enough to make any man fall in love with her. To suggest a cynical motive for a proposal of marriage would be hurtful and almost certainly untrue. 'No,' he said. 'No, no, no!'

That evening, over a game of billiards with his grandfather, Archie mentioned his sister's request. The tightening of the marquess's lips in annoyance confirmed his guess that Lucy had gone first to her grandfather for permission to marry.

'You told her not to be a little fool, I hope,' growled the marquess.

'Of course, sir. But I wondered – she's a headstrong girl – I wondered whether it might be as well to make her a ward of court.'

'Waste of money. Chancery proceedings would eat up a far larger fortune than Lucy can expect. That sort of business is for heiresses on the grand scale, with no relatives, or else quarrelling ones. To protect her from fortune-hunters. You and I can agree on Lucy's well-being, I take it. And what fortune has she got? On her twenty-first birthday she'll come in for a few pennies from the money I put into her mother's marriage settlement. As for the rest – if she makes a sensible marriage she can hope for a settlement of her own, and a bit more when I'm gone. But that's not money in her hands now. No call to let the Chancery get its hands on the family affairs. The Hardie boy won't give up his China ambitions just for the sake of the girl. He's due to sail soon – in October, I believe he said. We should be able to keep Lucy under our eyes until he's gone. After that – by the time he comes back in three years or so, she'll have forgotten him.'

'Perhaps it would be a good idea for her to accompany me to Scotland when I visit Aunt Anna next week; and to stay for a month or two.'

'Not Scotland!' exclaimed the marquess. 'Brougham may have put an end to all this wedding-by-handshake business at Gretna Green, but they still have some outlandish laws up there. She's over sixteen, so she'd only need twenty-one days' residence north of the border and she could marry any Tom, Dick or Harry without needing permission from anyone. Hardie's no fool. He'd be on to that fast enough. Certainly not Scotland. She'll do better here, where I can keep an eye on her myself. I'll put an end to any correspondence, for a start.'

Archie nodded his approval. 'You mentioned our mother's marriage settlement,' he said tentatively. 'When I was talking to Lucy just now, I saw no reason to speak of that. It seemed better to make her recognize that she could have no expectations at all if she were to behave foolishly.'

The marquess, concentrating on a successful series of cannons, made no comment, but from his manner seemed not to disagree.

'I'd like to go further, with your permission, sir,' said Archie. 'I think it should be made clear to both Lucy and Hardie that should this marriage ever take place, they couldn't expect you or myself to recognize it, and certainly they could never hope for any financial help – whether in the form of gifts or of legacies.'

'Doubt if that will make much difference,' grunted the marquess, marking up his score as the break came to an end. 'Young girls in love think they can live on air. And as for young Hardie – doesn't know his place, but that doesn't mean he's a fortune-hunter. Probably reckons he can afford to keep a wife – and so he can, no doubt, in a way. Not the way I want for Lucy, that's all.'

'Even so.' Archie pressed doggedly on. 'I would be glad to have your agreement on this, sir. If Lucy understands that both the men she should most respect are adamant in refusing permission for her to marry, she might think again. And the best way to indicate firmness would be in the way I suggest. It would be a support to me if I could have your word that if she is disobedient to your wishes you will give her nothing during your lifetime and leave her nothing when you die.'

'It won't come to that. You're right – when she sees that the two of us are of one mind . . . But yes, you can tell her that by all means, if she comes to you again. My word on it.'

178

Nine

On each of the first five days after his return to Oxford, Gordon received a letter from Lucy. She wrote of her love for him, and her plans and preparations; she asked how she could find a way to learn Chinese. The letters bubbled with her youthful vivacity, bringing a smile to Gordon's lips as he read them.

On the sixth day, however, her tone had changed, bringing a thoughtful frown to his forehead. Archie was being horrid and stubborn and had refused to give his consent to any marriage on her part. And her grandfather, who had by now returned from Scotland, was taking longer than usual to respond to her blandishments. He would come round in the end, of course, to give his own consent and order Archie to follow suit: Gordon was not to worry.

Midge must have taken note of the flurry of letters from Castlemere. No doubt at the time of her friendship with Archie she had learned to look out for the distinctive seal. She made no comment until the servants had withdrawn and her parents and Will Witney had all left the table. 'Is the marquess proving to be a demanding patron?' she enquired then as Gordon read the latest epistle through for a second time.

'I think I must expect that he will withdraw his patronage,' Gordon told her. 'Although not for any reason connected with the plants he instructed me to provide for his garden.'

'Why then?'

Gordon hesitated. Would Midge be upset if he told her what had happened? Well, she would have to know at some point. He gave a rueful smile as he confessed.

'I've had the presumption to ask Miss Lucy Yates if she will marry me. And she has had the sweetness to accept my proposal. She will be sailing with me to China.'

It was easy enough to interpret the expression on his sister's face. She was astonished – but she was also hurt. He hurried to make it clear that he had not gained the acceptance earlier refused to herself. 'His lordship is no more approving in this case than he was in yours. But there's a difference. Archie Yates depends on his grandfather to set him up in the world. Otherwise – heaven forbid! – he might find himself forced to work for a living. Without family approval, he has no hope of being able to support a wife. But Lucy . . . if Lucy is prepared to accept a more modest way of living than that of Castlemere, then she may accept the support of a husband and snap her fingers at her grandfather and brother.'

'My impression, when we met, was that she was strongly attached to them.'

'Yes. So we hope that they can both be brought round, if only by the realization that she cannot be turned from her decision. It's only the marquess, though, whose good opinion I would like. It would give me a certain satisfaction to marry Lucy *against* the wishes of her brother.'

'You're not, I hope . . .' Midge looked down at the table, her fingers playing with the unused cutlery. 'It was love for Miss Yates, I take it, which prompted your proposal? Not any wish to take revenge on her brother? Not anything to do with myself?'

'How can you think such a thing?' Midge's suspicions came so close to the truth that it was necessary for Gordon to be vehement. 'You've seen how beautiful she is.

You've learned from speaking to her how delightful her enthusiasms are, and how sweet her nature.'

Midge nodded her agreement, but did not abandon the argument. 'I also remember how clearly you set out your views on marriage to me. You would not dream of looking for a wife until after your return from China. And even then, you would first of all check all contenders for the post in terms of their suitability before deciding with which one to fall in love.'

'Was I so pompous?'

'Only because you were playing the part of the big brother. But that gives me the right, as little sister, to remember it.'

'Well, I was saying what I believed. To tell the truth . . .' Gordon hesitated before proceeding to an indiscretion. Midge would laugh – but why should he rob her of that amusement? 'To tell you the truth, I hadn't intended to make any proposal of marriage before I left. It was Lucy herself – '

'She asked you?' As Gordon had expected, Midge laughed delightedly. 'How my opinion of her rises! A young lady not just sweet and pretty, but prepared to speak her mind.'

'Not in so many words. She merely made it very clear that she wished to accompany me. And you see . . . I would have found it possible to sail off without saying anything at all of my feelings for her. Then at least I could have indulged in dreams that she might still be free when I returned. But once it had been put to me in such a way that I must say Yes or No – why, how could I say No and rob myself of all hope?'

'But you could just have asked her to wait for your return,' Midge pointed out.

Gordon shook his head. 'She loves me as an explorer

rather than as a wine merchant.' There was a silence between them as they both at the same moment realized the significance of what he had said. 'I must get to work,' he added hastily.

He spent that day at The House of Hardie, sitting at a table with Will Witney and going through the ledgers. Within a few weeks a new generation of undergraduates would arrive at the start of the academic year. Before that fluster of activity began it was as well to notice which of the old accounts were overdue for payment and to consider how best to treat the young debtors. Gordon gave the new manager what amounted to a thumbnail character sketch of each of his customers.

So efficiently had Will already taken over the office that Gordon wondered as their session ended whether there would be any place for himself in the business after his return from China. The Oxford establishment was now in good hands, whilst John Hardie himself would not expect to hand over the general management of the business for a good many years yet. Gordon could not extend his first expedition beyond the three years he had planned, because his patrons would expect him to return with their promised plants, but there seemed no reason why he should not contemplate a second exploration before too long.

It was not hard to guess what had led him to this thought. Did Lucy Yates realize that she would be marrying a vintner who would only for a very short period of his life be free to travel abroad? Gordon felt no false humility about his social position. Lucy might be the granddaughter of a marquess, but her father had been only an army captain at the time of her birth, and she had neither title nor fortune in her own right. She would not, in Gordon's opinion, be demeaning herself by marrying into a family which had earned a comfortable livelihood for all its members by two and a half centuries of honest hard work. She needed her family's permission to marry while she was still under age, because that was the law; but she was not being asked to bring a dowry with her.

So from Gordon's point of view there were no hidden problems – but had Lucy, he wondered, considered the life she would be expected to lead when she returned to England? He ought to bring her to see his home, to meet his family, but he had not even suggested such a visit. Was that because he knew that she would not be allowed to come, or because he was afraid that she might be dismayed by what she saw? Or could it be – something he had not dared to admit to himself – that he almost hoped she would be shocked, but only when it was too late for her to escape: when she was tied to the Hardies by marriage and estranged from her own family by disobedience?

His conversation with Midge at the breakfast table had found its mark. Gordon's desire for Lucy was genuine enough – but so was his belief that a female companion could only be an impediment to his travels; the two balanced each other out. Some extra emotion had been required to tip the balance, and there could be little doubt that Archie had provided this. Gordon did indeed feel a wish to score off that conceited and insensitive young gentleman – to hurt his pride by proving that an alliance with The House of Hardie was not after all unthinkable. What *was* unthinkable, as Gordon belatedly realized, was that he should sacrifice an inexperienced girl to such a discreditable impulse.

It was not an easy conclusion to draw; and Gordon did not come to it within a single day. His decision was made easier, though, by the fact that no further letters arrived from Castlemere. Lucy, he felt sure, had continued to write. What appeared as silence could only mean that her family was blocking all further communication. They would take precautions, as well, to prevent Lucy from running away, should she have any ideas of that kind. But since they would also have prevented his own letters from reaching her, she was more likely to be unhappily believing that he had forgotten her than making romantic plans for escape. It would be better for everyone if the situation were to be drawn to a tidy end. Without pausing to consider any longer whether he was regretful or relieved, Gordon sat down to write one last letter.

Ten

Lucy did not allow herself to become downcast by her family's opposition to her marriage. Her grandfather could not bear to see her miserable and would soon, she was sure, change his mind. Meanwhile, there was no time to be wasted if she was to be well prepared for the great journey.

During the eighteen years of her life at Castlemere Lucy had needed to make few decisions about her own affairs. Her grandfather issued orders and the machinery of the household ensured that they were carried out. If a dinner party was to be arranged, Lucy would discuss the menu with the cook and the flowers with the gardeners, but she was not required to solve any problems which might arise. She could order ices to be served on the hottest day of summer without needing to trouble herself about details – it was enough that an ice house existed and that somebody had presumably at the right time of year remembered to do whatever should be done with it. So it came as a surprise even to herself when she discovered that she was capable of being practical.

Another – more regrettable – discovery was that she could carry off deceit. It was only for a little while, she assured herself. As soon as her grandfather relented she would describe to him everything she had done, and they would laugh about it together. Concealment began even with the reading which encouraged her to make her plans. The adventures of Miss Marianne North, who had travelled all over the world, became her bible. Had the marquess realized that Miss North was an explorer, he would have frowned. But because the purpose of her explorations was to depict the plants she found in every country, Lucy could openly admire her botanical artistry – a skill of which no young lady need be ashamed.

Lucy's packing list began, in fact, with her painting equipment. Gathering together the most necessary items, she took note of Miss North's hints, collecting jars with tightly-fitting lids in which to carry water, and commissioning the estate carpenter to construct a light-weight folding support to replace her unwieldy easel. Complaining of a headache, she visited a pharmacist and spent a fascinating hour discussing with him the contents of a medical pack which, she said, was to be given to a friend just about to embark on a long journey. Together they envisaged every possible illness and accident and listed a cure for each – and, if possible, a preventive.

'And Keating's powder against fleas,' added Lucy, when it seemed that nothing could have been overlooked.

'And a poison for cockroaches?' suggested the pharmacist.

Lucy hesitated. 'We shall – I mean, he will be camping in the open as a rule. A poison is for use in a kitchen, I imagine. Besides, in some emergency, groping in the dark for a medicine . . .' She shook her head. 'No. No poison. The list, I think, is long enough already.' She left the pharmacist to collect all the items together and arrange directly for the local saddler to make a leather and canvas roll for them, easier to carry than a wooden box.

The pharmacist entered cheerfully into the spirit of the adventure, but Lucy found it more difficult to persuade the dressmaker that she was not joking when she asked for several divided skirts to be made for her. 'They are the latest fashion for playing games such as croquet and

186

lawn tennis,' Lucy assured her firmly and untruthfully. 'And they should be a little shorter than is usual.'

'In white, or in cream?' asked the dressmaker, preparing to measure Lucy in case she had grown taller since the most recent fitting.

'Two in black and one dark brown. One of the black ones should be of a thin stuff which will dry quickly if it becomes soaked. The others should be of the warmest possible quality, to wear in the coldest weather.'

'For croquet!' exclaimed the dressmaker. She had known Lucy all her life. In the end, of course, she always obeyed instructions. But there had been times when as a child or a very young woman Lucy had demanded something so unsuitable that a word of warning was necessary, and it must have seemed that this was just such an occasion. Lucy herself saw the absurdity of her request and burst into laughter – but without altering her requirements.

'Well, you must keep a secret,' she said. 'I intend to surprise my brother by abandoning my side-saddle. He will never be persuaded that a woman can ride as well over hedges as a man. I propose to appear at the hunt one day and amaze him by my new style of horsemanship.'

Part of her explanation was true, and the secret – although not of course the reason for it – was one which she was forced to share also with the grooms. But although they might gossip amongst themselves, there was no reason why they should discuss her affairs with the marquess – who would not in any case have listened to tittle-tattle. Lucy did not expect that she would need to ride fast in the course of the expedition. But she would certainly have to spend long hours in the saddle, and it was unlikely that a Chinese muleteer would saddle his animals in the manner taken for granted by ladies of quality. There would be new muscles to stretch and a new habit of balance to acquire. It was only sensible to practise now rather than to develop aches and pains at the outset of her travels with Gordon.

All this secrecy was only necessary in case Archie and her grandfather remained obdurate. She hoped she could change their minds, but it was impossible to be sure. For this reason, she hardly hesitated for a moment when Archie asked her – in the most casual of manners – when young Hardie proposed to set out on this jaunt of his. If she was indeed to be forbidden to marry Gordon, a close watch would probably be kept on her for the day or two preceding his departure. Truthfulness would be unwise – yet she was almost shocked by the facility with which the lie tripped off her tongue.

'On October the second,' she answered. It would not do for her answer to appear as offhand as the question, for then Archie would never believe her. 'And I do ask you again, Archie, before it's too late, to give me whatever this stupid permission is that's needed so that I can join him. It means so much to me, and so little to you. It will break my heart to think of him sailing out of Southampton without me.' The scrap of paper which she kept in a locket round her neck assured her that Gordon would be leaving the Royal Albert Dock in London by the P & O ship *Parramatta* on October 14th. If on the much earlier date she had mentioned she was to display an appearance of melancholy, this would surely put to rest any suspicions of an elopement.

The thought of an elopement was a recent one; previously she had assumed that such events took place only in novels. But she was not used to having her wishes thwarted, and a stubbornness of character which she had not known herself to possess made her determined to get her own way. Having not yet come out into society, she had no conception of how it might feel to be refused acceptance by that society. By the time the long expedition ended she would have passed her twenty-first birthday and would return from China as a married woman. What could be more respectable than that? Naturally she had complete trust in her fiancé as an honourable man.

It was worrying, nevertheless, that she received no answer to the letter in which she reported her family's opposition to him. Was he discouraged? Did he assume that under pressure she would change her mind? Lucy continued to write every day, and for the time being repeated her belief that her grandfather would eventually be persuaded to give consent. But time was passing. She continued to plead with the marquess and to make her quiet preparations, but her anxiety grew.

It was not until nearly the end of September that a letter was brought to her as she sat down to breakfast one morning. Recognizing Gordon's handwriting, she glanced to see whether her grandfather was watching her; but he, at the far end of the table, seemed absorbed in his copy of *The Times*. Lucy opened the letter and began to read.

'My dear Miss Yates.' The very opening came as an unwelcome surprise, for he had previously addressed her as 'My dearest Lucy'. But there was a further shock to come, when she read, 'I have been distressed to hear nothing from you since you wrote to report your brother's opposition to our marriage. But through my disappointment I have to recognize that you show good sense in accepting the verdict of your family, because it would distress me even more if I were to find myself responsible for you severing relations with your grandfather and brother.

'My love for you is unchanged. My heart will be yours for the rest of my life, and I shall make it my first business when I return to England to assure myself that you are happy. But that return will not be for three years. A young lady as beautiful as yourself will be courted during that long period by many suitors, better connected than myself and able to count on your grandfather's approval. I could not expect – and would not wish – you to turn your back on them in favour of a man who can offer you nothing but three years of neglect. And so I write now to release you from any promises by which you may have felt bound.'

There were a few other phrases at the end of the letter, wishing her well, but Lucy was too upset to read them. How could he give her up so easily? How could he accuse her of losing hope when she had written every day – sometimes twice a day – to assure him that she would get her way in the end? A possible answer to the second question presented itself to her mind almost at once, and this might provide an answer to the first. Blinking back her tears, she addressed the far end of the table.

'Granda!'

The wall of newspaper was lowered. 'Yes, m'dear?'

Without warning Lucy found herself unable to speak. Was it because she did not want her grandfather to hear her voice quavering with unhappiness? Whatever the reason, her silence succeeded in imposing itself on the marquess as a question.

'The young man shows good sense, Lucy,' he said. 'He's taken his time to come round to it, but what he says in the end is right. Three years is too long to mope along on your own. You'll soon forget him. So cheer up.'

Lucy's blue eyes opened wide and she slowly rose to her feet. There was no quavering in her voice now as she

190

spoke. 'How do you know what he says?' she demanded. 'Did you read the letter? You had no right even to open it. It was addressed to me. And have there been other letters that I've not even been allowed to see? You let this one through, I suppose, because it said what you wanted it to say, but what about all the others? And my letters to him – what happened to them? I might have sent Marie out to post them quietly in the village, but I didn't think that you would stoop to stealing them and . . . and . . .' Lucy could control her tears no longer, but by now they were tears of indignation as well as of unhappiness.

'It's for your own good, Lucy,' said the marquess, a trace of uneasiness in his voice. 'You're only a child. You haven't the judgement – '

'If you treat me as a child, how can I be anything else? You had no right . . . no right . . . you've ruined my life.' She ran towards him, angry and appealing at the same time. 'Granda, it might still not be too late. Let me see him – let me explain.'

'Don't be a little fool, Lucy. It's all for the best.'

Lucy stamped her foot in a show of petulance. But she was acting. Her anger was genuine enough, but already a plan of action had flown ready-made into her mind. She no longer cared about behaving deceitfully, because she had been deceived herself. It was necessary that the whole household should know that she was upset, and in a decline.

Not for a moment did she consider that there was any wish on Gordon's part to break their engagement. The interception of her letters had misled him into thinking her unkind, but she felt sure that his true feelings, like hers, were unchanged. So when she returned to her room there was no fear in her mind about the step she proposed to take.

'Listen carefully, Marie,' she said to her maid. 'For the next four days his lordship and my brother, if they enquire, are to be told that I'm confined to my room by nervous prostration. I don't wish to see a doctor. The cure for my condition is in my grandfather's hands, and if the opportunity arises you may indicate that I said so. Certainly you may say that I can't stop crying. I'll have all my meals sent up to my room, although I shall return most of them uneaten. On the fifth day – that will be October the third, will it not? – I shall appear again at meals. But I shan't need your help with my dress or hair for a few days, since I shall take no interest in my appearance. Instead, I shall require you to run some errands for me secretly.'

She set to work to write them down. Marie – who was as English as Lucy herself, adopting a French name only as a professional requirement – read through the list doubtfully.

'I shall lose my place,' she said when she had taken it all in.

'There will be no place for a lady's maid at Castlemere whether you help me or not,' Lucy said briskly. 'I shall send a letter of high recommendation to the agency, telling them that you are at liberty only because I am about to travel abroad. And the sum you need to buy my passage will take only a part of what the pawnbroker should allow you. I shall be able to make you a present. To compensate you for any delay in finding a new position. And as a reward for your discretion. Now, let us go through this list together and see that you understand all you are to do.'

It was less than an hour since she had been weeping in

her grandfather's presence, but within that hour she had become a different person. During her Eights Week visit to Oxford, Lucy had changed from a child to a young woman. Now, as she made her plans, anticipated difficulties and resolved them, another and more rapid change was taking place. A new spirit of independence had been born in her. She was no longer a sister and granddaughter, nor yet a wife. Instead – although it might be only for a short time – she was about to take charge of her own life.

PART THREE
The Great Adventure

One

The Royal Albert Dock was crowded with passengers and their friends and relations when Lucy arrived there early on the morning of 14 October, although the *Parramatta* would not sail until noon. Confused by all the bustle, she wished that her maid was at hand to help her find her cabin and settle in. But Marie's part of the plan kept her at Castlemere, to report that her mistress was confined to bed with a feverish chill. Archie by now was back at Oxford, and by great good fortune the marquess was spending a week in London, believing the crisis affecting his granddaughter to have passed. After three days Marie was due to rush downstairs to report that Lucy's bed had not been slept in on Saturday night. Her acting performance was unlikely to save her from dismissal but might, if luck went their way, lay a false trail towards a ship of another line, scheduled to sail out of Southampton on that day.

Before anything else, it was necessary to make sure that Mr Gordon Hardie had taken up his passage on the *Parramatta*. How ridiculous it would be if, while Lucy was running away from England for love of Gordon, Gordon should decide to remain in England for love of Lucy! But all was well. Not only had Mr Hardie already embarked; he had been allotted his seat at table. Lucy, glancing at the lists in an apparently casual manner, requested that the name of Miss Young should be written in for the same table.

She had decided to travel under an assumed name in

case the marquess, anticipating some such escapade, should have written to the shipping lines asking to be informed if any Miss Yates tried to book a passage. But as every stage of embarkation passed smoothly, she was able to feel with relief that she had been successful in deceiving her grandfather.

Marie, too, had done well in her allotted tasks. The most important of these were to pawn Lucy's jewellery, book her passage and make the arrangements for her journey to London; but she had also smuggled clothes and other personal belongings out of Castlemere, packed them, and arranged for their delivery to the ship. Lucy checked that one of her trunks was in the baggage room and a second one – not wanted on the voyage – was in the hold. Her cabin trunk was already occupying most of the floor space of the tiny room – only six feet square – which would be her home as far as Bombay: a home to be shared with a stranger who seemed already to have claimed the top berth. At any other time Lucy would have been dismayed by the cramped conditions. But today she was too excited and too nervous to bother about such details.

With no one to see her off, she began to explore the ship while most of the other passengers were on deck. The cabin offered only a small collapsible washbasin, so it was a relief to discover a row of marble and mahogany bathrooms. Mahogany was again in evidence in the saloon, a large and imposing room, ornate with carvings and columns and panelling, and with a wide gallery at one end, furnished as a music room. There was a smoking room, from which Lucy retreated hastily, supposing it to be for gentlemen only; a card room; a small lending library and writing room; and a ladies' saloon, already occupied by so many children and nursemaids that it seemed likely to prove the noisiest part of the ship.

That thought was interrupted by a greater noise: first a clanking, then a shuddering and creaking, followed by the steady thumping of the engines. It proved after all impossible to stay below deck at the moment of departure.

Most of the other passengers were waving to their friends on the dock. Lucy did not trouble to look down. Instead, searching the line of passengers with her eyes, she picked out the back of Gordon's head as he leaned over the rail. Her body flooded with love for him, so that for a moment she was unable to move. But what a risk she was taking – and without the approval or even the knowledge of the man she loved. If she had miscalculated, she was ruined indeed.

For almost an hour, as the *Parramatta* moved into the estuary of the Thames, she remained on deck. Returning eventually to the cabin, she found her travelling companion lying on the top berth, weeping noisily. The sobbing stopped as Lucy closed the door, as though it had been an indulgence to be allowed only until this moment.

'Are you unwell?' asked Lucy.

A plump, middle-aged woman, whose hair and eyes and clothes all seemed to have been bleached to a watery paleness, gave one last sniff and climbed carefully down from the berth.

'Just said goodbye to my children,' she told Lucy. 'Three years since I saw them last. Three years before I'll see them again. When I came home in June, they didn't know me. It's hard to realize that in a month or two they'll have forgotten me again. The stranger who came to visit.' She began to cry again. 'My four darlings!'

'Why must you leave them, Mrs – ?' asked Lucy.

'My name's Mrs Stewart.' More firmly than before, she pulled herself together and made a good attempt at a smile. 'You're Miss Young. I saw your name on the cabin list. Going out to get married, I wouldn't be surprised, a lovely girl like you. This is something you don't think about when you promise to leave your country and your friends and family behind you to start a new life with your husband. India kills children. For their own sakes, they have to come home. And then where does your duty lie? With the children, or with your husband? Some choose one and some the other. Whichever way you do it, you think you've made a mistake.' She gave a deep sigh. 'Time for tiffin.'

'Tiffin?'

'A light luncheon. We dine in the evening. Food every few minutes, you'll find, on these ships. Stops you getting bored. Makes you fat instead. Like to come with me?'

Lucy shook her head. She was frightened, she realized. Frightened of the first encounter with Gordon. In that moment of surprise, before he could bring his feelings under control, would she see delight in his eyes – or horror? 'I made a good breakfast,' she said. 'I'm not hungry yet. Thank you very much.'

'Well, then. I've left you those two drawers. For the rest, we have to use our trunks as wardrobes. When I come back, we'll walk together for a little if you like. If you're travelling alone, you may like to have someone my age to keep an eye on you. Not that I'd interfere, I don't mean. But you know what they say – that every voyage to India ends in at least one marriage. Something to do with the sun and the moon and all being cooped up together and needing a bit of excitement. If you've got a beau waiting for you in India, you won't be interested in a shipboard romance – but you might find yourself slipping into one all the same, and be glad of someone to check it. I shan't meddle unless you ask. But we shall get to know each other pretty well, I don't doubt, before we're through.'

Lucy was tempted to say at once that she was not proposing to stay in India, but merely to change ships at Bombay for the second part of her voyage to Shanghai. But she was not used to such a blunt style of speech from strangers and was disposed to be cautious until she knew Mrs Stewart better. She had expected to keep herself to herself, but clearly this would not be possible. Her fellow-passengers would be talkative and curious; she must think of some story to explain why she was making the voyage.

Considering this, and approaching the moment when she must come face to face with Gordon, her nervousness increased. There was no room in the cabin for two people at once, unless they were lying on their berths, so Lucy not only agreed that she and Mrs Stewart should take daily turns to be the first to dress for the evening meal, but offered to have the later turn on this first evening. As a result, most of the other passengers had already taken their places for dinner when she hesitantly approached her table.

'Ah! Our elusive tablemate!' The florid gentleman who rose to greet her obviously saw himself as the life and soul of the party. 'We all speculated throughout tiffin as to who would occupy the vacant place, but none of us could have imagined such a vision of delight. Allow me to introduce you to Miss Fawcett, Mr Hardie, Captain Hunter, Mr Elliott. And myself, of course. George Crichton, at your service.'

Lucy was standing almost immediately behind Gordon as these introductions took place. She smiled and nodded mechanically, but her eyes were fixed on the back of his head. He turned in his seat and began to rise as his name was spoken. Then, seeing her for the first time, his movement was arrested, as though he were suddenly paralysed in an uncomfortably bent and twisted position.

'I am Lucy Young,' said Lucy clearly. She held out her hand first to Gordon, because he was the nearest, but allowed him to touch her fingers only briefly before moving round the circle. 'Mr Hardie. Miss Fawcett. Captain. Mr Elliott. Mr Crichton.' The need to be polite in a social situation brought confidence flooding back to overcome her fear of what Gordon might be thinking. She took her seat opposite him and looked straight across the table.

How good-looking he was! Not handsome in the ordinary, smooth way in which the young captain to whom she had just been introduced was handsome. But his features were so strong and interesting, and his eyes so fiercely dark. Although she had made it clear that she was to be greeted as a stranger, she searched those eyes now for signs of welcome.

She could read nothing in them but incredulity. Through the whole of the first three courses he did not speak at all, as though the one question which he must not ask in company blocked him from attempting any other remark. His silence was not noticed in the general chatter as, within the first half-hour, Lucy learned that young Captain Hunter was on his way to rejoin his regiment in Peshawar, that Mr Crichton managed a tea plantation in Ceylon, that Mr Elliott served as a magistrate in Madras, and that Miss Fawcett was a missionary, returning to China.

Lucy herself spoke little. She was wearing one of the dresses in which previously she had entertained her grandfather's aristocratic friends, and Marie had taught her a simple but effective way in which to coil her long golden hair smoothly on top of her head for evenings. She wore no jewellery because everything she owned had been pawned to pay her expenses, but her neck looked even longer and more slender than usual for being unadorned. Candlelight, she knew, suited her complexion. She sat very straight, dominating the table by her beauty, so that even remarks which were not addressed to her were intended for her to hear.

Sooner or later her companions would begin to question her. She waited until the moment seemed imminent, with the serving of the second entrée, and anticipated it with a plea of her own.

'This is the first time I've made such a voyage. There's so much I need to know. Are there conventions to be observed – and mistakes which may be made by the ignorant, like myself? And how are we expected to amuse ourselves for so many weeks?'

'You may find, Miss Young, that the weather provides all the amusement you need for the first few days.' Miss Fawcett was over fifty and no doubt had suffered the batterings of the Bay of Biscay many times before. Her smile contained an advance dose of sympathy for the malaise to come.

'I'm sure Miss Young will prove to be a splendid sailor.' The fair-haired Captain Hunter, although in his twenties, had the fresh-faced complexion of a schoolboy. From the first moment of her arrival he had made no secret of his intention to bid for her company during the voyage, and now gave a wide grin. 'And if you feel boredom approaching, Miss Young, you'll need only to raise a little finger to find a host of admirers ready to entertain you.'

'I was seeking information, not compliments, Captain Hunter.' Lucy spoke primly, although not discouragingly, and was given the information she had asked for by Mr Crichton.

'I'm afraid Miss Fawcett may prove to be right about the Bay of Biscay,' he said. 'And even the Mediterranean can't be relied on for smoothness at this time of the year. But from the day we reach Suez you'll never have a free moment. You'll be required to take your part in all sorts of competitions – everything from cards to deck quoits. And even before that you must apply your needle to the making of a fancy dress, and practise your singing and playing for a concert. As for your first question, you should book a chair to be placed on the best part of the deck, even though it may be a week before you wish to use it.'

'But which *is* the best part?' asked Lucy. 'You see, I know nothing.'

As she had hoped, her companions were anxious to ply her with information drawn from their previous experience of travelling east. They would end the meal knowing little more about her than when she first appeared.

When dinner came to an end, Lucy's chair was drawn back for her by Mr Elliott, the magistrate: a serious man in his late thirties, who had spoken little more than Gordon during the meal. Out of the corner of her eye she noticed Captain Hunter advancing confidently towards her, and turned quickly in the other direction. Gordon Hardie moved just as fast, and reached her first.

'There's to be a concert by the stewards' band in half an hour, Miss Young,' he told her. 'Would you care for a brief promenade before that?'

'Thank you.' As he offered his arm, Lucy rested her fingers lightly upon it. That, at least, was all she intended to do. But in the weeks since their last meeting – the meeting at which he had asked her to marry him, and had kissed her – her love for him had been fired like one of those cylinders of steam which at this moment were

204

propelling the *Parramatta* forward. In her case, there was no valve to let the steam escape, and seeing her beloved again had brought her almost to the point of explosion. She had only barely managed to control herself throughout the lengthy meal, and now could do so no longer. Her hand gripped his arm with an intensity which must have been painful, but every other muscle seemed to be in spasm, preventing any movement.

It seemed that Gordon understood. He put his arm round her waist as though to steer her politely towards a door and propelled her out of the saloon and towards a secluded corner of the open deck. Other passengers were walking slowly up and down, but at this early stage in the voyage, when they were all strangers to each other, only their four tablemates were likely to be interested in the intensity with which these two gazed at each other.

Lucy was unable to speak. She had made her gesture and burned all her bridges behind her: she had no more courage left. It was for Gordon now to take her into his arms and assure her of all his delight and love. Her body trembled as she waited for his embrace.

'I don't understand,' Gordon said. 'Did you not receive my letter?'

Two

Even before he finished speaking, Gordon knew that he had made a mistake. Lucy's blue eyes, moist with emotion until that moment, narrowed and became distant. He should have talked of love, not of letters; he should have embraced her and covered her face with kisses. There could be no doubt at all that she had run away from home in order to be with him. She had risked everything he had told her not to risk – and it could only be for love. She must have expected him to be joyful, and instead he had asked for an explanation. What a fool he was!

He stepped forward towards her, his arms opening wide, ready to hold her close. But she stepped back, and there was a coolness in her voice as she answered the question in which he was no longer interested.

'Why yes,' she said. 'My grandfather allowed just one of your letters – if you wrote more than one – to reach me; after he had read and approved it. I hoped you would have guessed why you hadn't heard from me. But then, how could you be expected to realize that I could be treated in such a way, when I didn't suspect it myself?'

'It seemed to me that there was a message to be learned from your silence, whether it was deliberate on your part or enforced – that the wishes of your guardians were bound to prevail. How could someone who is only eighteen years old, with no experience of the world – '

'You should have given me credit for more determination,' cried Lucy with spirit. But it seemed that she was no longer hurt, for the sparkle was returning to her eyes.

'And it's only Miss Lucy Yates, I must tell you, who is a child of eighteen. Miss Lucy Young has announced herself as being twenty-one years old. I booked my passage under another name because I'm told that the *Parramatta* will call at Marseilles: some passengers to the East take the train across Europe to join the ship there, rather than experience the storms of the Bay of Biscay. Although I don't expect it, it's just possible that Archie may be despatched by that route to find me and take me back. But he would look for a Miss Yates – or he might enquire about you. So it would need to be clear that you are travelling alone and have developed no particular friendship with any other passenger.'

Gordon laughed. 'You mean that for the next few days I must behave coldly to you – the only man on board who doesn't realize his luck in sharing a table with such a beauty! Would your brother really go to such extremes? I'm truly sorry to have been the cause of a rift between yourself and your guardians.'

Lucy shrugged her shoulders. 'If there had been more time, my grandfather would have given in to my pleading. His only objection was on the grounds of my age – although he was also hoping that I might have a triumph in my London Season next year. I found Archie's objection more difficult to understand. I hardly expected him to care much about whom I should marry. But when he heard your name – '

'It's not to be hoped that he should care to have me for a brother-in-law,' Gordon admitted. 'At our last meeting – my visit to Castlemere – we had a difference of opinion. A violent difference of opinion. Since he was the one who knocked me down, it hardly seems reasonable that he should also be the one unable to forgive. But then, his behaviour has not been reasonable in any respect.'

'He knocked you down!' Lucy's eyes showed that she was recalling the scene. 'That time when your hand was cut? I noticed that your feelings were overwrought, but I thought . . . I didn't realize that you were angry.' She shivered as the ship changed course slightly, allowing the wind to penetrate their seclusion. 'Shall we walk a little? Or look for a sheltered place on the other side?' She led the way without waiting for him to answer or to offer his arm. 'What was the cause of your difference of opinion?'

'I'd just learned that your brother had made advances to my sister, giving her the impression that he had marriage ultimately in mind. Luckily, she was not too greatly misled – or so I believe. But the letter in which he later made it clear that there could be no possibility of an alliance between his family and mine was hurtful to her, to say the least.'

'So you wondered how he might feel if his own sister was to be hurt in the same way? A little tit-for-tat. How fortunate it must have seemed that an occasion presented itself so quickly.'

'Lucy, you can't believe – '

'Lucy?' The tone of her voice made it clear that if she had ever given him permission to address her so, she was withdrawing it now.

'Miss Yates . . . Miss Young . . . Lucy, you can't believe that your brother's behaviour has anything in common with mine. I told you in my letter how much I loved you, how much I shall always love you. It was for your own sake entirely that – '

'Was it?' asked Lucy. 'It seems to me that I've been quite as foolish as my grandfather thought. You never wanted to travel with a companion. It was unforgivably forward of me to suggest that I might accompany you. Whether it was politeness which prevented you from rejecting the suggestion, or a wish for revenge which encouraged you to accept it, hardly seems of much importance.'

'I was in love with you,' said Gordon. 'I still am. I underestimated your courage, perhaps. But how can you believe that I feel anything but delight – ?'

'I wasn't sure of that when I saw you this evening.'

'You must allow that I was surprised. And when you announced yourself under another name . . . You yourself have said that it would be unwise of me to pay too much attention to you at once.' They were still walking, close together but not touching except when the rolling of the ship caused one or other of them to stagger a little. But he was conscious of a lessening of her stiffness. She was ready, surely, to forgive his unforgivable reaction and to agree to what she had always wanted. 'I'll accept your instructions to remain reserved until we've left Marseilles. But after that, dearest Lucy, we must get married at once. Let me kiss you, my darling.' He could hear that the band had started to play. All the other passengers, grasping at every amusement on offer, would be back in the saloon by now to listen to the concert.

'I think it would be better,' said Lucy, 'if we were in a manner of speaking to start again from the beginning. As though we were *really* strangers today, and learning to know each other gradually as the voyage progresses, without any feeling of obligation on either side. So that if it seems to you, when you think about it, that I could only be an impediment to you on your travels, you will only need to keep silent and not to excuse yourself.'

'It's impossible to imagine such a thing,' Gordon protested. 'And your situation is such that anything but marriage is unthinkable. On a long sea voyage people accept unusual behaviour. No one may raise an eyebrow when you travel alone aboard ship, but it would be a very different matter if you were to arrive unescorted in Shanghai.'

'So you're prepared to marry me to save me from the consequences of my own rashness! You're too kind, Mr Hardie. Do you think I could spend the rest of my life knowing that I've burdened you with an unwanted wife? I doubt whether I shall have any trouble in providing myself with an escort whenever one is needed. I think marriage too important to be accepted as a form of politeness.'

Gordon was at a loss to understand how he had managed to put himself in the wrong for the second time that evening. Lucy must love him, or she would never have taken the huge risk of leaving home. And surely she must know in her heart that he loved her. It was true he felt a certain ambivalence about taking her as his companion on a dangerous expedition, and some of this feeling might have penetrated her consciousness. But he had made an honourable offer of protection, and she must realize that she had no real choice but to accept it.

Perhaps for the first time, he made an effort to understand her. It was not only her courage that he had undervalued, but her pride. For all her lack of a title, she was an aristocrat. Her disobedience to the marquess's wishes would rob her of any material legacy, but in her very cradle she had been heir to a centuries-old dignity and self-esteem. Because she was only eighteen, she might not yet feel secure in it, but that would make it all the more important for her to feel herself respected. Cursing his own insensitivity, Gordon took her by the hand and held her back for a moment.

'Lucy,' he said.

'Miss Young,' she reminded him. 'It seems to me, Mr

Hardie, that in this situation – of a group of people confined within a small space – it will not be easy to keep any secret. It would be unwise to think that we can step out of our roles even for a moment and expect to be unobserved.'

'But before we begin, may I not be assured that your feelings for me are unchanged?'

'I would have thought that my actions might speak for my feelings. It was not I, after all, who ended our engagement. But I accept that it has been ended, and that I have no claim on you of any kind. I notice that the concert has begun. But if you'll excuse me, I think I would prefer to retire early. The day has been a long one, and tiring. Goodnight, Mr Hardie.'

She was gone before Gordon had time to stop her. He was left with the irritating realization that he had completely mishandled what should have been a joyful and passionate encounter. And now he would have to play her game. He saw the sense of it, at least for a few days, but hoped that Lucy in turn would then admit that there was no point in continuing the pretence. Because after all – although it had been tactless of him to phrase it so baldly – she could certainly not be left to look after herself. He was in honour bound to marry her now.

Three

As the newest member of staff at Cheltenham Ladies'
College, Midge Hardie could not expect to be given a
working day off for anything less than a death in the
family; so she had not been able to wave her brother
goodbye when he sailed away on the *Parramatta*. Her first
free weekend came two days after he had left. She prided
herself on her energy as a rule, so was surprised to arrive
home feeling exhausted. Making a great effort to keep
awake throughout Saturday evening, she described her
pupils and duties with her usual liveliness; but afterwards
sank into sleep with the feeling that she would never want
to leave her bed again.

She had asked that no one should wake her in the
morning, but the clocks and church bells of Oxford did
not obey such instructions. One after another they called
her to service or marked the passing of another quarter-
hour. Midge lay on in bed. At first she was still heavy
with sleep and tiredness. Then her drowsiness became
pleasant, a luxury to be indulged. By ten o'clock she was
wide awake, and sufficiently relaxed to ask herself why
such a short term of employment should have caused her
to feel so tired.

She put the same question to Will Witney when, an
hour later, she at last went downstairs. Will sprang to his
feet as she opened the door.

'Your parents have gone off to church,' he said. 'From
what you told them about the number of times you have
to attend school chapel, they reckoned your soul wouldn't

come to much harm if you gave one Sunday a miss. Breakfast has been cleared, but shall I ring for some coffee for you?'

'Thank you.' Midge was interested to find that she had become a visitor in her own home, with Will acting as her host. But she made no comment on this and instead crossed to the window and looked out. To judge by the strength of the shadows, the Indian summer which had begun a week ago was not yet fading. 'I'll have it out in the garden – make the most of the sunshine before winter comes.'

'Good idea,' he said, tugging at the bell pull and giving the order. 'You looked pale last night. As though you could do with a bit of sun.'

'It's odd,' she commented, turning back to face him. 'I'm used to getting up early. I'm used to working hard. I chose to be a schoolmistress because I knew I should enjoy it. And I *do* enjoy it. But at the end of every day . . . I have to supervise an hour's prep after supper every evening, and I can hardly keep my eyes open, I'm so tired.'

'Any new job is a strain,' suggested Will. 'Getting to know a fresh lot of people and having to treat them right even before you know them. And wondering all the time whether you're up to the work. When I came to Oxford . . . So many mistakes to be made! As if I were on a tightrope above a pit of crocodiles.'

'I didn't realize,' said Midge, troubled. 'I ought to have been more . . . more . . .'

'More nothing.' Will brushed the apology aside. 'You were exactly what I needed. Your father and brother naturally had to keep an eye on me, to see that I got off on the right foot. But you simply took it for granted that I knew what I was doing. I was the Oxford manager, so I must be able to manage. You didn't even notice that I was a mass of quivering jelly my first day in the High Street. So it wasn't too long before I stopped quaking and became what you always thought I was – dignified, efficient, perfect!'

Midge knew that she ought to be ashamed. She had not noticed Will's problems because she had been too engrossed in her own. But his grin allowed of no apology, so instead she joined in his self-mocking laughter.

'You're right about meeting new people,' she agreed. 'Causing the strain, I mean. There are so *many* people in a school – colleagues and pupils, changing every forty minutes. Such a long day, and never a moment to oneself. That's the real shock, I suppose: never being alone. Well, I can enjoy an hour of that luxury now.'

He pulled a disappointed face. Had he hoped to accompany her into the garden, or was he teasing again, playing his comic act? She lacked the energy to find out, but instead made her way out through the French doors to the chair and table which were just being set out for her. Although she carried a book, she was too lazy even to read; content instead simply to sip her coffee and listen to the sounds of the garden.

This idyll was interrupted by a different sound – that of an angry voice in the drawing-room. It was not Will's voice, because she could hear him, more quietly, protesting. It seemed to Midge, as she listened, that she knew who it was.

Drawn by curiosity, although recognizing that she would be wiser to keep her distance, she walked towards the open doors of the drawing-room. As she had thought, it was Archie Yates whose wrath was breaking over Will's head. As Midge was about to step back, out of sight, he turned and saw her.

'Miss Hardie!' he exclaimed, his lack of politeness making it clear that he was overcome with anger. 'I must speak with your father at once.'

Midge looked at him in astonishment. Had he forgotten that this was their first meeting since the writing and reading of the letter which at the time had seemed to break her heart – the first meeting since the afternoon when he had carried her to his rooms in Magdalen? How was it possible that he could treat her as though she were merely a casual acquaintance? His anger must be great indeed if it could override in such a way what should have been at the very least a social awkwardness.

Well, if he could forget, so could she. 'I'm afraid my father's not at home, Mr Yates.'

'So your servants have tried to tell me, but I'm not in a mood to be put off.'

'My father doesn't play social games. If he's not at home, it means that he's somewhere else. If you have business with him, I suggest you make an appointment at his office tomorrow.'

'My business is not of that kind. Where is your brother, Miss Hardie?'

'He's abroad. Or at least, on his way.'

'And when did he leave?'

Really, thought Midge, this is insupportable. 'I hardly think that his travel arrangements are any concern of yours, Mr Yates,' she said coldly.

'He has run off with my sister. You'll allow, I hope, that *that* is my concern.'

Midge considered this statement in silence. At her last meeting with Gordon, just before she left to take up her post in Cheltenham, he had told her definitely that he had written to release Lucy from her engagement and would be travelling alone. Nevertheless . . . She turned towards

Will. 'Perhaps you would leave us to discuss a family matter,' she suggested.

The expression on Will's face changed from puzzlement to doubt, but he accepted his instructions and withdrew. It was odd, Midge thought, that had she still been in love with Archie she would have realized the impropriety of deliberately closeting herself with him. But because he was angry, and she no longer cared for him, there could be no harm in it. It was a good indication of the fact that she was cured of her attack of love.

She sat down and indicated a chair to Archie, but he was too perturbed to keep still.

'Well?' he demanded.

It was tempting to repeat that Gordon's movements were none of Archie's business. But Midge could tell that her visitor's anger was fuelled by genuine anxiety. Her willingness to be helpful did not, of course, make it any more possible for her to produce the information he was seeking.

'It's certainly true that your sister engaged herself to marry my brother,' she said. 'But when he learned that you and your grandfather were opposed to the marriage and had refused the consent that was necessary, Gordon wrote to release her from her engagement. He didn't think it reasonable that she should spend three years bound to someone who would be so far away for the whole of that time. That was the last communication between them.'

'It was certainly the last one that we were intended to see. But there must have been some later, secret message.'

'I think not. My brother and I are open with each other. I'm sure he would have told me of such a major change in his plans. And besides, my father saw him off.

He inspected Gordon's cabin and gave us a description of the gentleman who would be sharing it. You must be mistaken.'

'How can I have mistaken the fact that my sister has disappeared? She has not been seen by any member of the household except her personal maid since Wednesday night; and this morning it was discovered that the maid herself left Castlemere during the night. I received a message from my grandfather an hour ago. He is as certain as I am that Lucy has run away with your brother. You are not suggesting, I imagine, that she would do so without an invitation. Plans must have been made.'

'My acquaintance with your sister is limited to the afternoon which we spent together on the Magdalen barge,' said Midge. 'But my impression was of a spirited young woman with a fervent desire for excitement and, in particular, for travel. Might she not have made the plans herself?'

'She is eighteen years old!' exclaimed Archie. 'She knows nothing of the world. You cannot seriously be suggesting that she would leave her home and family, forfeiting any prospect of the kind of income and establishment to which her birth and beauty entitle her, and all without encouragement!'

'Young women in love have been known to behave foolishly.' The bitterness which Midge had done her best to control squeezed itself out at last and pulled Archie up short, as though until that moment he had forgotten that she had once been more to him than merely Gordon Hardie's sister. She shrugged her shoulders, dismissing the thought from her mind. 'Well, I'm afraid I can't help you, Mr Yates. I don't believe that my brother planned any elopement. But if Miss Yates has acted impulsively and thrown herself on his protection, he will see that she comes to no harm.'

'She has come to harm already, simply by placing herself in this position.'

Midge had had enough of the discussion. Her voice became even colder as she dismissed the subject. 'Then there's nothing more to be done, is there?'

'There's a good deal more to be said. How a man who had the blasted cheek to accuse *me* of not behaving like a gentleman in respect of *his* sister can then take it on himself – '

Midge stood up slowly and stared at him, hardly believing her ears. 'What are you talking about?'

'I'm talking about the way Mr Gordon Hardie arrived at Castlemere and tried to teach me my own business. I knocked him down for it – but I don't suppose he told you *that* part of the story.'

'He told me nothing of the incident at all. He was not authorized . . . He had promised to forget what I told him.'

'So he's not as open with you as you claimed! Well, next time you're in contact with him you may send a message from my grandfather and myself. To the effect that if Lucy thinks she can ever return to Castlemere or expect – '

'You may send your own messages, Mr Yates,' Midge interrupted icily. 'I'm not your errand-boy. You appear to have mislaid your manners. Kindly leave.' She rang the bell and waited in silence, as angry as himself, until he had been shown out.

When the door closed behind him, Midge was at first incapable of giving any further consideration to the unlikely idea that Lucy Yates had run away from home with the intention of travelling to China – and the even

218

more extraordinary possibility that she had made her plans without Gordon's help or even knowledge. Instead, she found herself trembling with emotion on her own account. How could she ever have believed herself to be in love with Archie Yates?

Four

Within a few moments of Archie's departure, Will Witney returned to the room, the troubled expression on his face contrasting oddly with his comic bottle-brush of ginger hair. Midge was in no mood to talk to him, or to anyone else, but could tell that he was resolved to interrupt her thoughts.

'I have to beg your pardon,' he said. 'Your visitor seemed in such a high old temper that I didn't like to go far away, in case you should need assistance.'

'Oh, I don't think it would have come to blows,' Midge assured him, still *distraite*. Then her cheeks flushed as she realized what his words implied. 'You mean that you overheard our conversation?'

'I felt that there might be a need to interrupt, so I listened, yes. Quite unforgivable, I see now. Will you forgive me all the same? I do apologize. I shall forget everything I heard straight away.'

'There's no need to do that.' Midge gave a careless toss of her head. 'Mr Yates told you what he thought had happened to his sister before you left the room. And for the rest – if you were left with the impression that I had once had a close relationship with Mr Yates, you would be right. But since that's entirely a thing of the past, I don't in the least mind your knowing.' She hoped, nevertheless, that nothing had been said which could reveal just how close the relationship had been.

'I'm glad,' said Will gravely. 'Glad that it's a thing of the past, that's to say.'

'What do you mean?' Had Midge been less distracted, she would have held her tongue – because even while she was asking the question she guessed what he meant, but did not want to hear him put it into words.

'I mean that I enormously admire you. No, I don't mean that at all. I mean that I'm head over heels in love with you. I see every other man in the country as a potential rival. So if one of them's been ruled out, that's marvellous news. Only a few million left to go. Your father said – '

'My father! You've been talking to him about me?'

Will looked momentarily abashed. 'Well,' he said. 'Fathers always have to come into this sort of discussion at some point. I know it's more usual for the lady herself to be sounded out first. But in this case – he's my employer, after all. He might have said, "You're getting above yourself, my lad. Hands off."'

'And what would you have done then?' Now that Midge had had time to recover from her surprise at the course of the conversation, and to shrug off the confusion aroused by Archie's unexpected arrival, she was prepared to give Will her full attention – relieved to realize that, at least on the surface, he was prepared to keep his manner light.

'It wouldn't have made much difference to what I *did*. Only to what I should say. Instead of "Would you be willing to marry one of your father's employees?" it would have to be "Would you consider marrying a man without a job?" Doesn't sound too good either way, does it?'

Midge could hardly prevent herself from laughing at his doleful face. 'And what *did* my father say?' she enquired.

'Nothing helpful. Just that you appeared to be a sensible sort of girl with a mind of your own. That he was reconciled to the fact that one of these days he'd have to pay all the bills for your wedding; but if you'd be willing to leave the choice of champagne to him, he was prepared in return to leave the choice of bridegroom to you. I have to admit, I took that as an invitation – no, that's a bit strong – as permission to try my luck.'

In the silence which followed Midge was conscious of Will holding his breath as he waited for the encouragement which she was not able to provide. She gave a little grimace of regret. 'I'm not sure that you've been wise in choosing today to raise the subject,' she said.

'I agree that moonlight in the conservatory would have created a better atmosphere; but it's a fortnight to the next full moon. I looked it up in the almanac. I thought this would be as good as I could hope for. Your parents out. Yourself tired and strained from your work, perhaps considering that there was something to be said for the life of a lady of leisure, with only a home to run. Although I've only got my salary – '

'I didn't mean any of that,' interrupted Midge. 'I was thinking of a time so soon after Mr Yates's visit.' She turned her head to look at him. 'A year ago I was – to use your own phrase – head over heels in love with him.'

'I don't care about that, as long as you aren't now.'

'No, I'm not. That's what bothers me. Within such a short time, to meet somebody I once loved and realize that I don't even *like* him. As things are, there's no harm done. But suppose I'd *married* him a year ago?'

'There are hundreds of answers to that,' said Will cheerfully, preparing to list them. 'The fact that you didn't marry him shows that your father is quite right in thinking that you're sensible. When you do decide to take the plunge, it will be with the right chap. And then – to be particular for a moment – there's no doubt that Mr Yates is a good-looking fellow. Tall, handsome, all that sort of thing. I can see that a girl – even you – might get swept off her feet without stopping to consider whether he might be a fool or a snob or an ugly customer beneath it all. But now look at me. No one's going to be swept off her feet by *my* face. And while Mr Yates is a rowing blue, I'm a cripple.'

'Don't be silly, Will.' Midge had never called him by his Christian name before, but she used it in her thoughts because she had so often heard her father and brother discussing him. Only when she saw the pleasure in his eyes did she realize that she had spoken it.

'Facts are facts,' said Will. 'Anyone who marries me will be marrying a lame man. But that's part of what I'm trying to argue. Anything you could feel for me would have to be for what I am, not what I look like. I've no fortune which might make my freckles seem invisible or sleek down my hair. I've got nothing to offer at all, really. It's all a great impertinence even to think of it. But I can't *not* ask. Will you marry me? Not at once, if you don't want to. If you feel that you ought to keep on working for a year or two, to make all your studying worth while . . . I wouldn't mind how long I waited, as long as I could be sure in the end . . . I can't live without you, that's what it comes to. For the next year or two I'll be in Oxford and you'll come home from time to time, I suppose. But then Gordon will return and I may be sent back to London.' He stopped, and let out his breath in a great sigh. 'Do please say you'll marry me.'

Midge stared at him with a troubled face. She liked Will. More than that, she admired him for what he had made of himself. He would be an easy man to love – but she didn't love him.

Everything was Archie's fault. Archie had taught her how it felt to be infatuated with the appearance of someone who was almost a stranger. Archie had given her the passionate excitement of a love which had nothing to do with liking. Archie had left her with a guilty secret which would have to be explained to anyone who expected that he would be his wife's first lover. And Archie had taught her that love was transitory. Had he been the only one to grow cold, it would just have meant that Midge was not capable of holding a man's affections. But her own love had died as well, and she found that far more worrying.

So her doubts now had many facets. She lacked the courage to open her heart to Will and to see whether love might grow simply as a result of that decision. Even if it did, she lacked the certainty that it would last for ever. She lacked confidence that Will himself would continue to love her once he knew her better. And on top of all that, she was genuinely unsure whether she wanted to live the life of a married woman. If she was finding it hard to come to terms with the career which she had chosen and worked towards for so long, could she be happy with an alternative which she had not seriously considered?

In the end, it was her very tiredness which supplied her with the strength to make up her mind. She had decided to be a teacher, and she must master that task before even considering a way of escape from it. How could she explain that to Will without hurting him?

There was no need to. He read it in her eyes, which must have shown compassion rather than love.

'Don't say it,' he begged. 'Don't say anything at all. I can't live with No. I might just be able to stagger on with a silence. Hope you'll change your mind one day.'

'It really *is* the wrong day,' Midge said. 'Nothing to do with you personally at all. I'm sorry, Will.'

As she turned away, she heard with relief the sounds of her parents returning from church. The episode could now be brought to a natural end by the need to tell them the news about Lucy Yates. But Will was standing between her and the door.

'Won't you kiss me before you go?' he begged. 'Just to show that you don't think I'm a monster.'

Midge had been trapped by kisses before. She shook her head and went quickly out of the room.

Five

Thirteen years earlier, as a runaway schoolboy of fourteen, Gordon had been reduced to a state of shivering
misery by the Bay of Biscay. He had hoped that his
subsequent three years of voyaging in the South Seas
might have cured him of seasickness for ever – or else,
that a steamer might not be as violently buffeted as a
sailing ship. But his hopes were disappointed. From the
moment when the *Parramatta* rounded Cape Finisterre he
was confined to his cabin. Only as the ship passed Cape
St Vincent and headed towards Gibraltar did his appetite
return. Either the sea was smoother now, or else he had
at last found his sea legs.

He had not been the only sufferer, he discovered, when
at last he presented himself at table again. The atmosphere in the saloon had changed markedly since the first
day out. Those few passengers who had remained on their
feet formed a select group, already friendly with each
other. They welcomed the others back without at once
admitting them to the new intimacy. At his own table, it
seemed that only Lucy and Mr Elliott, the magistrate,
had been unaffected by the rough sea. While only the two
of them were appearing for meals, Mr Elliott had naturally enough changed his place in order to sit next to
Lucy, and showed no intention of relinquishing it to Miss
Fawcett again. Captain Hunter, recovering a day earlier
than Gordon, had appropriated the seat on her other
hand.

Staying where he had first been set, Gordon told

himself that to stare across at Lucy was the greatest privilege – but could not restrain a feeling of envy as he saw how earnestly Lucy discussed the problems of India with Mr Elliott and how lightly she accepted Captain Hunter's flirtatious compliments. Mr Crichton leaned across to solicit her participation in the deck sports to be arranged that day, now that the sea was calm enough, and she made her selection from the events with laughing good humour. When Miss Fawcett arrived, the last of them all, to take her place at breakfast, Lucy was full of sympathy for her seasickness. Only to Gordon did she seem to have nothing to say – and that must be because he could think of no subject on which to open a conversation. It was a disquieting thought that she had first been excited by his stories because he was a traveller whilst she was obliged to stay at home. Now that she too was travelling, seeking her experiences at first hand, perhaps she found him less interesting.

After a brief stop at Gibraltar, it was not long before the *Parramatta* came within sight of Marseilles. Lucy retired to her cabin with a diplomatic headache, whilst Gordon, whose presence on the ship could not be concealed from anyone who studied the passenger list, leaned on the rail to watch the activity below. The boat train had already arrived from London, and the new passengers were waiting in a group. Neither the Marquess of Ross nor Archie was amongst them. Would Lucy, wondered Gordon, feel any regret that her family had, in the end, let her go? If that were the case, she threw it off as rapidly as her pretended headache when the engines once more began to throb and the screw to turn. It was more likely, he supposed, that she was triumphant at the success of her escape.

Certainly there was a new gaiety in her manner, as

227

though any uneasiness which she might have felt about her position had been thrown off. There could no longer be any danger in Gordon seeking her company, and this he did – but without great success. She was always, it seemed, engaged in one of the many activities organized by the entertainments committee – running egg-and-spoon races, playing deck quoits or softball cricket, singing and applauding in a concert, or chattering excitedly amongst the cluster of passengers who waited to discover the distance covered the previous day, and the winner of the sweep on it. In bad weather she joined in the tournaments of whist, euchre or cribbage – and when she declined to enter the chess competition, because she did not know the game, she immediately received half a dozen offers to teach her.

It was not surprising that Gordon found it so difficult to catch her alone. There were more than twice as many male passengers aboard the *Parramatta* as female – and, in addition, the ship's officers had time free for a good deal of socializing. Although Lucy was not the only unmarried woman aboard, she was undoubtedly the most beautiful. By the time the ship reached Suez, Captain Hunter, while continuing to flirt with her as though in fun, had become genuinely lovesick. Mr Elliott, whose character was more serious, affected to seek her out for the pleasure of her conversation; but his expression – when he was not in her immediate company but watching from a distance – revealed to Gordon that he too was enamoured of her.

These two gentlemen had enjoyed a start on the rest by virtue of sharing Lucy's table, but they were by no means alone in paying court to her. As well as her beauty, she had a touch of mystery to recommend her. Her story of relations to be visited in China could not be challenged, but was unconvincing. It was now taken for granted that she was travelling under an assumed name. Only a member of the aristocracy, rumour suggested, would make such a journey unescorted, and her clothes – well made of expensive materials – supported the theory that she was an heiress, the daughter of some noble line. Gordon alone knew the truth of her situation, and he remained as silent on the subject as Lucy herself.

As the ship approached Port Said, it was met by the coaling barges and a flotilla of tiny boats from which goods of all kinds were held up for sale, whilst small boys dived for coins thrown into the water. Larger boats appeared, to carry any passengers who wished to go ashore, and with some anxiety Gordon noticed that Lucy appeared to be dressed for such an expedition. He hurried to her side, but was annoyed to find that Mr Elliott had reached her first and was instructing her in the principles of barter.

'They would be astounded if you were to pay the price they first ask,' the magistrate explained. 'They'll demand at least twice what the article is worth, and will be highly delighted if they are paid in the end a little more than half that sum. So you should counter by offering to pay a quarter of the first price. They won't think you mean – it's the way the game is played. They'll start to come down a little, and you can increase your offer a little.'

'I shall watch you give a practical demonstration of your lecture,' said Lucy, laughing. 'But I shan't attempt the procedure myself. Although I want to walk through the streets, I shall take no money with me.'

'I've never met any young lady who, when it comes to the point, can resist the lure of shopping,' said Mr Elliott.

'You've met one now. On the return voyage it may be

a different matter, but for the moment I hardly feel the need of a rug or an Arab headdress.'

'May I also accompany you ashore, Miss Young?' asked Gordon. Until now he had refrained from intruding on her conversations with other passengers, but he was worried by the possibility that she might become lost and confused in this first experience of a foreign country.

'A pleasure, Mr Hardie.' Lucy smiled, although Mr Elliott did not look so pleased. Within an hour the three of them were making their way through a maze of bazaar streets, preceded by a crowd of small boys who demanded baksheesh for showing them the way, and importuned by others who sat on the ground displaying amputated limbs.

'I should after all have brought a few coins with me,' said Lucy; but the magistrate waved the beggars away.

'Their parents maim them in the cradle, so that they may make a living in this way,' he said. 'It's the same in India. I don't think it right to encourage the practice by giving to them.' He placed himself between Lucy and the beggars, and offered her his arm. There was only just room in the narrow streets for two together to pass the donkeys, laden with wide panniers on each side, which trotted up and down delivering goods. Gordon was forced to fall behind.

He watched the backs of his two companions with a growing feeling of irritation which he knew to be unreasonable. How elegant Lucy was! With her free hand she had lifted her skirts a little to keep them above the filth of the road; he could see her neat shoes, her slim ankles. She ought to have allowed Gordon himself to give her a first glimpse of a foreign country. Why was she walking with a stranger like this? She must have known that he regarded himself as responsible for her and was certain to offer himself as an escort. Why had she not waited?

Six

It had never been Lucy's intention to make Gordon jealous. Her feeling for him was straightforward. She was in love with him. She wanted to spend the rest of her life with him, to be wherever he was. If there were any complications, they were all on his side.

When, at Castlemere, he asked her to marry him, she took it for granted that he equally was in love with her, and continued to believe so even after the arrival of the letter which freed her from her engagement. But their first conversation aboard the *Parramatta* had sown such doubts in her mind that it was for Gordon now, she felt, to convince her of his love if in fact he still felt it.

A mere renewal of his offer of marriage would not be good enough. Whatever Archie might think, Lucy was sure that Gordon was indeed a gentleman, who would recognize his obligations towards her even though the difficulties of her situation were wholly of her own making. But just as she was not prepared to enter into a marriage intended only as a spiteful gesture towards her brother, no more was she going to let herself be married out of pity for a maiden in distress.

If, then, she took advantage of the free and easy atmosphere of shipboard life to encourage the advances of some of her fellow-passengers, it was not because she was a flirt and not because she wished to stir Gordon into jealous action. She was showing him that he could honourably withdraw without needing to feel that she was left unprotected. If, having understood that, he proposed marriage to her again, she would accept with joy. It was part of the game she was playing that he must not be allowed to guess at this in advance.

So, as the ship steamed cautiously through the Suez Canal and out into the stifling heat of the Red Sea, Lucy laughed and chattered and danced and played games as though she had not a care in the world. She was hardly prepared to admit even to herself the humiliation of her position. She could make herself independent of Gordon, if she chose, and so free him to continue his travels alone. But it could only be done by making herself dependent on someone else – someone whom she would not even love. It was the last thing she wanted to do.

As a girl in her grandfather's house, Lucy had taken it for granted that she would marry and have children one day. Until Gordon's arrival she had not thought of herself as a rebel; there was an appointed way of life for women, and she expected to follow it. The gesture of independence which had brought her to her present predicament was the only one she had ever made.

There was, moreover, no possible way in which she could continue to be independent. Mr Elliott had not believed her, and nobody else on the ship – except Gordon – would believe her either, but she was in truth penniless. All the most valuable jewellery which had belonged to her mother was still locked up in the marquess's safe, waiting for Lucy's twenty-first birthday. One necklace and a pair of ear-rings had been handed over in advance of that date so that she could dress the part of her grandfather's hostess with proper dignity. But by the time she had paid her expenses and rewarded her maid out of the pawnbroker's money, she was left with little more than the price of a single ticket to Shanghai. There would be an opportunity, when it was time to change ships at Bombay, to trade in her forward ticket for a return to England, but that was her solitary option. If she did return to England alone, she risked finding herself disowned by her family, and without doubt her reputation would be ruined. If, on the other hand, she continued on to Shanghai, landing without a penny to her name, what would become of her?

In her mind she ran through the short list of possibilities without flinching. She loved Gordon and she needed Gordon, but that must not be admitted until he had decided, without being swayed by pity, that he still wanted her for his wife. If he made no such decision, she could leave the ship at Bombay as the fiancée of someone else. Or – this startling idea was one which had only recently occurred to her – she could continue to Shanghai and offer to help Miss Fawcett with her mission work in return for board and lodging.

As the days grew hotter and hotter, Lucy began to spend more time in conversation with the missionary, fanning herself in her deck chair whilst her admirers, hoping to be noticed, loitered up and down the deck in front of her. It was embarrassing to hear Miss Fawcett talk about the 'rice Christians' – the Chinese converts who were motivated less by the love of Christ than by the offer of free rations. Uneasily Lucy wondered whether her own motives for the conversation might not be equally worldly.

'Are you talking about China? May I join you?' Most of the passengers on the *Parramatta* were travelling only as far as India, and had little interest in places further east. But Gordon, of course, was as anxious as Lucy herself to hear the missionary's experiences.

'Miss Fawcett has been telling me the most terrible things!' exclaimed Lucy. 'Did you know, Mr Hardie, that daughters are so little valued in China that when a girl baby is born she may be exposed at once on a bare hillside to die of cold?'

'I've heard the story,' said Gordon. 'Is the Church able to do anything for these unfortunate children, Miss Fawcett?'

'My own mission is on the edge of a small town. We've established some trust amongst the people. They'll bring babies to us which once they would have exposed, knowing that we'll take responsibility for them in our orphan compound. But in the countryside . . . Each month either my colleague or myself travels round the villages to preach the Gospel and offer whatever medical help is within our competence. It's part of our daily routine to search the nearby hillsides before dawn, listening for a cry and looking for a movement. But in almost every case, of course, we come too late.'

'Oh!' Lucy buried her head in her hands, feeling faint with horror as her imagination pictured the tiny naked bodies, stiff with cold. She was only just aware of Gordon hastily moving away and returning.

'Drink this water, Miss Young. You're too hot. Perhaps you should lie down in your cabin for a while.'

'My cabin is even hotter than the deck.' She sipped the water gratefully. 'Thank you, Mr Hardie.' After another drink, she tried to explain. 'I find the thought sickening. That a man should kill his own child, and the mother should allow it to be done.'

'She'll do it herself,' said Miss Fawcett bluntly. 'Within an hour of the birth she will leave her bed and go out into the night rather than burden the family with another mouth to feed – a girl who will never be of any use to her own parents, although when she marries she may act as a slave to her mother-in-law.'

'I can't understand it,' said Lucy. 'I can't even understand how someone like Mrs Stewart, in my cabin, can have children and then send them away. To bring babies into the world and then not care for them . . . Why – ?'

'I think we should speak of a more cheerful subject,' Gordon interrupted. 'Miss Young, I understand that a dance has been arranged for tonight. May I be allowed to partner you for the first dance, and the last, and as many as possible in between?'

'It's not to be a formal dance, I think.' Lucy spoke abstractedly, needing a moment to change to a mood of frivolity. 'I shan't have a programme.'

'You mean that I must jostle in the crowd of all your other admirers and trust to catching your eye? Well, I'll accept that as long as you give the same answer to everyone else, making no promises.'

'I'm happy to promise you a dance, Mr Hardie.' The happiness was sincere, and she allowed it to show in her eyes. 'And now that you put the thought of dances into my mind, I ought perhaps to look out a dress. Everything becomes so crumpled when there's no room to hang it up.'

She left Gordon to continue talking to Miss Fawcett while she herself went down to her cabin. There had been a baggage day in the Canal, when passengers were allowed to bring up from the baggage room items which they had not packed in their cabin trunks but would need now that the weather was so hot. Lucy had taken the opportunity to extract the dress which had been made for her to wear at the Magdalen Eights Week Ball.

'How lovely you look!' exclaimed Mrs Stewart later that evening. She had undertaken the role of lady's maid, claiming to be proud that the most sought-after passenger on the voyage was her cabin-mate. With her help Lucy had woven her long golden hair into an elaborate crown on top of her head and had been buttoned into the balldress which fitted tightly round her slender waist.

There was no full-length glass in which Lucy could study her own appearance; but as she shook out the fullness of her gossamer-light skirts, she remembered how she had looked at herself when she put on the dress for the first time, in an Oxford hotel. How young she had been then – and how nervous, hoping that the unknown partner whom Archie had arranged for her would not find her dull. Within an hour, as Archie's friends clustered round her, she had understood that she was beautiful, and had needed none of the champagne which flowed so freely to intoxicate her with the gaiety of the occasion.

Tonight she hoped that she would look beautiful again. But although she could be sure that, as before, she would never be left without a partner, on this occasion she was interested in one man alone. She needed the prospect of general admiration, but only in order that Gordon Hardie would be spurred by it to realize that he did not want to let her go.

Seven

It did not at first seem that Lucy's hope was to be realized. All through the dinner which preceded the dance, Gordon stared at her – with admiration to start with, but later with a troubled expression. He did not ask her for the first dance after all, nor the second, nor even the third. Instead, he stood alone in the gallery above the saloon, watching as she danced first with Captain Hunter and then with Mr Elliott and again with Mr Elliott. Lucy was conscious of his gaze, although she tried to restrain herself from looking up at him. The consciousness made her more vivacious, more determined to show by her smiles that she was not pining for him. But beneath the smile lay disappointment. When would he come down and ask her to be his partner?

The fourth dance was a reel. Lucy did not know the steps, but the ship's purser promised to teach them to her as they went along. She enjoyed the exercise and was flushed and laughing as the dance ended with a wild galop. And then – at last – Gordon was approaching her.

'May I have the honour, Miss Young?'

'I think I must have a rest. That was so vigorous! But if you're willing to sit out . . .'

'Of course. Let's go out on deck, then.'

Before climbing the steep and narrow steps Lucy gathered up her voluminous skirts with one hand, keeping the other ready to hold the rail in case there should be a sudden shudder even in the calm of the Red Sea. She shook them free again on reaching the deck. The sound of the music followed them up, becoming fainter with each step they took.

Even so late, the evening was hot, with no breeze except that stirred by the ship's movement. Lucy needed no shawl to cover her bare arms – and yet, compared with the fierce midday heat, there was refreshment in the air. She breathed it in deeply, leaning against the rail and looking down at the rippling silver path which led towards the moon.

'It's a very romantic picture.' Gordon spoke from behind her. 'A beautiful woman in a beautiful dress, shimmering in the moonlight.' The words suggested a compliment, but Lucy's ear was sensitive enough to recognize a criticism. 'You've brought with you a wardrobe fit for the mistress of Castlemere. I wonder what setting you envisage which will do it justice in the future.'

It did not need much intelligence to understand what he was implying. Should she defend herself, or stand on her dignity? She chose to tell the truth, and with spirit.

'I've brought with me almost everything I possess – or at least, everything which it was possible to smuggle out without attracting attention – because when I return to England I shall have no claim on anything that I left behind. I learned from my maid that a long voyage such as this imposes a social life in which some attention to dress is expected. I didn't have this gown made for a shipboard dance; but since I already own it, this seems an occasion on which to wear it. At the end of the voyage it may be packed away in a trunk and left in the shipping office until I need it again. I have another trunk, marked NOT WANTED ON VOYAGE, which contains riding clothes and painting equipment and everything I could think of which might be required for a rough journey – together with straps and covers so that the trunk itself

238

need not be carried. I've noticed before that you seem to think of me only as a pampered child. I must ask you also to give me credit for some practical common sense.'

'You're being very severe on me.'

'Well, it's very provoking of *you* to think that I might have been expecting to climb a Himalayan mountain in a ball gown.'

'I can imagine, though, that you could find other places in which to show it off. At Captain Hunter's regimental ball, for example. And please don't protest' – for Lucy had opened her mouth to speak – 'that he doesn't want to marry you. Everyone on the ship knows that he's prepared to die for love of you.'

'Captain Hunter is young and impressionable,' said Lucy with all the dignity of her eighteen years. 'But he knows – and so do I, as a soldier's daughter – that he can't marry without the permission of his colonel, and he will certainly not be given that before he's thirty.'

'In the case of Mr Elliott, though, there's no such problem.'

Lucy looked directly into Gordon's eyes. 'Mr Elliott is a widower,' she told him. 'His wife died in childbirth, together with her baby, three years ago in the south of India. Before she died, she had already miscarried four times. Mr Elliott has told me frankly that when he returned to England on leave this year, it was in the hope of finding a second wife. But when it came to the point, he felt unable to bring out a young girl to a climate and a country which she would not be able to imagine before she left England. He feels that a woman who expects a baby even in a hill station of India is in almost as much danger as Captain Hunter on the Frontier.' Lucy flushed slightly as she spoke, knowing that it was unladylike to discuss babies with a gentleman.

'He tells you this, no doubt, in the hope that you – having been apprised by him of the dangers – will give some indication that you are prepared to take the risks he offers.'

'Yes,' agreed Lucy honestly. 'I think he would ask me to marry him tomorrow if I allowed him to feel sure that his offer would be accepted. The reason why I haven't given him the kind of indication you mention is because I don't think it becoming for a young woman to attract offers of marriage which she doesn't intend to accept. It's not because I think the risks too high. Just consider for a moment, Mr Hardie, the courage of Mr Elliott's wife in enduring one miscarriage after another and all the time knowing the danger.'

'Certainly in a tropical climate – a country with poor hygiene . . .'

Lucy shook her head impatiently. 'My own mother died when I was born,' she reminded him. 'A young woman in good health, with the best medical attention that money could buy. You know, Captain Hunter has managed to persuade himself that no Afghan rifle will ever point directly at his heart – and perhaps that's courage of one sort. But it seems to me that every woman who marries is exposing herself to the *certainty* of great pain, and the likelihood of death.'

'Perhaps they lack the imagination to realize that. Or they may fear loneliness even more.'

'Perhaps, in some cases.' Lucy allowed her voice to express her doubt. 'What I'm trying to say is that I believe women have as much courage as men. Less strength, no doubt, but equal endurance. They are able to do what is expected of them. A woman in England is expected by her husband to shriek at the sight of a mouse but to endure without complaint the pain of having a baby every year, and she fulfils both those expectations. If she were given a different pattern to follow, she would take the mouse to bed with her as a pet, and think nothing of it.'

'I understand you at last. You're telling me that you are as able as myself to swing across a deep ravine on a rope and to listen to the howling of wild animals outside your tent without a trace of anxiety.' Lucy flushed. She had intended to make herself clear, but not by using words so baldly. She lowered her head, retreating from the position which Gordon had correctly understood.

'What I'm telling you is that if Mr Elliott should make an offer of marriage to me, I should reflect only that he is kind and honest and clever, and not that it might be dangerous to be his wife.'

'That's not the answer I wanted to hear,' said Gordon. 'I want you to say, my dearest Lucy, that you will share all the dangers of my journey with me.'

He stretched out a hand towards her, but Lucy shook her head.

'I've already said that once, and it was a very forward thing to do then. To say it again would be unforgivable. The best I can do is to quote my grandfather who has complained for years of my stubbornness. When I've determined on something, I don't easily change my mind.'

'When will you marry me, then?' asked Gordon.

Above Lucy's head, the star-speckled heavens seemed to rise into a high, wide dome, allowing all the anxieties which had been pressing down upon her to float away. She laughed with relief as well as delight. 'Whenever you like,' she said. 'Oh, darling Gordon, whenever you like.'

At last, after so long a period of uncertainty, she could enjoy his kiss. Close together, they began to dance to the sound of the music which percolated faintly up from the music gallery. Her filmy skirts swirled around her feet, making her feel that she was treading on air, hardly attached to her own body. Gordon was extricating her from a predicament, but that was not the only reason for her relief. He was doing it because he loved her, and for that reason only. She felt completely sure of that.

Mrs Stewart was already lying in her berth when Lucy returned to the cabin that night. 'Have you had a triumph?' she asked.

'I've had an offer of marriage,' Lucy admitted.

'And accepted it? In spite of my warnings to you about shipboard romances.'

'We're to be married before we reach Bombay. I understand that while he's at sea the captain of the *Parramatta* is like a king: he has the power to do whatever he chooses. So if he will oblige, Miss Young is to be buried at sea.'

'And a Mrs Elliott will step ashore? I must congratulate you, my dear.'

'Thank you,' said Lucy. 'But not a Mrs Elliott. A Mrs Hardie.'

She laughed to see the surprise on her cabin-mate's face; but she herself was to be surprised before the voyage ended. Sometimes as a girl she had tried to envisage her own wedding, wondering whether it would take place in the Castlemere chapel or in some large London church. Not in her wildest dreams could she have imagined then the ceremony which took place on the day before the *Parramatta* arrived at Bombay. Confessing the secret of her real name, she had asked Miss Fawcett and Mrs Stewart to act as her witnesses, and Gordon had called on Mr Elliott and the lovesick Captain Hunter – but as she stepped out on to the deck which was normally reserved for games, she found that all the passengers were crowded round to take part in the service. The captain, in his white tropical uniform, stood behind a table, with the ship's purser on one hand and an army chaplain, who had volunteered to preach a sermon, on the other.

Lucy walked slowly across the deck to stand beside Gordon. On the previous day he had teased her with the accusation that no doubt she had packed a wedding dress in her trunk. That would have been going too far, but it was true that she had brought with her one of her prettiest white summer gowns and had deliberately not worn it earlier in the voyage. She felt like a traditional bride, even though the setting was so unusual.

The captain coughed and opened his service book. 'By virtue of the authority vested in me,' he began – but Lucy hardly listened to the words. Gordon was holding her hand, pressing it as though to assure her of his love, and she cared about nothing else. It was curious, she thought, as the stewards' band played and the passengers roared out one of the hymns she had chosen – it was curious that in the novels which she had liked to read at Castlemere, a wedding ceremony was always presented as the end of the story, as though nothing else was likely to happen to the hero and heroine. But it seemed to Lucy, as the ship steamed steadily across the Indian Ocean, that she had reached not a happy ending but a happy beginning.

Eight

As the ship which had brought Mr and Mrs Hardie on from Bombay sailed up the Huangpu River to berth at Shanghai, Lucy voiced her disappointment. She had expected China to greet her with tall pagodas and dragon-decorated temples, with narrow streets and low houses. Instead, the tall and solid offices and hotels which fronted on to the river could have formed part of any European port.

'That must be the Bund,' said Gordon, reminding her that, although this was not his first journey out of England, he had never visited China before: everything would be as strange to him as to herself. 'After the Opium Wars, the Chinese were forced to allow trading concession areas to several European countries. The real China isn't far away – we shall be in it tomorrow. It may not be a bad thing that for today we shall be dealing with British banks and customs officials, and staying in a British hotel.'

Their first visit was to the office of a shipping agency. Gordon had already explained to Lucy how important the agent would be to them. He would receive and keep any letters which might arrive from England until notified of a base camp to which they might safely be forwarded. He would store whatever luggage would not be needed on the expedition, and to his office Gordon would send batches of seeds and plants – some to be despatched immediately to England and others to be kept safely until the Hardies were ready to return home. He would hold the money which Gordon had brought out with him, and in return would make funds available at appointed places along the expected route.

Lucy sat quietly while all these details were discussed. How businesslike her husband was, and how authoritative! Naturally she left all the arrangements to him, but when the discussion of the journey became more detailed, she leaned forward to listen, so that she would not need to ask too many questions while they were travelling.

'You'll do best to go as far as Chungking by river,' the agent said. 'It should take about six weeks. I'll arrange that for you and send the tickets round to your hotel. There's a Jardine Mathieson steamer leaving tomorrow evening. That goes as far as Hankow; you can change to a smaller boat there. When you leave the river, you'll have no trouble finding coolies. Pay them by the journey and change them often – about a week's travel for each gang, so that they don't find themselves too far from home at the end. Once you get right into the interior and start to explore, that'll be a different matter – you'll want a team to stay with you for a season. You'll have to bargain for that yourself with a local muleteer. But while you're still on the beaten track, five shillings will hire you a coolie for a week; he'll find his own food out of that. For yourself, you'll want a pony. A coolie will do your haggling for you, but don't pay more than about fourpence for ten miles. You change ponies at each village – they just go back and forward over the same stretch. For Mrs Hardie, I suggest a sedan chair.'

'I can ride!' protested Lucy. She had not meant to speak, but felt the need to make it clear from the start that she did not expect special treatment. Probably, she thought, she would be far more at home on horseback than would Gordon.

'I'm sure you can, Mrs Hardie. It's a question of

dignity, though. I might have suggested the chair even for your husband if he'd been alone. The Chinese set a lot of store by status. When you arrive at an inn for the night, you'll get the best room if you come in a chair. Or at a ferry – there could be a hundred people waiting to cross the river, but the chair will go on first. It's your choice, of course.'

'You were speaking of pence and shillings.' Now that Lucy had found her voice, she began to take part in the discussion. 'But we surely don't – '

'Oh no, no. I'm going to give you the kind of money you'll need now. On the steamer you can use Mexican dollars. One dollar a day each will buy you foreign chow. Chow is food, Mrs Hardie. But as a rule you'll be dealing with Chinese cash.' He pulled a bag out of a drawer and tipped out a shower of tiny copper coins, some of them strung on to leather thongs through the holes in the centres.

'How much are they worth?' Without needing to be told, Lucy realized that Gordon did not object to her asking such questions. He had been confident as he made all his business arrangements; but, knowing as little about these small matters as she did, he was perhaps glad that she should be the one to reveal ignorance.

'Forty cash equals one English penny – and that penny will go a long way here. Forty cash will take you a mile in a sedan chair.'

Lucy was relieved to hear all this. One of her worries had been that by her presence she would be adding too much to Gordon's costs.

'Talking of money,' added the agent. 'I don't know how you'll feel about this. Your steamer passage from Shanghai to Hankow will be twenty-eight dollars each, if you travel as Europeans. If you put on Chinese dress, you'll

246

pay only a quarter of that – and the same will be true everywhere you go.'

Gordon burst out laughing as he waved a hand in Lucy's direction. 'How many blonde Chinese women are there who are as tall as my wife, and with such large feet?'

Lucy, who was proud of the smallness of her feet, was about to protest, but remembered just in time that Chinese girls had their feet bound to keep them tiny.

'It's hard to explain. If you ask me to kit you out, I can get you a hat, for example, with a false pigtail fastened to it. No one who sees you wearing that is *really* going to believe that you're Chinese. Yet in some odd way he'll accept that by putting on the clothes you're making a gesture of conformity. In your own clothes, I can promise you, once you leave Shanghai you'll be followed everywhere by crowds shouting "*yang kweitze*" after you.'

'What does that mean?' asked Lucy.

'Foreign devil. I'm only talking now about the Yangtze valley, where there's a lot of anti-foreign feeling. When you get further west, near the frontier, any kind of stranger is such an unusual sight that it won't matter whether you're a foreign or a Chinese stranger. The frontier itself is only an invisible line, of course, but you must stay on the right side of it. Tibet is closed to foreigners. If the Tibetans find you in their territory, your guides will be beheaded and you yourselves will be beaten and tied and thrown into a river.' The agent paused to emphasize the solemnity of his warning, before continuing in a brisker manner. 'Anyway, what you wear is up to you. I'll send a couple of outfits round. You can try them on in your hotel room and see what you think. Now, I suggest that you should go straight away to register at the British Consulate. That will enable you to get a special Chinese passport, permitting you to travel through the country. After that, I should think you'll be glad of a rest.'

Two hours later Lucy and Gordon stepped together up the wide staircase of the Palace Hotel. It still seemed odd, after seven weeks at sea, to be treading on an unmoving surface – so odd that Lucy found herself rolling slightly as though this were necessary to maintain her balance. After the cramped conditions in which they had lived at sea, their room seemed enormous, with a huge four-poster bed and wardrobes built on the same scale. But for the moment Lucy did no more than glance around. She had a question to ask her husband on a matter which could only be discussed in private.

'Gordon, while we're here, I'd like to write to my grandfather, so that the letter may be sent off by the agent.' He gave her a questioning look, and she hurried on. 'I want to tell Granda that I'm married. He will have been very much upset by my disappearance.'

'And you think he'll find it comforting to know that you are Mrs Gordon Hardie?'

'Yes. It will make it possible for him to speak of me to his friends, if he wishes, when otherwise he might be too ashamed even to mention my name.'

'I suspect that it may require more than a certificate of marriage to appease him. Of course you may write, Lucy, and for your sake I hope that you can persuade him to love you again. But I think you'll be unwise to count on his forgiveness.'

'Well, I shall send just the one letter – and give him the address of the agent here so that he may reply if he chooses.' Lucy could not believe that her grandfather would remain cold for very long. 'But once the letter is despatched, I shan't think of him, or my life in England, again.' She walked across to the window and stared down into the street below. In this European area, only the wide straw hats and running bare feet of the rickshaw coolies told her that she was in China, but that was enough. She clapped her hands with excitement as she turned back to face her husband.

'So, our adventure is beginning!' she exclaimed.

'Something else may begin as well,' said Gordon. 'An adventure of love as well as of travel.' He gestured with his head towards the bed. 'Now at last we can be man and wife.'

Lucy looked at him uncertainly. It was one of the consequences of running away from home that she knew nothing about marriage. Had her life gone according to her grandfather's plan, she would have been presented at Court by one of her aunts who would also have organized her London Season and accompanied her through its social events. And when she became engaged to be married – the expected conclusion to the Season – the same aunt would no doubt have told her what to expect on her wedding-day. By depriving herself of the Season, Lucy had also deprived herself of what might be necessary information.

It had been impossible, after the captain of the *Parramatta* had married them on board, to change their cabins, for the ship had a full passenger list. But when they boarded their second ship at Bombay, they naturally as a married couple shared a cabin. It was, if anything, even tinier than the one on the *Parramatta*, with two very narrow berths which folded up against the wall during the day. On their first night aboard, Gordon had tried to sit on the edge of her berth while he kissed her but, finding there was no room, had given a rueful laugh before climbing up to his own bunk. In the days which followed they had kissed and embraced in a way which would certainly not have been proper for an unmarried couple and Lucy, blissfully happy, had assumed that this was what marriage allowed. From Gordon's look now, as he held a hand out towards her, it seemed that there was more to come.

Whatever it might be, she trusted Gordon to know best, and felt herself once again overcome by love for him as he took her into his arms. Looking into her eyes, he gave an odd laugh.

'What is it?' asked Lucy.

'Just for a moment I was reminded of my sister. When Midge was your age, her eyes shone as brightly as yours are shining now. But by the time I left home, when she was twenty-one, somehow it seemed to me that the sparkle had faded. I'd like to add one more wedding vow to those I've already taken. I promise that I'll try always to keep the brightness in your eyes.'

It would not be a difficult promise to keep, Lucy thought as he kissed her again. If her eyes were sparkling, it was with the delight of loving and knowing herself to be loved in return; and her love, she was sure, would never fade.

Nine

One of Midge's duties at the Ladies' College was to coach and supervise hockey on Saturday afternoons. In compensation for this, she was excused the Sunday supervision of her pupils as they wrote their letters home and went for walks in crocodiles. So when her father wrote to propose a visit, she was able to offer some free time on a Sunday afternoon. It was a treat to sit down to tea and cream cakes in a hotel lounge and enjoy a gossip about the family and Oxford. Midge assumed that her father's reason for coming was to assure himself that she was happy and well cared for in her work; but it was not long before a different topic was raised.

'When you were home last time, for half-term, did young Will Witney have a word with you?' he asked in a tone of voice which was too casual to be convincing.

'If you ask that question, you obviously know that he did,' said Midge. 'I hope you haven't been discussing me again.'

'Only from a practical point of view. Your mother said to Will that she hoped he'd spend Christmas with us. He hasn't got anywhere else to go since his own mother died, so we took it for granted. But of course he knows that you'll be coming home for the holiday. He started mumbling about not wanting to intrude on a family Christmas, because you mightn't want to have him around. I thought I'd better just find out how things are between you.'

If Will himself had hinted at the situation, it would hardly be betraying a confidence to confirm her father's suspicion. 'He asked me to marry him,' she admitted. 'You knew he intended to, didn't you?'

'He was a bit bothered about it. Because of his position in the firm. He's still bothered, if it comes to that, because he hasn't given up hope yet. He's afraid you may be thinking – well, you know the sort of thing. Apprentice boy makes good by marrying master's daughter. It may be my fault to some extent. When I offered him the Oxford job, I made it clear that it was only for three years – just till Gordon got back again. We didn't talk about what might happen after that. I wanted to see how he got on, and where else there might be room for him.'

'You mean,' said Midge carefully, 'that he thinks that I think that he only proposed marriage to me in order to make sure that you don't throw him out when Gordon comes home? You're not suggesting, are you, Father, that I should accept his proposal simply in order to demonstrate that no thought could be further from my mind?' Although the subject was a serious one, she could not help laughing at the absurdity of the idea.

"Of course not,' said Mr Hardie. 'I'm the one who's going to do some demonstrating. He's a good man, Will. We're lucky to have him. I'm prepared to tell him straight out that if he goes on as well as he's going now, there'll always be a place for him in the business.'

'And you're also going to tell him that you've made the same announcement to me. So in the first place he doesn't need to marry me to keep his job, and in the second place I shall know that that's the case and therefore take any proposal that comes as being sincere. There's one extra point, of course. I can turn him down without having to worry that I may be losing him his job by doing so.'

'I don't suppose you'd ever have considered that feeling

sorry for him was a good enough reason for getting married.'

Mr Hardie could see the ridiculous side of the conversation as clearly as Midge herself, but now he looked at her seriously. 'He'd make you a good husband, Midge. Just because he comes from a poor family doesn't mean –'

'Who cares about family?' demanded Midge. Her first love affair had ended because Archie's family was too good for her, and now she was supposed to consider the fact that Will's was not good enough.

'Most mothers and fathers do,' said Mr Hardie mildly. 'What I'm trying to tell you is that we don't. We both like Will. If you feel you could love him . . . Well, that's for you to decide. The only immediate question is, what do you feel about him spending Christmas with us?'

'I didn't hear that question,' Midge replied. 'If I were to say that of course he must regard our home as his own, since he hasn't any other, he might think I meant something more by that. It's for you and Mother to decide – and for Will himself to be sure that if he stays through the holiday it's just as a lodger and not as a prospective son-in-law.'

'Do you mean – ?'

'I don't know what I mean,' said Midge honestly. 'I shan't know what I feel until I hear what I say.'

She used that little piece of whimsy as an excuse for changing the subject, but of course it was not true. If Will was likely to propose to her for a second time, she must consider the possibility in advance and decide what she felt. Not now, though, when she had so short a time with her father. 'Have you heard anything from Gordon, about Lucy?' she asked.

'It's too soon yet. We weren't expecting him to write

253

before reaching Shanghai. If there's some special news to tell, he might send a letter from Bombay, but he'll only just about be arriving there now. We can't expect to hear for five or six weeks yet. Upon my word, I don't know what girls are coming to these days. Leaving home to run off with someone the family disapproves of. Or else leaving home to run away from someone the family would like to have as a son-in-law.'

'I didn't –'

'Of course you didn't.' Mr Hardie's eyes twinkled as merrily as his daughter's. 'We'll say no more about it. Tell me about the Ladies' College.'

There was plenty to tell. For the rest of their time together Midge chattered about Miss Beale and the formidable discipline she imposed, and her efforts to improve the curriculum against the wishes of the girls' parents. Midge herself had to teach a new course called Chronology, which covered the whole of world history. Since her studies at Oxford had ignored any country outside Europe which was not part of the British Empire and any period before the Roman invasion of Britain, she was finding it a struggle to keep one lesson ahead of her classes. The pleasure of the struggle showed in her increasing animation as she described the subterfuges with which she concealed her notes or dealt with awkward questions. By the time her father had to go, they had been laughing together so freely that Midge had quite forgotten the earlier part of the conversation.

She had no reason to recall the subject until the Christmas holiday began. There had already been a moment at half-term when she felt as though she were a visitor in her own home, and Will a member of the family. On her second return, in December, this impression was even stronger, for it was clear that Mrs Hardie, with both her children away, had begun to treat the lodger as though he were her own son. Midge was happy to join in the spirit of this arrangement by starting to treat Will like her brother.

Like most families, the Hardies had established an unchanging timetable for each Christmas Day. They continued the pattern this year, with Will taking Gordon's place. All together they went to church, walked to give themselves appetites, ate too much food and drank carefully selected wines, gave presents to the servants and exchanged others amongst themselves. Another part of the day had always been devoted to the playing of schoolroom board and card games, with a good deal of mock cheating and laughter. This custom too was continued, with Will proving himself to be as quick a learner here as he had been in business and education.

He was quick, too, in grasping the game that Midge was playing. By her friendly informality she was making it clear that she did not regard him as a suitor. To avoid spoiling the festivities, he made no comment on this over Christmas. It was on the last day of the year that Midge, just about to change for a New Year's Eve party, heard him calling her.

'Have you seen this?'

He was standing at the entrance to the morning-room. Out of polite curiosity Midge went to see what he had to show her, and found herself without warning in his arms. Surprise snatched away her breath, while the strength of his embrace made her feel almost too weak to stand on her own feet. He was kissing her as only Archie had ever kissed her, his body trembling with the urgency of his need to prove how much he loved her. Yet when at last he let her go, it took him only a second or two to recapture the humour which was so much part of his character.

Instead of explaining or apologizing in words, he pointed up to the lintel of the door, to which was fastened a very small bunch of mistletoe. She had never noticed it there before. Clearly he had set the stage himself for his gesture.

'Tradition excuses me, you see,' he said.

'Is that what you wanted me to look at?' Midge, still breathless, tried to speak calmly.

'Only after I'd put it to its proper use. I just wanted you to know – *really* know – that I love you. Last time I asked you to marry me, you said I'd chosen the wrong day. Could this be the right one? New year starting tomorrow. New life, all that sort of thing. There's nothing I want more – nothing I want at all – except to marry you. You're behaving as though I'm your brother, and that's very kind of you, I suppose, but I'm not your brother and I don't want to be. Will you be my wife? Please!'

Ever since the half-term holiday Midge had been trying, without great success, to decide what she would say if Will repeated his proposal. When it came to the point, she found that she could answer without hesitation.

'I'm sorry, Will,' she said. 'If I were going to marry anyone at all, I'm sure I couldn't find a better husband than you. But I'm not going to marry. I just don't want to.'

'I know you're a freak among women.' Will was desperately trying to keep a joking lightness in his voice. 'But you can't be as much of a freak as that. One day . . . I told you before, I'll wait.'

Midge shook her head. 'You mustn't do that. I read through the wedding service, Will, after we spoke of this before. All those promises – I can't make them. I want to be free to take my own decisions. To work for my own living. Not just because someone allows me to, but

256

because no one has the right to stop me. I'm terribly sorry. This has nothing to do with you, really. I'm choosing a different way of life.'

For a little while longer he tried to persuade her, but the pain in his eyes was too great for her to bear. Although he might not suspect it, Midge knew how it felt to be overcome with love for someone who did not return that love, and to feel that life could never again hold any happiness. As soon as she could, she escaped to her bedroom. She had meant everything she said, but that did not prevent her from feeling anxious. The freedom to live her own life would carry with it responsibility for all the mistakes she might make. She would have no husband to guard her, or sympathize, or set things to rights. There was no reason why a woman should not be capable of managing her own affairs as competently as a man; but Midge knew only a few – her fellow-teachers, for example – who attempted to do so. She suspected that it was because they had never had the choice.

She had told Will that her decision had nothing to do with him. Was that true, she asked herself suddenly; and the answer came as a surprise. If she succeeded in finding happiness in the life of a spinster – she faced the word boldly, knowing that amongst her friends it was the one to be dreaded, the one which carried the most contemptuous meaning – it would be because she had chosen it so deliberately: and the proof of that lay in the knowledge that for her there *had* been a choice. It was Will's proposal which had strengthened her confidence. Sometime, when the hurt had faded and he was happily married to someone else, she must tell him that.

In the meantime, there was bound to be some embarrassment, she reflected, as she set about her preparations for the party. Even if Will ceased to lodge with the

Hardies and found a home of his own, they were certain to meet frequently. She must think of a way to make their first encounter as friendly as possible – light-hearted without being heartless.

In the event, her father set up the occasion without realizing that there was a problem to be resolved. Later that night Midge was delivered home in her host's chaise, in high spirits after a party which had reunited many of her friends from school and university days. She found her parents and Will waiting up, with bottles and glasses to show that they, like herself, had begun their celebration as all the bells of Oxford chimed in the new year. But one bottle was unopened. Mr Hardie eased out the cork even before she had time to take off her evening cloak.

'We needed you here for one last toast,' he said. 'To Gordon!'

'To Gordon!' But that was not enough, Midge thought as she lifted the champagne glass to her lips. 'There may be another Mrs Hardie by now, for all we know,' she reminded them. When, after Archie's visit, she had discussed his information with her father and mother, they felt it as certain as she did that Lucy Yates's disappearance must be linked to Gordon's departure. And although Midge still believed that Gordon had not expected it, he must have found pleasure in such proof of Lucy's devotion. He might leave her in Shanghai for her own safety rather than allow her to travel to the wild mountain country, but he would surely have married her first – and not only for the sake of protecting her reputation. Lucy was beautiful and spirited and adoring: what more could any husband ask?

'You're right,' said Mr Hardie. 'I'll amend the toast. To absent friends, and all those we love, wherever in the world they may be.'

Once again all four of them raised their glasses, murmuring the words of the toast. It was easy to tell how Will was interpreting those words. When he looked longingly at Midge, she responded with an open, unaffected smile. Her thoughts and love, like those of her parents, were projected over a far greater distance. Where was Gordon now? Was he alone? Was he happy? Was his expedition going well? They must still wait a long time before they could expect to hear.

'Happy New Year, Gordon!' they wished him in unison.

Ten

'It's surely not possible!'

Had the words which sprang to his mind reached Gordon's lips, they would still have gone unheard above the crashing tumult of white water. On either side of the gorge, black rocks rose as sheer as pillars for a thousand feet or more, cutting out all sunshine and allowing no trace of life except for an occasional fern precariously rooted in a crevice. Through this narrow gorge the Yangtze River tumbled down in a mile-long cataract. The agent in Shanghai had talked of 'rapids', but it seemed to Gordon that what he saw ahead could only be described as a gigantic waterfall. And yet the heavy junk, travelling against the current, was expected to reach the top of it.

The first part of the journey from Shanghai had proceeded smoothly enough. Two steamers in turn had taken Gordon and Lucy up the Yangtze as far as Ichang. It was easy to accept the fact that the higher reaches of the river were not navigable by steamers – but more difficult to believe that even a junk could traverse the next four hundred miles to Chungking in safety. Some inkling of the problems ahead was revealed in the information that the junk would take at least thirty days to make the journey upstream, but no more than three to return.

One such returning junk was rushing towards them at that moment, careering from side to side as the pilot shouted orders and the hundred oarsmen struggled to control its direction. At any minute, it seemed to Gordon, the unwieldy vessel might hit one of the huge boulders which littered the edges of the gorge, narrowing the channel still further, and made invisible by the constant spray. The wooden carcasses of earlier casualties, caught briefly between the boulders before being battered to pieces, made it clear that the dangers were not imaginary – and the presence of a bright red official lifeboat, fully crewed, was only partly reassuring.

Lucy came to stand beside him on the deck. She slipped her hand into his – but only out of companionship, not in fear. With the boat tied fast in the comparatively calm water at the foot of the cataract, they watched the preparations being made for the ascent. On board, the crew were sacrificing a fowl, whose blood was smeared over the bow of the junk. Meanwhile, a hundred or more barefooted coolies appeared, scrambling down over the boulders from the top of the cataract, ready to fasten their tow-ropes and help the crew to haul the boat up.

After a great deal of shouting, everything was ready. With the couplings of the thick tow-ropes over their shoulders, the coolies moved off, singing a raucous chorus which helped them to keep a steady pace as they clambered over the slippery rocks. Several minutes passed while the long lines were paid out. When at last the junk was untied, the towing gangs were almost a quarter of a mile ahead.

Gordon thought it unlikely that safety could be guaranteed in any part of the boat, but the high half-deck was as good a place as any. If any calamity were to occur, the passengers' quarters below the deck would become a death trap. Still holding Lucy's hand, he felt through his body every movement of the vessel as it first fell back a little, then checked, and at last began to move steadily forward. There was a band of coolies on each bank, taking and releasing the strain so that the junk could zigzag past pointed rocks on the river bottom. But then the river bed narrowed still further, the long bowsprit pointed more sharply upwards and all the coolies pulled together, gaining a yard and holding it, and pulling again.

Suddenly a shout went up from one of the crew who remained on board. Thick and strong though the tow-ropes were, they were being rubbed against the boulders, and one of them had frayed more than half-way through. Gordon could not judge what the effect of a breakage would be, but the anxiety of the Chinese sailors was infectious. His eyes and the whole of his concentration were on the rope. For that reason he was not alert to the moment when they came to the foot of the last and highest torrent.

A fall of water cascaded on to the junk with such weight that its bow was briefly submerged. The tow-ropes continued to tug upwards and, as the front of the deck rose to the surface again, the water rushed towards the stern. Gordon was knocked off balance by its power. Struggling to keep his head above water, he came to rest, bruised but safe, against the wooden rail. He pulled himself to his feet again, spluttering and staggering, and looked round anxiously. Where was Lucy?

The scene on the deck was chaotic. Sailors shouted urgently to each other whilst passengers, dripping wet, scrambled up from flooded cabins. A mist of spray blinded him, and the tilt of the ship and buffeting of the water made it hard to maintain balance on the wet deck. All the time that he was searching, the junk was continuing its creaking journey up the cataract. Gordon called his wife's name, but knew that the word would be blown away before anyone could hear it.

He found her at last, prone on the deck, clutching a rope whose other end was secured to a mast. As she struggled to regain her feet without letting go of the rope, a new surge of water sent her slipping back again and she lay still for a moment, regathering her strength. Then, as Gordon slithered towards her, she raised her head and with great determination began to pull herself hand over hand by the rope until she could grasp the mast.

'Lucy! Lucy, my darling!' Gordon helped her to stand and pressed her back against the mast, encircling her with his arms to hold her close to it. How beautiful she was! Her sodden clothing clung to the shape of her slender body and the flattening of her long golden hair by the water served only to reveal the perfection of her features. 'I love you so much!'

'I know.' Her smile, free of any anxiety on her own account, took his love for granted. She had never doubted it.

Yet she should have doubted it. Even while Gordon continued to press his body against his wife's, pinioning her to the safety of the mast, his desire was compounded by shame. Although he had been swept off his feet by his first sight of her youthful loveliness, it was not so much love as anger which, a year later, had prompted his first proposal of marriage. He had released her from her engagement only partly out of concern for her future, and had married her in the end because by her actions she had left him no choice. However brave a face she put on her situation during the voyage to India, the fact remained that she had to be rescued. Recognizing his responsibility, he had shouldered the obligation. The service conducted by the captain of the *Parramatta* might almost be described – although not in the usual sense – as a shotgun marriage.

None of that meant that he found her anything but lovable. Someone so young and trusting and open in her affections could hardly fail to rouse a man's protective instincts. She was the most beautiful woman in the world, and she was his! Yet he had agreed to let her face three years of danger in his company. 'I should never have allowed you to come on such a journey,' he said, between kisses.

Lucy's eyes twinkled with a mischief as calm as though she were sitting on a sofa in Castlemere instead of being buffeted by a torrent which threatened to rush their vessel back down over the rocks.

'My memory is that you *didn't* allow me to come,' she said. 'I have only myself to blame for an unwanted cold bath.' The smile died from her face, and her expression became troubled. 'You made it plain to me that you considered the journey too hazardous. And it was later in the expedition that you expected the dangers to begin, so I suppose today must be considered one of the safe and easy days. I've been selfish – not realizing what an encumbrance I might be to you. I determined from the very beginning that I would never complain and never hold you back. But I realize now that there could be accidents – events which might not be my fault, but which mean that all your risks are doubled. You were right to think that I could have no understanding of the handicap I might be to you. I'm sorry.'

'Sorry? Oh, my dearest, how could I have been happy apart from you for three years? How can I thank you enough for taking a step that I had no right either to ask or to expect? All the happiness I can ever hope for is bound up in my love for you and yours for me.'

What he said had not always been true, but it was true as he spoke the words. He kissed her again, pressing her head back against the mast. His heart and his breathing both stood still; and so, briefly, did the junk. They had reached the top of the cataract. For a moment or two longer the bowsprit continued to point upwards, until the stern too was hauled clear. Then the bow crashed down into the level water. Its shuddering vibrated through every timber until, for the first time in six hours, there was calm.

The stillness brought with it a kind of silence. The waters of the Yangtze were still hurling themselves down the cataracts not far away, but the sound was distanced by the knowledge that all danger was past, at least for today. The coolies ceased to sing as they tied the mooring ropes and released the tows; and the crew, who had been shouting at each other without pause all day, collapsed into exhaustion.

They had reached a wide, calm stretch of water, whose smooth surface showed no sign of the racing current deep below. Instead of the bare cliffs which walled the narrow gorge, the river banks were flat and green. There was space for a village, the home of the towing gangs. In the distance, though, the land rose again, first in a vista of jagged black mountains and then, more distantly, to a range of high, snow-covered peaks.

As Gordon and Lucy walked hand in hand to the front of the junk, Gordon gave a sigh of expectation and pointed to the far mountains.

'That's where we're going,' he said. 'To the land of the lily.'

'The lily? I thought – '

'You thought we had a list of plants to search out and collect. Azaleas, clematis, primulas, alpines, rhododendrons. And a hope of finding plants which still have no name because they have never been brought to Europe. All that's true. But there's one thing I've set my heart on finding for my own sake, not for my patrons.' He described Merlot's lily to her, as many years earlier Sir Desmond Langton had described it to him. 'Over there, in the high mountain valleys near the frontier with Tibet – that's where we shall hunt for it.'

Together they looked westward, gazing at the mountains. The sun was setting, flooding the dark Yangtze water with crimson and purple. Gordon became aware that Lucy was shivering, and put his arm round her shoulders.

'We must change our clothes,' he said. 'After emerging unscathed from a waterfall, it would be humiliating to die of a common cold.'

Lucy nodded and began to move towards the lower deck. Gordon himself lingered for a moment longer. He felt physically and emotionally exhausted by the excitements of the past few hours, and yet, strangely, a warm glow of satisfaction was invading his body. In the course of the day he had recognized a new love, but without needing to surrender his old one. Lucy had become part of his life in a way which he had not earlier believed possible. But the ambition which had driven him for so long was not destroyed by the discovery. Very soon now, all his plans and hopes would be put to the test. For ten years he had dreamed of the moment when he would catch a first glimpse of the mountains of western China. It was a moment to be savoured. They were still many miles away, but the mountains were there, waiting.

Eleven

Lucy clung to the saddle of the mule, determined not to collapse. She had assured Gordon that she could ride, and it was no idle boast. At Castlemere she could happily spend all day on her riding mare; or keep up with the hounds on her hunter just as well as Archie, however high the hedges or rough the ground. But by 'riding' she meant an activity in which she was almost one with the horse, controlling it but at the same time becoming a part of it, so that their joint energy was channelled into a single flow of movement. Sitting on a mule for twelve hours a day was a different matter entirely.

It would have been more comfortable to walk from time to time – but also more dangerous. The mountain paths were rough and narrow. On the occasions – fortunately rare – when they encountered travellers moving in the opposite direction, it could take an hour or more as well as much argument before a passing place was found. Rocks fell from the sheer cliffs above; stones crumbled into the precipice below. A false step would allow no second chance. Although – after a daily demonstration of bad temper and refusal to move had been overcome – the mules appeared to plod along mindlessly, they were surefooted. Lucy knew that she was safe from anything but a landslide, but the knowledge did not help her to feel comfortable.

Their weeks of travelling away from the busy trading routes of China and even deeper into the mountain wilderness had brought her embarrassment as well as physical discomfort. As long as they remained on the plains, they had spent each night at one of the inns which awaited travellers in each small town. Built round a courtyard, with a kitchen and eating-room fronting the street and stalls for mules and horses along a second side, such an inn provided plentiful accommodation for guests; and although much of it was communal, there was always one 'best room'. Lucy had to endure staring and even touching as she passed through the public quarters, but could then enjoy a night's privacy with Gordon, sleeping on a *kang* – a stove bed, heated from below by glowing coals.

Since leaving the plains, however, conditions had necessarily become more primitive, whilst privacy had almost entirely vanished. It was clear from the sour smell of their clothes and skin that the men whom Gordon hired to act as guides and porters never washed at all, but instead rubbed rancid butter into their skin to protect it from the elements. A blonde woman was an object of such intense curiosity to them that they stared at her intently, not disguising their wish to see as much of her own skin as possible. So Lucy was forced to perform her ablutions as best she could inside the tiny yak-skin tent which was only just large enough for two people to sleep in, and did not allow either of them to stand up. The rivers whose clear water might have tempted her to a more refreshing immersion proved always to be flowing straight from a glacier or snowfield and so were icy as well as dangerously swift.

Even Lucy's most private functions would have come under interested scrutiny had Gordon not always placed himself on guard, forbidding his men to turn their heads on pain of forfeiting a day's pay. There was nothing evil in their wish to stare, he assured his wife, only curiosity.

Lucy believed him, but still felt embarrassed when she had to bring the caravan to a halt – for just as the mountain paths were too narrow to provide her with seclusion, so also they made it impossible for her simply to fall back for a few moments and take her place in the line again later. This was an aspect of travel which her heroine, Miss Marianne North, had never mentioned in the books which described her adventurous explorations. But the mortification which Lucy felt when she first needed to appeal to Gordon grew less with each day that passed.

They had reached the mountains which separated China and Tibet by the middle of March. This was the area in which Gordon expected to make his discoveries. Within a week or two the first buds of the earliest rhododendrons would begin to open, even in the snow. For the next six months he would keep a careful log of his position and everything he saw, so that they could return later to collect seeds which had ripened and dig up dormant roots. The prospect ahead was one of ceaseless trekking, with only occasional breaks to pick up more stores.

Lucy had known in advance about the discomforts of travelling and camping. She had resolved never to let a single word of complaint pass her lips. What she had not been prepared for was the effect of the altitude. Well aware that the mountains through which they must travel were some of the highest in the world, she had not realized that even the valleys would often be higher than mountain peaks in other countries.

Although they remained on the Chinese side of the frontier, as their special passports required, their mule-teer, Sati, was a Tibetan. Disregarding frontier lines drawn on a map, he had spent his life trading across the mountain area. He and his coolies, born and brought up at altitudes of over twelve thousand feet, were so well acclimatized to the thin air that they suffered in an opposite way from the two Europeans, feeling discomfort in the lower-lying plains of China. But their mules showed by the blood which trickled from their nostrils that they were near the limit of their endurance. If animals native to this part of the world began to gasp for breath and stagger under their loads, it was hardly surprising that the English couple should be affected.

The first sign of something unusual had been laughable. Lucy had smiled to see Gordon's dark, curly hair suddenly standing on end as though in an illustration for a ghost story. But within a few moments his nose began to bleed and her amusement turned to anxiety as the flow of blood resisted her efforts to check it with packs of snow. He was attacked, too, by severe headaches and spells of vertigo. It was the mountain sickness, Sati assured them. There was no cure except to move slowly and with as little exertion as possible.

Lucy was unaffected at first and, as Gordon gradually became acclimatized, they both felt fit and energetic. Then she in turn fell victim to the sickness. The precipitous country through which they were passing was enough to induce vertigo by the merest glance downwards, but Lucy felt giddy from the moment she awoke in the morning – unable to steady herself because of the sensation that she was floating above the solid earth. She found herself retching without being able to vomit. Gordon was solicitous, and the fact that he had been a sufferer himself made it easier for Lucy to avoid feeling guilty about her weakness. But she had always enjoyed good health. It was difficult now not to be impatient with herself.

It was no doubt the mountain sickness which robbed

her of her appetite, but the only food available was not of a kind to tempt her to eat. Lucy herself had never learned to cook, so it was just as well that meals were included in the service which Sati and his men provided. As soon as a camp site for the night had been chosen, Gordon would produce his flint and steel and ceremonially provide the spark to light the night's fire. Often the flames had to be fuelled by pats of dried dung, for there was little wood in the higher areas; but a greater problem was the low boiling point of water at such altitude. The Tibetans were as anxious as Lucy herself for a drink of tea, and a Chinese tea brick was the first item to be unpacked. But the beverage had to be stewed rather than infused; it was some time before Lucy became reconciled to its strong tang.

As for food, there was little variety of ingredients and less of taste. Whenever, in the lower valleys, Gordon succeeded in shooting game for the pot, the meat would be cooked in the rancid butter which the Tibetans loved. To them, every year of its stored life increased its attractiveness, but the stench nauseated Lucy even before the food touched her lips. By contrast, the dried barley and beans which provided the bulk of their rations were boiled to a tasteless mush. Lucy could force herself to eat only a little. She never complained about this, but her lack of appetite, and subsequent failing of strength, made her more susceptible to the extremes of climate which must be faced in every twenty-four-hour period. By day, as the sun blazed down through the thin air, the temperature reached 120°, whilst at night it fell below freezing point. And all the time a fierce wind blew, arid by day and bitter by night. Even in the quilted coat which she had bought locally, she shivered after the sun went down; and even under a wide-brimmed hat and wearing her thinnest,

271

loosest clothes, her body seemed to swell with the heat during the day.

As the weeks passed, she found herself considering a question for which no book of etiquette had prepared her. Would it matter, she wondered, if she were to remove her corsets? Polite society would hardly care if she were to relax her standards in the wildness of China, but would such slackness ruin her figure for the rest of her life? By the end of April she gave up the struggle. Like her husband, she had at last become acclimatized; but, as her appetite returned, her body felt even more swollen than before. Without saying anything to Gordon, she ceased to wear the corsets.

By now the excitement of the search had infected her as strongly as Gordon. Her eyes were keen, and often she was the first to see some flash of colour in the crevice of a rock, or far below at the foot of the valley. It had proved impossible to explain to their guide precisely what the purpose of the expedition was, for how could Gordon hope to describe plants whose most important characteristic was that he had never yet set eyes on them? He had made a drawing of a lily, hoping that it might bear some resemblance to the flower which above all he longed to find – but just as he had earlier discovered that Sati was incapable of interpreting a map, so the muleteer's puzzled expression as he stared at the drawing showed that the marks of pencil on paper meant nothing to him at all. The map problem could be solved simply by specifying a village or pass as destination and trusting the guide to find the best approach to it. But where new plants were concerned, the two Europeans had to rely on their own eyes and botanical knowledge; and already they had enjoyed many successes. Azaleas and rhododendrons came into flower – and to Lucy, who had only seen one or two solitary specimens, it was a revelation to come across a valley carpeted with them. Her only disappointment was the difficulty of using her water colours at such altitudes, for the water evaporated on the brush before she could touch the paper. Driven by necessity, she evolved a new way of working, making sharp drawings in pencil and pressing an example of each blossom for a few days until camping on lower ground made it possible to add the colour wash.

It was in May that she began to suspect what might be happening to her. The disturbance in the normal rhythms of her body she had first thought to be an effect of the mountain sickness. To be unexpectedly freed from a monthly process which would have caused discomfort while riding the mule and embarrassment in evading the eyes of the coolies came as a relief. This led her for some time to put to the back of her mind its possible explanation. But one day she felt a movement inside her body which could not be mistaken. It was the movement of a child.

Once again, Lucy had cause to regret the lack of a mother and her abrupt departure from home. No one had ever talked to her about having babies. Still, she had grown up surrounded by dogs and horses, and the conversation of the grooms had none of the polite restraint of her female relatives. It did not take much imagination to deduce that she must be pregnant. What she did not know – and could not guess – was how long the process would take.

Would Gordon know? But at the very thought of asking him Lucy was overcome with guilt. She had vowed never to let herself become an impediment to his journey and what could be a greater impediment than a baby? On the Castlemere estate she had carried parcels of food and

273

clothes to new mothers often enough to know that a woman needed a midwife for a birth, and a period of rest in bed after it, and that the baby itself, once delivered, must be kept warm and comfortable and frequently fed. None of this was compatible with the conditions under which they were travelling. When the time came, she would have to find somewhere to stay, and Gordon would feel obliged to stay with her. His plans would be spoiled. A whole season of seed-collecting would be wasted. He might even feel that she ought to return immediately to England – or at the very least to Shanghai, where there would be a European doctor. And he would, of course, insist on accompanying her. She was realistic enough to recognize that it would be impossible for her, a foreigner and a pregnant woman, to travel two thousand miles across such inhospitable country unescorted.

Gordon had been planning this expedition for ten years. He had put all his savings into it, as well as the money provided by patrons who had received firm promises of what he would bring them in return. He had also invested something far more important than money. The whole drive of his enthusiasm and ambition and determination had centred on this one great opportunity which could never be expected to recur. And she, who would do anything for him and had wanted only to share in his adventure, was to be the one to ruin it.

All that evening she sat in silence. Usually the meal at the end of the day was a noisy affair. Because of the lack of fuel, only one camp fire could be sustained for the whole party, so the Tibetans gobbled their food on one side of it whilst Gordon and Lucy sat on the other, discussing the day's discoveries as they ate. Then, while Gordon made detailed notes in his daily log and Lucy made pencil drawings, the coolies would pull out their opium pipes and puff peacefully away until it was time for them to take up the extraordinary posture in which they slept, keeping the main part of their bodies above the frozen ground by resting on knees and elbows, with their heads tucked in between their arms – a draping of all available furs and blankets giving them the appearance of a small flock of sheep.

Gordon and Lucy, changing their clothes inside the tent, one at a time for lack of space, would settle down more comfortably, close together on a mattress of furs and with more furs to cover them. They were still on their honeymoon: usually this was a time for joy. But on the night after Lucy first felt her child's movement she lay awake for a long time after Gordon was asleep, weeping silently so that her husband should not stir and suspect her unhappiness. How unfair it was, when she loved him so much, that she should be the one to bring him distress! Soon she would have to tell him her suspicions. She would see disappointment in his eyes – perhaps even anger. Would his love survive the news?

Throughout her life, Lucy's emotions had developed with a steadiness deserved by someone whose nature was affectionate and brave. Her love for Gordon was as smooth and deep as the waters of the Yangtze River which poured into the ocean. But now her body was shaken by an emotion she had never experienced before: of anger as turbulent as those same Yangtze waters when they surged down the rocky cataract of the Hsintan gorge. There was no person against whom that fury could be directed – not even herself. As much as Gordon, she was a victim of a situation which she would have avoided had she only known how to do so. She longed to have children – Gordon's children – one day. But not here. Not now.

Twelve

Gordon listened to his wife's news with a dismay which he struggled to conceal. He could tell from Lucy's expression that she already knew what his true reaction was certain to be. Instead of displaying the proud happiness of a mother-to-be, she was close to tears.

Try as he might, he could not quite bring himself to console her by expressing delight, but he did succeed in smiling. 'When is the baby due?' he asked.

Lucy's face flushed to a bright red. 'I don't know,' she confessed.

'But surely . . .' He checked himself. During the six months since they left Shanghai his wife had endured the hardships of the journey with a cheerfulness which made her an ideal companion. Her behaviour was that of a mature traveller, but in reality she was little more than a child, abruptly removed from a sheltered life. The problem was that Gordon himself knew little more than Lucy about periods of gestation and the process of childbearing.

He was silent for a few moments while he tried to puzzle it out, dragging up from his memory all the smutty jokes and rhymes over which he, like any other small boy, had once sniggered. There was just one which seemed to be relevant – a girls' skipping song which the boys at his first school had appropriated as they hit a rubber ball in the air on the edge of a cricket bat.

'A day to bake a lardie cake.
A week to eat it, maybe.
A month to tell I love you well
And nine to make a baby.'

It was hardly scientific statement, but it seemed possible, and he could recall no more precise facts. Reminding himself of the date of their arrival in Shanghai, he did a quick calculation in his head.

'The beginning of September,' he said, with more confidence than he felt. 'It could be later, but that's the very earliest. Three months ahead. No need to worry yet. You must get as much rest as you can. I'd planned to climb to the head of the valley tomorrow, to look for more primulas, and I'll still do that, while you relax here. It will give me a chance while I'm walking to think about the future. By the time I get back in the evening, I'll have everything sorted out.' He leaned forward to kiss her on the forehead. 'Nothing to worry about.'

He could hardly expect her to believe his assurance. Lucy's own mother had died in childbirth. That could be a terrifying memory for a young woman with no female companion in a country which was primitive and dirty and hostile to foreigners. Nor would that be the greatest of her worries, for Lucy was neither cowardly nor selfish. The tears trembling in her eyes had undoubtedly been for him rather than herself. He would have to reassure her on that score as well – but it was not something he could do on the spur of the moment, for his own disappointment was too great. There would be no chance now to complete his project.

Next day he set off from their lakeside camp with his pack empty of everything except collecting bags and trowel. The wind which screamed through the high valleys at every hour of the day or night was behind him today, raising his spirits by the ease with which he was able to climb towards the head of the valley. He heightened this mood of contentment by deciding to put the new problem out of his mind until the return journey. As the sun rose higher in the sky he began to climb, and was rewarded by the sight of the plants he had expected to find: rainbow edgings of colour along ledges hardly wide enough to take his feet.

The task of digging out a selection of plants to be dried, and marking those to be collected later, when their flowers had faded, demanded his full attention. When he had finished, he sprawled beside a tumbling stream to refresh himself.

The scene as he looked down towards the camp was a beautiful one. So dark and still was the lake that it reflected a perfect panorama of the surrounding mountains. These were impressive enough, but above them rose an evener high and more Olympian range – so high that they disappeared into a cloud and then rose above it, the snowy peaks seeming to float in the air. He had not come to China to admire scenery, but he felt the need to imprint the magnificent view on his memory. It would have to last him through a lifetime of selling wine in Oxford.

Sighing, he stood up. He must make his way back to the encampment. But his eye was caught by a flash of colour high up above the head of the valley, in a place so steep that the stream fell as a waterfall. Was there time to investigate? He knew that it was vital in such rough terrain to reach camp before sunset, but could not resist the prospect of another discovery. Climbing faster than was altogether safe, he came within an hour to what he had seen – a solitary clematis clinging to the skeleton of a wind-sloped sapling. The plant was heavy with buds, but only two had so far opened, revealing blossoms of such a clear, bright blue that Gordon gasped in wonder. No specimen that he had ever seen in England had flowers of so pure a colour. They were the colour of Lucy's eyes. They were beautiful.

Panting in the thin air, Gordon picked one of the two blossoms so that Lucy might paint it quickly, before the colour faded. Then he spent twenty minutes building a cairn of light-coloured stones, to help him identify the position from a distance. By the autumn its bright beauty would have disappeared, leaving little more than a twig to show where it had bloomed.

The autumn. By then he would be a father. Would he ever be able to return to this valley? He had gone through the routine of marking the primulas as though his plans were unaffected, but now he must give proper consideration to the future. Climbing down the steep cliff on which the clematis was growing, he scrambled as fast as the wind allowed along the rocky side of the valley, dropping a few inches of height in every yard he covered.

The camp was in sight all the way. Drawing nearer, he could see Lucy, who had been sitting near the edge of the lake, packing away her water colours as the light began to fade. Perhaps she too had been attempting to preserve a view which she might never see again. She stood up and walked towards their tent. How was it that he had failed to notice, until she had told him last night of her condition, that her tall, slender figure had thickened and her feet no longer stepped gracefully but were set wide apart in an ungainly movement? It could only have been because he was pleased with her for abandoning without complaint the elegant clothes to which she was accustomed and wearing instead a shapeless tunic over wide

279

trousers by day, and an equally shapeless quilted garment by night.

The change that he *had* noticed was in her face. The delicate, pale complexion which had been part of her blonde beauty had become reddened by the sun and weathered by the wind. She had not complained about that, either. He must remember that her enthusiasm for this adventure had been almost as great as his own. It would be unkind to talk of his disappointment and make no allowance for hers.

Without that thought – and the memory of the clematis – he might have made a decision that would have been unselfish but wrong. As it was, by the time they had eaten their meal of broth with barley doughballs, apricots in honey and a sour cheese, he had made up his mind what to say. Sati and the coolies shared the warmth of the camp fire with them, but not their language, so the conversation was private.

'There's no time for you to return to England for the birth,' Gordon said. 'And I don't think you should attempt even to reach Shanghai. Even though the journey down the Yangtze would be much faster than coming up, it would be no more comfortable, and I'm sure that you ought not to exert yourself. So our best plan is to make tracks to the nearest mission station. I believe the China Inland Mission requires its missionaries to have some medical experience even if they're not qualified. You can stay at the mission station until the baby is born and for whatever time is necessary afterwards. You'll be safe and well looked after there. I shall feel able to leave you in good hands for a few weeks in the autumn while I return to collect seeds or roots of the plants we've noted in this area.'

'Yes,' said Lucy quickly. 'I'd like you to do that very much.'

'Then we needn't make any more decisions until we know how strong you and the baby feel. But the first thing we must do is to unpack the chair from the heavy baggage, so that you can be carried.'

'Oh no!' exclaimed Lucy. 'I'm perfectly well.'

'I know you are, dearest, and as long as you feel strong enough to walk, that can do no harm. But I don't think you should continue to ride.'

'Why not?'

Gordon burst out laughing. 'What an ill-educated couple we are! How disgraceful it is that I should know so much about the propagation of plants and so little about babies. If I'd had an elder sister with a family, I might have picked up more information. But my mother would never have discussed such a subject in front of her unmarried children. Just once, though, I remember her commenting that our neighbour might be expecting a further increase in his family, because his wife had given up riding again.'

Lucy made no further objection to his suggestions – but although they had agreed on a plan, it was not easy to put it into effect. The mountain area held few inhabitants, and no missionaries. Three weeks of travel were needed before the mule train was able to round the barrier presented by the towering twenty-two thousand feet of Gongga Shan. Once over the last high pass, they could look forward to a less arduous passage through the foothills, following the tumbling course of the Min Jiang River towards Suifu, where some of the comforts of civilization might be found. That, though, was still many days' journey ahead. Gordon watched anxiously for any indication that his wife was tiring. She obviously felt more nervous at being carried along the mountain paths by two coolies in the chair than on the back of the sure-footed mule, but continued to smile cheerfully and to walk occasionally when the ground was level.

Gordon himself made no further stops, even when they passed through inviting groves of pristine rhododendrons, although each evening he devoted more time than usual to the charting of the area they were crossing. It was on the last day of June that they reached the head of the pass and turned their faces to the south.

'It will be softer going now,' he said reassuringly. 'Look, there's the river.' He pointed to a silver ribbon of water winding through the valley below. There was a village on its bank, not too far away – little more than a huddle of huts inside a mud wall, but holding out the hope that the muleteer might be able to purchase rice and fresh provisions to vary the diet of beans and barley on which they had subsisted for so many weeks. They could not expect to reach it that night, since the track was steep and winding, but with luck they might come to it before the second evening. Gordon nodded to himself in satisfaction and took a few steps forward, to the very edge of the pass: a position which allowed him to glance back at the mountain they were about to leave. He turned his head to the left.

For a moment, a long moment, he could not speak. Then he stretched one hand out behind his back for Lucy to clasp. It groped through the air, not reaching her, but he could not bring himself even for a second to take his eyes off what he had seen, lest it should disappear like a mirage.

'Lucy!' he whispered. 'Lucy, come and look at this!'

Thirteen

Lucy was looking down at the village which her husband had pointed out to her. She was careful never to express opinions on such matters, in case they should appear to be complaints, but in truth she preferred to sleep in a tent, in spite of the extreme coldness of the nights. The villages were dirty and smelly. The straw mattresses of the beds they offered were full of biting insects. And the villagers were always unfriendly and often actively hostile. On the first occasion when she had been called a foreign devil by passers-by, she had assumed that this was an automatic reaction to any stranger, meaning nothing personal. But since then there had been other cries, and one of the missionaries with whom they had stayed had reluctantly translated them. Burn her. Child-eater. Lucy was used to being liked. It was unpleasant to find that no amount of smiling or polite behaviour could prevent her from being hated just because she was not Chinese.

Sati and his men treated her differently. As Tibetans they had no great respect for the Chinese and seemed genuinely loyal to their temporary employers, despite difficulties of communication. Brought up, as she had been, in a great house which was run by a small army of indoor and outdoor servants. Lucy had an instinctive ability to command without offending. Because she was used to unobtrusive service, it had taken her a little while to overcome her distaste for the almost aggressive curiosity with which the Tibetans watched her. But just as she had earned their respect by her dogged endurance of the discomforts of travel, so she had grown to appreciate their honesty and reliability. Lucy was an aristocrat by birth and it was a mark of her breeding that she found it easy, once a good relationship had been established, to be friendly and firm at the same time. She trusted the men, and was at ease in their company. It was another reason for preferring to camp at night.

But she made no comment, and in her silence became aware of Gordon's stillness.

'Lucy! Lucy, come and look at this!' His voice was so intense but so soft that she thought he must have caught sight of a bird or butterfly which must not be disturbed. So she turned slowly and crept rather than walked to join him.

Gordon was no longer looking south towards the river, but had turned his head to one side. Lucy followed his gaze with her own, and drew in her breath sharply. Now she understood the tone of awe in which he had spoken.

What she saw was a cleft in the rock which was not large enough to be called a valley. A gorge, perhaps, rising for two thousand feet or more from a point below the level of the pass on which they were standing. In any case, the word was not important. All that mattered was that the gorge was curtained and carpeted with lilies in full flower.

For a second time Lucy gasped with amazement and was made almost dizzy by the rich perfume borne towards her on the wind. Her eyes widened as she studied the lilies. They were four feet tall, and from each long, elegant stem hung half a dozen long flowers, their ivory-white petals tinged on the outside with pink. A deep gold in the very centre of each trumpet revealed itself only as the swirling wind turned the plants in the direction of the two watchers. Lucy had never seen anything similar before. This, surely, must be the lilium which Gordon had described to her – the plant which had been discovered eighty years earlier but which had failed to make a safe passage to Europe and could never be found again.

'Thousands!' exclaimed Gordon, his voice husky with awe. 'There must be thousands there. And nowhere else. It's unbelievable. Just think, Lucy, if we hadn't turned back to come this way . . . Or if we had followed this path a few months later, when the flowers had died down and the bulbs were hidden below the ground. If it were not for our baby, Lucy! Oh, how I give thanks for the grace of God and the demands of our baby!'

He turned back to face Lucy, and it seemed to her that he was almost crying with excitement and delight. She was accustomed to the bright eagerness which was always in his eyes, and the alertness of his strong-featured face. But never before had she seen this expression almost of wonder. A weight of guilt flew from her mind and body as she understood that this discovery had by itself made his expedition worth while. Even if, through her fault, they had to cut short their time of travel, he would go home happy as long as he could take the lilies with him.

'We must stay near here,' she said. She knew that this season, while they were in flower, would not be the right time to dig up the bulbs; he would need to wait until the autumn.

'Yes. How it all works together for the best. You need to rest and I need to wait. I must collect a few now, though. So that you may have a flower to paint, and I can consider whether they will propagate best by seeds or by scales from the bulb.' He looked again towards the gorge. 'The first part of the climb will be difficult. It will take me several hours to explore the area. I can rejoin this track at a much lower level. But even the track is very steep. You, Lucy, should take the descent carefully. Would you be willing to go ahead with Sati and the baggage, leaving me and one coolie to make the climb? We'll fix a place where you should wait for me to catch you up.'

Lucy nodded her willingness. 'As long as the place cannot be missed,' she said.

'Well, we can see from here.' He called Sati to join them, and began to explain what he wanted in a mixture of gestures and the limited pidgin vocabulary which they shared.

'Follow the track down with your eyes,' Gordon instructed Lucy when the discussion was over. 'Can you see that brown line where the path reaches the river? That's a bridge, and Sati says it's the only one within miles. There's no possibility of mistake.'

Straining to see, Lucy was able to make out the thin line of the bridge, shimmering in the arid heat, many hundreds of feet below. On the further bank of the river, at a lower level still, was one of the first grassy patches they had seen for some days, suggesting a flat space which, beside water, should be an ideal camp ground.

'That's where I'll join you,' said Gordon. 'We'll stay there for the night.'

'You'll be sure to come back before it gets dark?'

'Of course.' Gordon kissed her in reassurance, but Lucy could feel his body trembling with eagerness to be off – and she herself felt such relief at his discovery that she would not allow another word of doubt to cross her lips. She watched as he confirmed the arrangement with Sati, chose one of the coolies to accompany him, buckled on his own backpack and, with a last cheerful wave, disappeared over the edge of the cliff.

Lucy dared not watch him go, knowing that she would become dizzy and nervous. Instead, she took her seat in the wicker chair and gripped its edges tightly as the coolies stooped to pick up the long poles between which it was suspended.

Lucy hated the chair – especially when, as today, she was being carried steeply downhill. Even on level ground the short quick steps of the coolies set up a swaying motion, and her feeling of insecurity became even greater when she felt herself tipping forward. But she recognized that she no longer had the stamina to make a full day's journey on her own feet and, more decisively, the changing shape of her body had affected her natural sense of balance. On a mountain track with a sheer fall on one side her lack of steadiness would be a danger. Common sense told her that she must accept the arrangement which her husband had made.

At three o'clock that afternoon the mule train reached the bridge which Gordon had pointed out from above. Lucy stared at it in dismay. The river here was still falling steeply from its source in the mountains and had cut out a gorge as steep-sided and deep as the higher one which Gordon was at that moment exploring. So the bridge – if it could be called a bridge – was sixty or seventy feet above the water. It consisted simply of two long ropes suspended at infrequent intervals to support a footway of narrow planks which seemed not to be in any way secured. Even before anyone had set foot on it, it swayed in the wind in an alarming manner.

Lucy got out of the chair. If the coolies were to carry her across, they would need both hands to hold on to the side ropes. The poles, resting on their shoulders, would raise Lucy high above the level of the ropes. Should she fall, there would be nothing to save her.

Why should she fall? Although the coolies occasionally stumbled on the stony mountain paths, they would be cautious in making such a crossing. But she herself might become dizzy and overbalance.

Sati observed her nervousness and misunderstood its exact cause. He led one of the mules across to show that the apparently fragile construction was stronger than it appeared. The heavily-laden animal plodded stolidly across, head down, placing one leg in front of the other in a straight line along the centre of the planks. There was nothing to be afraid of. And yet she was afraid.

Why, she wondered, should pregnancy have this effect on her? During the seven months since they set out from Shanghai there had been several moments of real danger and she had faced them with courage, even a kind of excitement. They were part of the great adventure which she and Gordon were sharing. During the past few weeks, although conscious of a new nervousness, she had almost managed to control it. But now, faced with the need to take a step forward, she was unable to do so.

Sati led forward another mule and indicated that she should ride it across, but Lucy shook her head. On its back, as in the chair, she would be too high. She could trust the animal, but not herself.

The muleteer had one last solution to offer. He tied a rope around her, under her arms: the loop was loose but the knot was firm. The words he spoke were presumably intended to reassure her that even if she were to slip, he would not let her fall far.

Lucy stared at him for a moment. Had she come face to face with such a man in England, she would have assumed him to be a brigand. His face was scarred and, although his high cheekbones and Mongolian cast of face gave the impression that he was always smiling, the narrowness of his eyes made the smile appear a sinister one – an impression strengthened by the way in which he had pulled down the ear-flaps of his felt hat. The problems of communication were so great that she could have no true idea of what he was thinking. Yet she must trust him. His agreement with Gordon had involved him not only in providing mules and hiring men, but in purchasing supplies and making all practical arrangements, and he had been both efficient and honest in this. It must be assumed that he knew what was for the best. In any case, somehow or other the river must be crossed. She told herself that she was being weak and cowardly and altogether despicable, and stepped on to the bridge.

It was like walking on a hammock. With each step the structure not only swayed but shuddered. Lucy took a tight hold of the waist-high rope on either side and inched her way forward. At first she held her head high, fearing that if she looked down, the emptiness below would increase her terror. But the roughness of the footway and the gaps between the planks forced her to watch her feet. Although she knew that to move fast would be safer, she continued to inch forward at a snail's pace, not daring to take the weight off one foot until she was quite sure that the other was steady. Sati walked backwards in front of her with only one hand sliding casually along the rope bridge, the other grasping her halter as though she were a recalcitrant mule to be brought safely across.

She was within ten feet of the further bank when the bridge began to sway violently. The plank on which she was treading tilted upwards and then lurched down again, and at the same moment the muleteer yelled out at the top of his voice. Was his grimace one of fury or fear? It might only mean that one of the other mules had been led on to the bridge too soon, against his instructions, but in a moment of panic it felt to Lucy as though the flimsy structure was about to collapse. What good would Sati's rope do her then, if he too was flung down into the gorge? She hurled herself forward, panting in her anxiety to reach the land. But she had been right to distrust her own sense of balance. Her right foot slipped off the plank and, before she could recover herself, she was down on her left knee, with the whole weight of her ungainly body following her dangling foot sideways and down.

The bridge did not collapse. Sati did not let go of the rope, for she felt it bite in under her shoulders. Nor did she herself release her grip on the two side ropes of the bridge although, as she slipped, her arms were jerked upwards, above her head. She was conscious of a new shuddering as one of the coolies ran to hold her from behind and, with Sati's help, to raise her to her feet and carry her to the end of the bridge. But by now she had ceased to worry about falling. She had a new fear instead.

They reached the bank. 'Missee alrightee?' asked Sati, grinning with success. Lucy did her best to smile. She leaned against the steep wall of rock – for the track on this side was as narrow and precipitous as the other – and tried to bring herself under control while the rest of the mule team was led across. She was not all right. As she slipped, and as her arms jerked upwards, she had experienced an agonizing pain. It had lasted only for a second, and she hoped that it might be explained by the strain on some muscle. But her body told her, as she waited, that the pain would come again.

Within moments it returned, squeezing her as though in the jaws of a man trap. She slipped to the ground as if only on hands and knees, like an animal, would she be able to endure it. For a while, in the bustle of reorganizing the mule train and starting it on its way down, her distress went unnoticed. By the time Sati came to look for her again, she was in tears.

It was not so much the severity of the pain which upset her as its significance. Ignorant though she might be about childbirth, the one fact which every young woman knew was that it was painful. The only possible explanation for the feeling that her body was being stretched and squeezed and torn into pieces must be that the baby was about to arrive. Gordon had promised that there should be at least two months to wait, but Gordon must have been mistaken.

So what was she to do, with no woman to help her, no husband at hand to comfort her, surrounded by men whose manners were rough and whose clothes were dirty? How could a baby born on a mountainside in such conditions survive even for an hour? There would be no hot water to wash him, no way to keep him warm when the sun set and the temperature fell below freezing. She cried from a feeling of helplessness – and with anger at finding herself trapped in such a situation.

When the pain came again, she struggled to control her groans. An Englishwoman ought not to let a native see that she was suffering. But Sati, uncouth though he might seem, was not to be deceived and crinkled his wind-tanned forehead in worry. 'Beebee?' he asked, rocking his arms in the gesture which Gordon had used when teaching him the new word to explain their change of itinerary.

Lucy nodded her head. She could not afford to refuse any help. She had read about countrywomen who gave birth to their babies in a ditch and went straight back to work, but her upbringing had been of a different kind. The memory of her mother's death was enough to remind her of the dangers. She tried to ask that someone should be sent to fetch Gordon without delay, but was unable to interrupt the excited discussion as all the men, in a cluster, argued about what should be done.

In the end she was given no choice. The poles of her carrying chair were used to make a litter on to which she was strapped with blankets. Two coolies set off with her at a run, with two others trotting behind, ready to take their turn with the burden. Down the mountain path they went and past the flat meadow on which the camp was to be pitched. Lucy tried to stop them there, but they took no notice. They had been given their orders by Sati and it soon became clear that they proposed to run on towards the village which had been visible from high above.

Lucy gave up, resigning herself to the jogging of the litter and the spasmodic swelling of her body, which pressed against the straps holding her firm. Under the blankets her fists clenched with each new pain – but between them, she was able to stroke her own abdomen, sensitive even through layers of clothing to the movements of her child. Often during the past month, feeling the baby's kicking, she had smiled to think how fit and active he seemed to be. But now his movements frightened rather than reassured her.

'Wait a little,' she pleaded to her baby. 'Please wait.'

Fourteen

Gordon sighed with contentment as he rested in the valley of lilies. Surely this must be the happiest day of his life!

Throughout the years of dreaming and studying and planning which had preceded the expedition, he had done his best not to make his expectations too specific. The purpose of his venture was to discover something new – something which could not be imagined because it had never yet been seen outside its native habitat. Nevertheless, as a runaway boy, one of the earliest lessons he had learned from the botanist who befriended him was that discoveries are made by people who know what they are seeking.

It was that same botanist who had told him about the lost lily. Merlot's lily, he had called it. Vividly Gordon recalled the excitement with which he had listened to the story. From that moment onward he had longed to become the man who would find the lily again and this time bring it safely back to Europe. But others had had the same ambition. Naturalists had been searching for it for years without success. To have proclaimed such a rediscovery as his principal goal would have doomed his expedition to failure. So he had made no mention of it to any of his patrons.

This restraint made his triumph all the sweeter. The lily would be his own. He could name it, breed from it, sell it if he wished or else keep it for himself to be the envy of every other horticulturist. With a second sigh of satisfaction he lay back, intoxicated by the heady perfume of the flowers and his own sense of achievement.

It was all because of the baby. Remembering his reaction of dismay on first hearing Lucy's news he was momentarily ashamed. He had even felt angry with her, as though it were her fault, instead of experiencing the joy with which a man ought to greet the news of a new life.

He knew that joy now. His feelings for the baby and the lily merged in a swell of possessive love. For Lucy, the conditions of the birth would be hard, but he would give her every assurance that he wanted the baby.

The wind changed, wafting the scent away and reminding him by a sudden edge of coldness that he ought not to delay any longer before making his way to the camp. In his excitement he had climbed to the head of the valley of lilies. Now, with more difficulty, he began to make his way down. In his pack were a dozen of the precious bulbs, and a bunch of the flowers for Lucy to smell and to paint.

The descent took longer than he had expected. The sun had set behind the high mountains long before he reached the bridge, and darkness was falling as he made his precarious way across it. But the camp could not be more than half an hour or so away. Lucy would be worrying – so Gordon began to sing, loudly and untunefully, gesturing his coolie companion to join in so that Tibetan and English notes mingled in discord. Hearing them coming, Lucy would be laughing and teasing when they arrived, instead of anxious.

The camp, as they approached in the gathering darkness, seemed smaller than usual and there was none of the usual bustle associated with the cooking of the evening meal. Gordon's mind began to twitch with anxiety. 'Lucy!' he called.

Two coolies came running, chattering an explanation which he could not understand. They addressed themselves to his companion who nodded but was unable to translate.

Not for the first time, Gordon cursed his inability to speak or understand Tibetan. When preparing in England for the expedition, he had tried to teach himself Mandarin Chinese from a book – but on arrival in China quickly discovered it to have been a waste of time. With no teacher to guide him in the sound of the language, he had failed to master the tones which allowed every word to have several different meanings, and could only with difficulty make himself understood. He could get the gist of what officials asked or ordered; but the poorer people conversed in their local dialects – and Tibetan, of course, was different again. By miming and the use of pidgin he had established sufficient communication with Sati to cover the normal requirements of travel. But without Sati he had suddenly become deaf and dumb.

Gordon needed only a moment to check that Lucy was not in either of the two tents. He returned to the three coolies to struggle with an interrogation. 'Where missee gone away?'

The question was understood because it was expected, but could be answered only with gestures – vigorous jabbings of fingers in the direction of the village below. Sati, it appeared, had also gone that way. Only as Gordon made a show of losing his temper did one of the men produce an explanation. He had forgotten the word, but remembered the mimed gesture which Gordon himself had earlier used for the expected baby. He crossed his arms in front of his chest and rocked them.

'Baby?' checked Gordon. 'Missee gone baby?' Unless there had been an accident, no other explanation was possible; he accepted it at once. Striding past the tents, he searched for the continuation of the mountain track which led down to the village.

'*Kabadar, kabadar!*' The coolies ran to tug him back, shouting their warning of danger. Gordon disregarded it at first, but before he had gone a hundred yards was forced to stop. Although the gradient of the descent was less severe here than it had been higher up, the path was still only a corniche – a narrow ledge hacked from the mountainside with a precipitous drop on one side down to the falling river. Even by daylight, care would be needed in following such a track. On a night when there was no moon, only a fool would go further. He would gain little time by groping his way through the darkness, since he could travel at ten times the speed next day. Besides, if Lucy had been taken to some isolated house in the valley, before reaching the village, he might go past it without realizing it was there.

So common sense held him back. He shared the meal which the coolies prepared and then left them to their opium pipes and retired to his tent – too worried to write up his notes; too worried even to sleep. What was happening to Lucy at this moment? Where was she? How was she? He ought to be with her. Even though he could do nothing to help with the birth of the baby, she should have been comforted by the knowledge that he was close at hand. And the villagers would feel no great respect for a foreign woman. He ought to be at her side to provide authority and make decisions.

As he tossed through the night his anxiety increased to a deeper fear. Suppose Lucy should die! In such a remote country area she would be fortunate if there were even a village midwife who could be summoned. Certainly there would be no trained medical help. So many things could go wrong. He could hardly bear to think of the pain which she must be suffering – but when he tried to put that out of his mind it was replaced only with the thought of his own pain if he should lose her. So great was his desolation that it was almost as though the loss had already occurred. Terror froze his body into a tense immobility, while his heart pounded erratically. If he had lost his darling, how could he bear to go on living?

Instead of growing steadily, the love he felt for his wife seemed to have increased in dramatic leaps. At their first meeting he had been instantly attracted by the beauty of her face. Once he was married – almost against his will – her body had aroused his desire, which fed on the adoration with which she gave herself to him. Her courage and cheerfulness throughout their travels – especially during the dangerous Yangtze ascent – had given him a new reason to love her, as a companion. In short, he could have had no complaint about the way everything had turned out, except that it had been as she, not he, had planned. No doubt a good many marriages took shape in very much the same manner. It was only because Gordon so much prided himself on his strength of purpose that a trace of regret had remained to mar his honeymoon delight.

The regret inevitably increased when Lucy's pregnancy threatened to destroy all his plans. But the excitement of finding the lily had brought him triumphantly to terms with that. Only a few hours ago he had believed himself to be the happiest man in the world. And now, without warning, his happiness was at risk again, threatened by the possibility of Lucy's death. All his doubts and hesitations were swept away by that danger. He could think of nothing but the fact that without Lucy his life would not be worth living.

The next morning, long before it was fully light, he left two of the coolies behind to pack up the camp and hurried away with the third towards the valley. A three-hour scramble brought them to the edge of the cultivated land. The track broadened and was crossed by what – to judge from the mule trains which were on the move in both directions – was a considerable highway. The route that Gordon had been following for the last three weeks was chosen for its directness rather than for ease of travel – and, in any case, its starting point was in a wild area which no ordinary traveller would have cause to visit. Now they had met the high road along which enterprising traders carried their goods between Tibet and China.

There were no buildings beside the road, so Gordon, crossing it, pressed on towards the village he had first glimpsed from high above. It was walled against dacoits and unfriendly neighbours and all the valley's inhabitants had chosen to live in security behind the walls, rather than in the countryside around. Only the dead rested outside.

Passing through the graveyard, Gordon made for the nearest gate. He was still a little way away when he saw Sati emerge on horseback, coming to look for him. Although the Tibetan put out his tongue in the usual form of greeting, his expression was sombre. Without speaking, he turned his horse round and led the way back through the gate.

The first building inside the wall was an inn. Its public rooms were crowded, but the chatterers fell silent as Gordon followed Sati through. He had become accustomed to a demonstration of curiosity when arriving at such places. Crowds, sometimes hostile, would gather to stare; it was usual for him to be pointed at, touched, questioned. But today, it seemed to him, the polite bows of the inn's guests expressed not interest but sympathy. A hundred eyes pierced into his back as he approached the door of the inn's principal guest room. He was the only man there who did not know what he was going to find.

Fifteen

of the better moment away it turned and turned away. A hundred eyes peered into her face at his inquest, and the mirror of the lamp. The inquiry good room. He was the body from there was the not know what he does really to do.

Tears trickled down Lucy's face as she lay in the darkened room and waited for Gordon to come. He would not be long; she was sure of that. There had been a moment in the early hours of the morning when, between her pains, she had been afraid – afraid that he would hurry too fast through the darkness to catch her up, and would fall, leaving her alone in this barbaric place, so far from home; and alone in the world, with no one to love her. But then the pain had consumed her, leaving no room in her mind for any other emotion; and now she was too unhappy to feel fear.

She sniffed; but that did nothing to check the flow of tears. It was impossible to dab her eyes dry, because her hands were not free. The old woman brought by the innkeeper's wife had first of all helped with the birth and then, when it was all over, had strapped her body to a flat wooden board, winding a kind of bandage tightly round and round from shoulders to ankles, as though she were being prepared for burial. She could move nothing but her head and toes; could hardly even breathe. From time to time she slipped into sleep or faintness. And each time, as she regained consciousness, the first question she asked was the same: 'Where is the baby?' But no one understood.

The door opened and closed again. It was too dark to see who had come in, but she recognized the perfume of lilies which she had seen in the gorge only twenty-four hours earlier. 'Gordon?' she asked weakly.

In a rush he was beside her, dropping the flowers and kneeling on the floor so that his hands could grip her shoulders.

'Lucy, darling, how are you? I've been so frightened. Oh, my dearest, I love you so much. Dearest, dearest Lucy.' He pressed his face against hers, and Lucy could feel that he was crying. Their tears mingled, but only Gordon's were tears of relief.

'I want to see the baby,' whispered Lucy. She ought first of all to say how glad she was to see him, and reassure him on her own behalf; but her anxiety about the baby was too great. 'I heard a cry. Just one. Then they took her away. To wash, I thought. But they won't bring it back.'

'I'll go and see.' Gordon kissed her all over her face. 'They have different customs, I expect. And didn't understand you. But how are *you*?'

'I'm tired. But I shall be all right. The baby – '

'Yes, I'll go.'

He was away far too long. Lucy tried to comfort herself by imagining possible explanations. Perhaps the new-born baby had been put to a wet nurse and was at this moment being fed. But then, why had Lucy's own breasts been bound so uncomfortably tightly? Although in England she might not have chosen to feed her own baby, in the present circumstances it was the obvious – the only – thing to do. Although her mind would not accept it, her heart already knew what news Gordon would bring.

When he returned at last he tried to find her hand and hold it, but was frustrated by the bindings.

'I'm sorry, dearest,' he said. 'The baby's dead.'

'It can't be. I heard the cry.'

'She was born alive. A little girl. But she was very small. Too small to live. I think I was right when I said that September was the earliest time for her to be born safely. This was too soon. It was all my fault. You shouldn't have had to travel in such a rough way. I should have found somewhere you could rest.'

'How could you, when I didn't tell you until we were in the mountains?' Lucy began to cry again. 'Oh Gordon, I know you didn't want the baby. And I didn't either, not at first, not here. I knew it was spoiling everything for you. But when I felt her move, and when I heard that cry, I wanted her then. I ought to have looked after her better before she was born. I'm not fit to be a mother. It was my fault that she died. She died because she wasn't wanted enough. But she was, really. It was just, just . . .'

'Be quiet,' said Gordon gently, drying her face. 'This was an accident of travel, nothing else. No one is to blame. We can feel a little sorry for ourselves, but that's all. I know that you want to have a family, and I want your babies as well. Nothing has been spoilt. The baby brought good fortune to me, although only pain to you. We shall have more children, Lucy. There's plenty of time ahead of us. Just as long as you are well. That's all that matters.'

'I'd like to see her, Gordon. They took her away so quickly.'

'I wanted to see her as well. I asked. But she's been buried already.'

Lucy felt herself becoming upset again. 'She should have had a Christian burial. She was born alive.'

'I've found out from the innkeeper where the nearest mission house is,' Gordon said. 'As soon as you're fit to travel, we'll take you there on a litter. The innkeeper's wife has gone to find a woman who will travel with us, to look after you. You'll be better cared for at the mission station, and we'll ask one of the missionaries to say a

302

prayer for the baby. Probably they travel around the area from time to time. When one of them next comes this way, he could say the funeral service over the grave.'

'She should have a name,' said Lucy.

Gordon nodded. 'We could call her Lily, and remember her by the valley of lilies.'

'No,' said Lucy. 'I want your lily to be a happy memory for you, not a sad one.'

'Then I tell you what,' said Gordon. 'I shall name the lily after our *next* daughter. The beautiful, golden-haired girl who is going to be born in England in two or three years' time and who will grow up to be as tall and slender and lovely as her mother. I would like to call *that* daughter Grace – and give the name to the lily at once. So I'll leave you to christen your first-born.'

'Rachel,' said Lucy. Rachel had been the name of her mother, who had also died too young.

'Rachel,' agreed Gordon.

Named, the baby seemed to become a person instead of only a ghostly cry in the night. Lucy struggled to bring her unhappiness under control and put everything that had happened behind her. 'I want to leave now,' she said. 'Straight away. As soon as you've found a nurse.' She could feel that she was bleeding, but was too embarrassed to mention this to Gordon. 'First of all, I need to get out of all this strapping and have my arms free. And I'd like something to eat.'

'That's my brave darling.' Once again, Gordon covered Lucy's face with kisses. 'I love you,' he said.

The journey to Suifu, the nearest settlement of any size, was smooth and comfortable. There was a well-made stone road for the first section, and the last day was spent aboard a river boat. Lucy felt her strength returning with every hour that passed. She was young and healthy; and the baby had been small. At first she had to force herself to put on a show of cheerfulness; but by the time they arrived at the compound of the China Inland Mission her smiles had become sincere.

The English missionary, Mrs Dennie, welcomed her compatriots with delight. The prospect of company was especially welcome because her husband, a doctor, was away on a three-month tour of the frontier villages, she told them. When Lucy learned that he would probably have been not too far from the village of Jinkouhe at the time when her baby was born, it was hard not to wish that she had known this in time to send for his help. With more expert care, perhaps even a premature baby might have survived. But she had promised herself that she was not going to make Gordon unhappy by any signs of mourning for her little Rachel.

'I act as a teacher here,' Mrs Dennie said. 'But I used to be a nurse. You must stay as long as you need. I shall be so pleased to have someone to talk to.'

Safe and comfortable at last, Lucy allowed her mind and her body to relax. Gordon too, after so many months on the move, was in need of a rest. Although July and August were hot months, the river breeze made the heat bearable, contrasting with the scorching winds of the high mountain valleys. He and Lucy engaged a teacher to help them with their Chinese, and delighted the small boys of the mission school by joining in the daily practice of the tones needed to make their vocabulary intelligible.

Lucy spent another part of each day with the class of girls. There were fewer of these. They were all foundlings, Mrs Dennie told her. Some, wrapped in brown paper, had been left as babies outside the door of the mission once the townsfolk had come to believe that the foreigners did not live up to their reputation of eating children.

Others had been found naked, lying exposed to the elements amongst the graves outside the city wall. Dr Dennie, when he was at home, explored the area at first light each morning in case there was a living child there to be saved. Lucy remembered how shocked she had been on board the *Parramatta* when she first heard Miss Fawcett describe the ruthlessness with which Chinese parents rejected girl-babies as useless and unwanted. She was glad that these bright-eyed girls, with their unbound feet, had been saved to grow up as Christians.

The room provided for the visitors at the mission was barely furnished, but whitewashed and clean. Lucy herself was able to feel clean for the first time in many weeks. She ate regular meals, including the fresh fruit and vegetables which had not been obtainable in the mountains. For a second time within a few months her clothes began to feel tight round her waist – but by now she had had a woman-to-woman talk with Mrs Dennie. The information which her own mother had not lived to give her, Lucy acquired from the motherly missionary. So instead of wondering whether another baby might already be on the way, she unpacked the bag in which her corsets had been stowed away and enlisted Mrs Dennie's help in lacing them for the first time.

Even after a great struggle it was clear that she had lost her eighteen-inch waist. Lucy was panting and Mrs Dennie was laughing when at last the fastening was secure.

'What would the Chinese think of this!' exclaimed the missionary. 'We upbraid them for deforming their daughters' feet by binding the bones tightly, yet we are doing much the same to our own rib-cages.'

'With less success,' laughed Lucy, hardly able to breathe in her strait-jacket after so many weeks in which

305

her body had been unrestrained. Yet she took it as a sign that her recovery was complete. That evening, tentatively, she broached the subject of the future to her husband.

'We agreed that you would go back alone to the mountains when the time came to dig up the bulbs and plants that you've marked,' she reminded him. 'When we made that plan, of course, it was with the thought that my confinement would be in September – and that afterwards I should have to care for a baby.'

Gordon took her hand in his. 'And now you are thinking that you are well and free and would like to accompany me.'

'I don't want to hold you back in any way,' Lucy said. 'If I make you slow, or worried, or make it necessary to take too many men or mules, or if you think there are climbs too steep for me . . .'

'You climb like a mountain goat,' Gordon assured her. 'Speed is not important. This time we shall be spending several days in each area. I shall be glad of an assistant, because there will be so much marking and listing and wrapping to be done. And if I leave you behind here, even in such good hands, I shall worry about you every day and night. There's nothing I want more than to have you beside me – for every hour for the rest of my life. So please come back with me to the mountains, Lucy.'

Lucy's heart swelled until she felt that it must surely burst. She had never loved anyone as she loved Gordon. Her inexperience had made it hard for her in the past to be certain that he loved her. On three or four occasions she *had* felt certain – and yet within a short time some new expression of his love made it appear that the earlier experience had been incomplete. There had been moments of doubt, when she felt that she had forced herself upon him and that he was only making the best of a situation he would have preferred to avoid. He might have felt that he had no choice but to marry her, but she had given him a choice of a kind now, and his answer was all she could have hoped for.

Nor was it an answer only in words, for he opened his arms to enfold her. She had heard him tell her before that he loved her, but this time his voice expressed an appeal as well as an assurance, justifying her trust. The sharing of sorrow had made them one person in a way that love alone could not. Lucy looked into Gordon's black eyes as he kissed her, and saw there the promise of happiness for the rest of her life.